MURDER & BILLY BAILEY

NIKI DUPRE MYSTERIES BOOK 3

JIM RILEY

FRIDAY NGHT

BILL *BILLY* BAILEY watched film with the quarterback and receivers of Central High School's epic win over the top ranked Zachary Broncos the past Friday night. The comeback win marked the most important victory in his tenure as head coach.

At only twenty-eight years old, many questioned his credentials for the position. That win over Zachary quieted most of those critics. The crowd roared onto the field after the game, astounded at the turnaround in the football program over the course of one season.

Three quarterbacks and eight receivers joined the Bailey and Jimbo Wax, the offensive coordinator, in the film room this Monday afternoon. Mistakes had been made and for the Central Wildcats to go far into the playoffs, those must be corrected and eliminated.

The door burst open.

"Hey, you can't come in here," Bailey said, shielding his eyes from the bright lights in the hallway.

"Coach, I believe we can."

Bailey recognized the Sheriff's deputy that was talking.

"Arnette, what is this all about?"

"Bill Bailey, you are under arrest for the rape and carnal knowledge of a minor."

Bailey gasped, not believing his ears. The two deputies grabbed him, one by each arm, and hurled him against the wall. Arnette slapped the cuffs on his wrists. They dragged him out of the room.

"Jimbo, call my wife. Call Sara Sue."

2

MONDAY AFTERNOON

SHERIFF'S OFFICE

LESS THAN AN HOUR LATER, Bailey wore an orange and white striped jumpsuit, emblazoned with the letters EBRSO stitched across the back. Those were the initials for the East Baton Rouge Parish Sheriff's office. He received his Miranda rights and was strip-searched prior to donning his present attire.

"What is this all about? What is going on here?" He asked of every officer within hearing.

They ignored him. Bailey had never been arrested before. The worst offense the coach ever committed was forgetting to put on his turn signal. He got a warning, but no ticket.

The coach settled and sat quietly in the jail cell. He wondered why he was in a cell by himself. The one adjoining his held six prisoners, each clad in the same orange and white jumpsuit he wore. This was the first time that Billy could remember he had absolutely nothing to do.

He looked at the stark furnishings. A stainless toilet with a water tap on top. The steel bed with an ultra-thin mattress had more stains and holes that solid covering. A single sheet rolled up on one end of the bed was too short for his 6'4" frame.

The tinted window to the outside was only four inches wide with steel grating stretching from the top to the bottom. He could see it was still daylight outside, but could discern no shapes.

Billy thought about Sara Sue. What did she think when told of the charges? They were high school sweethearts, both attending Denham Springs High School, less than fifteen minutes from Central.

Sara Sue was the head cheerleader, captain of the softball team, and star of the girls' basketball team. Bailey played the three major sports, earning all–state awards as the quarterback for the football team and ace pitcher for the Yellow Jacket's baseball team.

They both attended LSU, Bailey earning a degree in kinesiology and Sara Sue getting her degree in the entrepreneur program. He wanted to coach, and she wanted to own a personal business. After graduation, she started a temporary employment agency, furnishing workers ranging from warehouse laborers to accountants.

The couple had no children, opting to get their careers established before parenthood. They began talking about a family, even discussing potential names for their children.

Now the rising star in the high school coaching ranks sat in a dark and smelly cell with his career and his marriage in jeopardy. He taught Sunday School at the Baptist Church at the corner of Joor and. Hooper.

What would the seventh grade boys in his class think? What would the football players he loved and coached think about the man who always stressed character and integrity over all other traits?

His future—Wait, what future? Was twenty years behind bars at the state prison in Angola considered a future? Bailey realized why he was in a cell by himself. He had heard stories

4

about what happened to rapists and child molesters in prison. He was about to live that story unless he was separated for his own safety.

Bailey tried to lie on the steel cot. There was no comfortable position for his tall body in the short bed. The room was cold. Frigid cold. The short-sleeved jumpsuit provided almost no warmth. Billy pulled thin sheet over him and closed his eyes.

The coach tried to make sense of the day's events. Who had accused him of rape? Who had accused him of having carnal knowledge? Was it the same girl? Was it a girl? Could he afford bail? He and Sara Sue had sunk what little savings they had into Sara Sue's business.

The Wildcats Temporary Agency was only beginning to turn cash flow positive, generating a little more revenue than operating costs. It was not in a financial position to afford the hefty requirements of bail.

Then two deputies appeared outside the cell. They replaced the handcuffs and put leg irons on each ankle. He shuffled between them to a small conference room. The deputies put a belly chain around the coach and fastened it to a link under the table.

They left him without explaining the move. Then he heard people approaching. He twisted much as he could with the constraints restricting any movements. Sara Sue came in, mascara running down her cheeks. A tall, elderly gentleman dressed in an expensive blue suit followed her.

EAST BATON ROUGE PARISH JAIL

SARA SUE STEPPED toward Billy to hug her husband, but a grunt from a guard stopped her.

"No contact with the prisoner," he said.

"I'm sorry," she said through her tears.

She sat in a chair on the other side of the table with the gray-haired gentleman. The elder fellow addressed the guards.

"I would like to have privacy with my client, please."

Even though he stated it in non--threatening terms, the guards quickly assented and left the room.

"Honey," Sara Sue began. "This is Durwin Kemp. He is the best lawyer in the state."

Bailey, through reflex, tried to extend his hands, but the restraints prevented him from raising them.

"It's okay," Kemp said. "We aren't supposed to make contact, anyway. I'm pleased to meet you."

"Look, Mr. Kemp. I don't know what you charge, but I know that we can't afford you. I'm on a high school coach's salary, and Sara Sue is just getting her business off the ground. We don't have a lot of money."

Kemp's smile never left his face. But in his eyes, there was a steely focus, like a panther right before it struck its prey.

"I hate to tell you this, Bill. You can't afford not to have my services in the position you find yourself."

"But—" Billy protested.

"It's okay, Honey," Sara Sue interrupted. "I'm taking care of it."

Billy was incredulous.

"How? Where did you get the money?"

"Niki Dupre is helping us."

In Billy's muddled mind, he recognized the name, but could not place it with an actual person.

"Who?" He asked.

"Niki Dupre. She's the famous private investigator who solved the Spirit Island case."

"How does she know us?"

"She's a client of mine. She is so busy she hires temps from me to type up her reports. She's wonderful. I want to introduce y'all when you get out."

Kemp spoke. "Miss Dupre has agreed to pay my fees for your case for as long as you need me."

Bailey shook his head. "How much are your fees?"

Kemp glanced at Sara Sue. She nodded.

"I charge one hundred thousand dollars for a retainer. That is only to assess the validity of the charges against you, and attempt to get you bail. OF course, any further actions on my part will require additional fees."

"Of course," Bailey says sarcastically. He looked at his wife.

"We can't ever pay this back. We can't do it. What if I go to jail? How will you ever get that kind of money?"

"Are you guilty?" Kemp asked.

"No. Hell, no," Bailey shouted in the small room.

"No need for profanity, Bill. I understand the English language. A simple 'yes' or 'no' will suffice," Kemp said.

"No. Is that simple enough? And don't call me *Bill*. I go by *Billy*. All my friends call me *Billy*. I preferred you called me that."

"Okay, Billy. If you aren't guilty, why are you charged for these egregious acts?"

"What egregious acts?" Billy asked. He turned to Sara Sue. "Baby, I can't let you go into debt like this. It has to be a simple mistake by somebody."

Sara Sue started to reach her hand across the table but pulled it back.

"We aren't going into debt. I would if that is what it takes, but we don't have to do that."

Confusion clouded Bailey's face.

Sara Sue continued, "Niki is paying for Mr. Kemp's services. Whatever they end up being, no strings attached."

"Why? I don't even know her," he wondered.

"But I do. I can't say that we are best friends, but she was in the office when the sheriff called. I didn't know what to do."

Tears streaked down Sara Sue's face, the angst over their situation almost too much to bear.

"I'm sorry, baby. I'm really sorry, but I still don't even know what I'm being accused of doing."

Kemp cleared his throat.

"Do you know a young lady by the name of—" Kemp checked the piece of paper from his briefcase. "Flavia Foster? Miss Foster is a student at Central High School. A senior. Age seventeen."

"I know her. I mean, I know who she is. I've never had her in one of my classes. I teach trigonometry as well as coaching."

"Do you often stay late at the school after football practice?" Kemp asked.

"Every day. That is when I review film. I look at the day's practice and whatever tapes we have of our next opponent. That usually takes at least two hours."

Sweat formed on Bailey's brow. His hands, though constrained, shook.

"Were you alone during these film sessions?" The attorney asked.

"Most of the time. Sometimes Jimbo will stay and help me break down our opponent's schemes."

"Jimbo?"

Bailey explained. "Jimbo Wax. He's our offensive coordinator and assistant head coach. He's very good at spotting trends based on formations."

"I don't understand, Mr. Bailey. I was not a member of a football team. What do you mean?"

Bailey sighed, wanting to return to the conversation about the charges against him. But the lawyer was going through this methodically.

"Formations. An offense can line up in several ways. The standard once was two wide receivers, a tight end, a fullback, and a running back. Five different skill positions plus the quarterback."

Kemp took notes and nodded but said nothing.

"Now, teams will line up with any combination of those five skill positions. One of the most popular is three wide receivers, a tight end, and a running back. Though they may be five wideouts and no running backs."

"Okay," the attorney said, indicating for Billy to continue.

"The quarterback can take a snap under the center, standing right behind the guy who snaps the ball or he may back up and take it. If he backs up, that's called a shotgun formation."

"Sounds complicated. I would imagine all these different

9

formations can cause a bit of confusion for the opposing team," Kemp said.

Bailey chuckled.

"To say the least, that's where Jimbo helps. In high school, when a team lines up in one particular formation or another, they tend to run certain plays from the different formations. If we know which play the opposing team will run, then we can adjust our defense to stop it."

"Fair enough." Kemp flipped to the next page of his tablet. "Did anyone else join you in the film sessions?"

"Sure. Sometimes one or more of the players volunteered to stay. I really don't encourage their participation, though. It's more important for them to keep up with their studies."

"Anyone else?" Kemp asked.

Billy became frustrated. "Look, if you have a question, then ask it. Quit beating around the bush."

"All right. Did Miss Foster ever accompany you in these film sessions?" Kemp did not look up from the tablet in front of him.

"What?" Below blurted. "Why would a cheerleader want to watch film of our opposition? Are you crazy?"

Kemp remained calm. "So, you are aware that Miss Foster is a cheerleader at the school. I thought you said previously that you did not know the young lady."

"I said I didn't know her well. I damn sure know that she's a cheerleader. I have eyes and I have a brain."

Kemp was nonplussed. "Do you know the names of all the members on the cheerleading squad?"

"Yes. No. I don't know. I never gave it much thought." Sweat poured off Billy forehead.

"But you know that Miss Foster is on the squad? Is that right?"

"I've already answered that," Billy's voice raised in tone.

"Why wouldn't I? She is probably the prettiest student in school."

"Hmm," Kemp mused. "You think she is attractive? Is that what you said?"

"Sure," Billy answered. "Wait. Not like that. I'm not a dirty old man. She is attractive, but not in the way you're insinuating."

"I'm merely restating your words, Mr. Bailey. You are the one that said the young lady was pretty."

"She—I—" Billy did not care for the direction of the conversation, particularly in front of his wife. "Is all this necessary?"

"Sir, what we've been through so for is child's play compared to what the prosecutor will ask. It's better if I know how you will answer the questions before he asks them."

"But you're twisting my words. You're making me sound like a pervert."

The attorney looked at the sheaf of papers in his briefcase. "The prosecutors believe you are a pervert, Mr. Bailey. The alleged facts in this case assert that you are a pervert, Mr. Bailey."

"What alleged facts?"

"Miss Foster had informed the officers she accompanied you after practice in these film sessions, and you seduced her on several occasions." Kemp looked at the papers.

"I what?" Bailey exploded, rattling the restraining chains.

The guard opened the door to the small conference room. "Everything okay?"

Kemp held up one hand. "Everything is fine, officer."

The guard stepped back outside and shut the door.

"Mr. Bailey, if I am to be of service to you, then you must remain calm. Theatrics will not help you or your case."

Billy steamed. "But she is saying she and I had sex during the film sessions. That's preposterous. I mean, it's just crazy."

"Does that mean that you never had sex with Miss Foster after practice?" Kemp asked.

"Hell, no. Of course not. She's lying. I don't know why she's lying, but she's lying."

"Can you prove that she is being untruthful?" The lawyer now studied Bailey's face.

"Sure. I mean, no. I can't prove I was alone if I was by myself? But she's lying." Billy realized how much trouble he was in.

He looked at Sara Sue.

"You believe me, don't you? I need to know that you believe me."

"Yes, I do, Honey. I wouldn't be here if I didn't believe you and believe in you."

"Thank you."

The coach appreciated his wife more in that moment than ever before in their marriage.

He turned to Kemp. "How do we prove she is lying?"

Kemp hesitated. "It will be difficult, I'm afraid. Just from a preliminary review, Miss Foster seems to be a popular student of impeccable character. Most people will tend to believe her, including a jury."

"But she's lying. I don't know why, but she's not telling the truth."

Kemp nodded. "And that is precisely the problem, Mr. Bailey. Why would she lie and offer false allegations? What does she have to gain with such accusations?"

"She—She—" Billy hesitated. "I don't have any idea. Other than saying *hello* in the hallway when she passes, I've never spoken to the girl."

"That's the other problem." Kemp stared at Bailey's face.

"She is a girl. A minor. We will not have the same leeway in direct examination we would have with an older woman. There are certain boundaries that we cannot cross."

Billy's heart sank. He could not imagine a worse situation than this.

"What do we do? If we can't call her a liar to her face, and tell the world she's a liar, what can we do?" His voice sounded that of a defeated man.

"The first thing we can do is ask the judge for bail."

"When will that happen?" Bailey asked.

"If we're lucky, we'll get in front of him tomorrow morning. We'll be able to present our side then. Do you have a passport?"

"Yes," Billy answered. "Why?"

"One condition of bail will be that you surrender your passport to the court. It does not want you to flee the country."

Billy bared his head on his chest. "I'm not going anywhere. How much will bail be?"

"Have you ever been in trouble before? Any other accusations like this, even as a juvenile?"

"No. Never. Of course not. I'm not a pervert."

Kemp held up a hand.

"If you aren't telling the truth, the judge will know. It is better that I find out from you rather than finding out from him."

"I told you. I've never been accused of anything close to this before."

"Good." Kemp seemed lost in thought for a moment. "Based on my experience, you will get out on bail. That's the good news."

"And the bad news?" Although Billy was not sure that he wanted to hear any more bad news for the day.

"The bail will be set between a quarter of a million and a million dollars. Maybe a little higher, but not much."

Billy shook his head, his mind heavy. "It doesn't matter. I can't afford either of the amounts you mentioned. We're wasting our time even going through the motions. I suggest we cancel the hearing."

Kemp formed a weak smile. "The money has been guaranteed, Mr. Bailey. It is already pledged."

Billy could not believe the words he thought he heard. He stared at the attorney, a puzzled look across his countenance.

"Miss Dupre will pay for your bail."

"But—" He looked at Sara Sue. "What is this all about? I don't even know the lady."

Sara Sue wiped her tears.

"I know her. If she told Mr. Kemp she will post the money, then I believe it will happen. At least, you'll be out of jail until the trial. We'll have that time together."

Billy turned to the attorney. "How long before the trial?"

Kemp hesitated. "It depends. At this point, I don't know what evidence they have. It may take some time to review the evidence and build a case to refute it."

"Then get me out," Bailey blurted. "I will find out what is happening and why. I'll make that little liar tell the truth."

"No. You can't do that. You can't go anywhere near the victim, the alleged victim. That will be a condition of your release. If you violate that order, you will land back in jail."

"But we have to get her to tell the truth. I can't teach and coach with this hanging over my head. What will the students and players think?"

"I can't control that," the attorney replied. "Neither can you. You won't be coaching or teaching until this matter is concluded."

"I have to work. We have bills to pay. I'm not running from this. I will tell everyone that I am innocent." Bailey's face turned beet red.

The attorney pulled another sheet from his briefcase. "I spoke briefly with the president of the Central school board. If you continue your work at school, there will be inevitable inadvertent meetings between you and the alleged victim. It's not that big of a campus."

"You were talking about my future without consulting me? Is that legal?"

"Very much so. I am your attorney, and I must act for your benefit. In this instance, I did that."

Billy fumed. "And what did you and the president decide? That my career is over?"

"You will be suspended with pay for the duration of the case, including any appeals should the jury returned an adverse verdict."

"You mean a guilty verdict, don't you?"

The lawyer nodded.

"But I'm not guilty. Now I have to sit at home watching Gilligan reruns while that liar goes on with her life as though nothing has happened. That's not fair."

"You can help your case by telling our investigator everything you know. Don't hold back anything, no matter how embarrassing it might be," Kemp advised.

"I guess this Dupre lady is picking up the tab for the investigator." Disgust poured off of every word.

Kemp chuckled. "In a way, yes. Miss Dupre is the investigator for this case."

4

EAST BATON ROUGE PARISH JAIL

BILLY WATCHED the attorney pack all the papers back into his briefcase. Sara Sue dabbed at her eyes as Kemp escorted her from the room. Bailey could only twist his body and watch them disappear, the thick gray door slamming behind them.

The burly guard entered, unshackled the coach, and led him back to the dim cell. Bailey almost broke down when the iron clanged together.

"Hey, pervert," a man in the next cell call to him. Bailey glanced up to see a large Mexican man staring at him. The prisoner must've weighed well over three hundred pounds, probably closer to four hundred. Tattoos ran down both arms and around his neck. Billy guessed there were more under the orange and white jumpsuit.

But a pair of them caught his attention. Beneath his left eye were two dark teardrops. Bailey did not know much about prisoners or prison life, but he knew that each of these tattoos signified a death at the hands of the prisoner.

"What you looking at, pervert?" The man sneered.

Bailey did not answer. He laid down on the steel bed and stared at the ceiling.

"We got something for you, perv. They ain't gonna keep you by yourself forever."

Bailey tried to focus on what he did not know. He could come up with no reason for a teenage girl to fabricate a story against him. What did she have to gain? Why was Niki Dupre doing all the things she was doing for him? He tried to recall ever meeting the detective, but John David a blank.

"The guards, they ain't gonna protect you. They don't care what happens to perverts that do little girls. They ain't gonna say nothing. They ain't gonna report nothing."

Billy's mind wandered. If this was how he was to be treated in the local jail, what would he be facing when he went to the state penitentiary in Angola? How long would he have to endure the torture? Should he end his life now?

"Hey, perv. I'm Tyrone. But you can just call me *Honey*. I ain't had no white boy in a long time."

Bailey tried to shut out the man's voice, but he was only a few feet away. Then another voice chimed in with the first. Much of the same that came out of the first man was echoed by the second. Then a third man joined the first two. Then Billy's mind became a blur, the voices becoming more and more faint until he could no longer hear them.

5

LOUISIANA STATE COURTHOUSE

"WHAT ARE the charges against the defendant?" The judge asked the bailiff.

"Six counts of rape against a minor, and two counts carnal knowledge of a minor, Sir."

"Has the defendant been advised of the charges against him?" The judge asked.

"Yes, Your Honor," Kemp spoke.

Billy Bailey remained seated beside his attorney. Sara Sue sat in the first row of seats in the gallery. She was sitting next to a long–legged strawberry blonde who Billy had never seen before. He would have remembered. He thought she might be a television reporter given her photogenic face.

Behind the district attorney sat almost twenty men and women. Billy recognized some of them from meetings he held with his students' parents. Others he did not recognize. It was clear, however, which side they supported. It was not his.

"Is the defendant prepared to enter a plea?"

"Yes, Your Honor," Kemp replied.

"Does the defendant plead guilty or not guilty?"

"Not guilty, Your Honor."

A groan erupted from the crowd behind the district attorney. The bailiff glared at them.

The judge hammered the gavel three times.

"There will be no demonstrations from the members of the gallery. If anyone does not think I am serious, they will find themselves as a guest in the facilities adjacent to this courtroom for contempt."

The prosecutor, a thin, middle–aged lady with premature graying hair and Durwin Kemp remained standing, undisturbed by the judge's reprimand.

"Plea is accepted as *not guilty*. Does either party have any briefs or petitions to be submitted today?"

"No, Your Honor," the lady replied.

"None for the defense, Your Honor," Kemp said.

"Bail recommendations?" The judge asked.

"The state recommends that defendant be retained without bail due to the seriousness of the charges and the supporting evidence, Your Honor." The prosecutor cited without emotion.

"The defendant has led an exemplary life, Sir. He has a wife and a home in this community. He is not a flight risk. Defense recommends a bail of one hundred thousand dollars."

"Nice try, Mr. Kemp," the judge smiled.

Billy's heart sank. Sara Sue wailed behind him. When he turned at the sound, he saw the young lady put a comforting arm around his wife. Then the judge surprised him.

"Bail will be set at eight hundred thousand dollars. Any objections?"

"No, Your Honor."

"None from the defense, Your Honor."

6

BATON ROUGE

NINETEEN MINUTES LATER, Billy Bailey walked out of the parish jail into the waiting arms of his wife. The leggy blonde stood behind her.

They hugged and kissed and hugged some more. Then, as if an afterthought, Sara Sue nodded toward the other lady.

"This is Niki Dupre. She will be the investigator for Mr. Kemp."

Billy extended his hand. "I'm glad to finally meet you, Miss Dupre. I saw you sitting with Sara Sue in the hearing, but I didn't make the connection. When she was telling me about you, I imagined someone older."

Niki grinned. "Sorry to disappoint you."

Billy blushed. "I didn't mean it like that. I'll be eternally grateful for what you have done for us. I don't know how to thank you."

"Win the state championship when you get back on the sidelines. I'm a Central alum. Wildcat for life."

"Geez. I haven't even thought about football since the deputies came into the room. I usually—"

"I understand. And call me Niki. We have a lot of work to do and not much time to do it. I need to get with you as soon as possible."

Billy hesitated. "I've got to go by my office to—I don't guess I have to go by there. I'm unemployed at the moment."

"Technically, you're still employed, Billy. The school board put you on administrative leave with pay. One condition is you avoid going to school grounds or attending any meetings where any student might be present."

"But I teach Sunday School at the church. We have a lot of Central students attending services."

"I'm sorry. I know Brother Kevin. I'll call him and explain the situation. He can arrange for a substitute teacher until we get this cleared up."

The private investigator made Billy feel more comfortable. Her ease and confidence were infectious.

"I have to ask you a question, Niki," he said.

"Don't worry about it. I'll be asking you a lot of questions."

He cleared his throat. "All this you're doing for me. I mean, you're almost a million dollars in the hole. I am truly thankful. But I need to know why. Why are you helping us so much?"

Niki laughed.

"I'm not out all that money. Unless you go to Belize and hunt sand crabs. When you show up for trial, I'll get the money back."

"I thought the court kept ten percent. At least that's what I had heard."

"You're thinking of a bail bondsman. They'll put up your bail if you pay them ten percent. If you and Sara Sue went that route, you wouldn't get that money back."

"But you're still out the money for the attorney. I don't understand why."

"Why don't I treat you guys to a brunch at Frank's? It's only about fifteen minutes from here. I'll answer your questions then."

7

FRANK'S

Sara Sue barely touched the sunny-side up eggs, bacon, ham, and buttermilk biscuits. Niki nibbled at the veggie omelet on her plate, but did not touch the stack of pancakes.

Billy wolfed down a western omelet, two biscuits, and pancakes smothered in Maple syrup. When he looked forlornly at Sara Sue's plate, she shoved it to him.

"Sorry," he explained. "But what you hear about prison food, it's all true. I wasn't sure what it was they gave us last night when I saw it. After I tasted it, I thought of roadkill soaked in ammonia."

Sara Sue laughed. "Maybe I could actually lose some weight on that diet. Nothing else seems to work."

Niki reassured her. "You look great. Don't change a thing."

Billy swallowed half a biscuit. "You said you would tell me why you're helping us so much."

Niki hesitated. "Your wife is my friend. She is also a fine person. She doesn't deserve to go through something like this. She deserves justice."

Sara Sue looked down, unable to maintain eye contact with

her husband or the detective. Billy still maintained a confused look.

"But you don't know me. Why are you assuming I'm innocent?"

Niki looked straight in his eyes, her sky-blue orbs unwavering. "Because I know Sara Sue. She would not be married to you if you were that kind of man."

Billy sat back in his chair. Sara Sue glanced up, and he whispered, "Thank you."

"Now," Niki said, "we need to talk about the case. We can do it here or go back to my office. We'll have more privacy there."

Billy cut a sausage patty in half and engulfed it. When he finished, he addressed her question.

"Let's do it here. I doubt if there is anyone left in Central who hasn't heard about my situation by now. I'm sure the rumor mill is rolling."

"True. I'm glad you realize what you're up against. This won't be easy on either of you."

Billy grabbed Sara Sue's hand. "I hate this is happening. But I did nothing to cause it. At least, thanks to you, I'm on the outside where I can help however I can."

"The best way to help me is to answer every question I ask honestly and completely. My first question is whether you want to do this in front of Sara Sue or would you prefer to be alone. Remember, I need the whole truth."

Billy straightened up. "I have nothing to hide. Let's do it."

"Let's start with Flavia Foster."

Niki watched Bailey's reaction to the mention of the cheerleader's name. He displayed no signs of deceit.

"Okay, shoot."

"The basics. You know her?"

"I know who she is. We don't have a close relationship. We don't have any kind of relationship."

Niki took a few notes. "When was the last time you talked to her?"

Billy looked up at the ceiling. "I don't know. I might have said *hi* to her in the hallway last week. Or it could have been the week before."

"Did you ever talk to her after practice?"

"No. Never." Billy stated firmly.

"Were you ever alone with Flavia in the film room? After practice? On a weekend? Ever?"

"No. Never." The coach was again firm.

"After the win last Friday night, did you have any contact with Flavia?"

"Do you mean when we all rushed onto the field?"

"Yes. Did you talk to or touch Flavia during the celebration after the game?"

"Geez." Billy brought both hands over the top of the said. "Honestly, I don't know. I was hugging everyone who got close enough. Players, parents, band members, other coaches. I might have hugged a cheerleader. I don't remember."

"Do you know LaDonne Elgin?"

"The name rings a bell, but I can't place it at the moment."

"Think hard. LaDonne Elgin. Do you know her?"

"LaDonne Elgin. LaDonne Elgin." He repeated more to himself than to Niki or Sara Sue. Niki waited, in no hurry to jog his memory.

The coach finally answered. "I'm sorry. I can't recall where I've heard that name before."

"She's a cheerleader, too."

"LaDonne. Of course. The Mexican girl. I mean, Latino. Yes, I know her. Why?"

"Let me ask the questions. Did you have any contact with LaDonne after the game Friday night?"

Billy replied. "Like I said before, I was so excited. We just beat the number one team in the state. My boys came through. That was all I was thinking about. I don't remember seeing LaDonne after the game, but I could have."

"How well do you know LaDonne Elgin?"

"Not as well as I know Flavia, which isn't saying much. I know her name is LaDonne just from listening to the guys talking in our locker room. They talk about all the girls, especially the cheerleaders."

Niki paused. "Do you participate in those discussions?"

"No," he exclaimed.

"Remember, I need the truth. It is all gonna come out, anyway. You might as well tell me now."

Billy sighed. He glanced at Sara Sue before answering. "I might have made a comment or two. You know, guy talk. I try to build camaraderie with the boys."

"Did you ever make a comment about Flavia's looks or parts of her anatomy?"

"No way."

Niki remained silent. Suddenly, Billy's chair became extremely uncomfortable. He fidgeted and squirmed like a four–year–old accused of taking a cookie with crumbs all over his shirt.

His voice was much softer when he spoke.

"I may have said something. But it was generic boy talk. I didn't mean anything by it."

"And LaDonne Elgin? Did you have the same generic comments about parts of her anatomy?"

"I—I guess so. But I was only adding to what the guys were talking about. Looking back on it now, it sounds stupid and immature, but at the time, I didn't think anything about it."

"Do you often discuss young girls' private areas without thinking about it?"

"Hold on," Billy showed his agitation. "It's not like that. I don't go around ogling little girls and then talking about them. The boys were talking about them, so I—I—"

"You jumped in and added your comments. Is that what you are trying to say?"

Billy face fell. "I guess so. How did you hear about that? It wasn't in the public. It happened in the locker room."

"It's part of the prosecution's case. Some of your players remember the conversations."

"And they told that—the prosecutor?"

Niki nodded. "The guys, at least some of them, are close friends with those girls. They are more than willing to testify on their behalf."

"Geez," he exclaimed. "They turned on me. I wouldn't have thought they would."

Niki put down her pen. "Don't blame them. In their eyes, they are defending the girls, their classmates. They don't see it as attacking you."

The big brunch no longer sat well on Bailey's stomach. He wished he had eaten less.

"But they were offhand comments. I meant nothing by them."

"When your words are printed, sometimes they don't look like what you think you said. In a situation like this, they can be damning."

"What do we do? I can't take them back."

Niki picked up her drink. "We have bigger problems than your locker room comments. The problem is those will be presented to the jury as part of your character, to tear down your image."

Sara Sue started to speak, but decided against it.

"What could be worse than that?" Billy asked glumly.

"Let's go back to the celebration after the game. What did you do? Please be specific."

Billy buried his head in his hands for a few minutes. After searching the recesses of his memory, he spoke.

"I jumped up and down like a kid. I hugged Jimbo Wax. He was standing next to me when the horn sounded. Then I hugged Floyd DeGeneres, our defensive coordinator. After that, the other coaches, then a bunch of the players. We all ran onto the field. I hugged our quarterback, a couple of the offensive lineman. Then the fans made it out to the middle of the field. I kept talking to and hugging every one of them. Somewhere, I took time out to shake the Zachary coaches' hands. Then I went back to the celebration."

"You didn't mention either Flavia or LaDonne in your recollection. Was that on purpose?"

"No—Yes—I don't remember either of them specifically. You keep talking about those two girls. Did they say something? Did they accuse me of something?"

"Quite a bit," Niki responded.

"What? What did they say that I did?"

Niki glanced at Sara Sue. "Are you sure you want to hear this?"

Sara Sue nodded, her lips quivering.

Niki continued. "Both girls told the authorities that you improperly touched them. They said you groped them."

"That's a downright lie. I was excited about the game but I never touched either of them in an inappropriate place, as you put it."

"Are you saying that you definitely did not touch those girls' breasts or bottoms?"

Digital almost choked. "No way. I'm not a pervert getting my jollies by feeling up the cheerleaders. Come on now. I'll testify in any court in the world I never touched them, at least not the way they are describing it."

"I wouldn't do that if I were you," Niki sighed.

"Why not? I'm telling the truth."

"If you don't tell the truth, I can't help you. You know that, don't you?" Niki held her gaze.

"I am telling the truth. How many times and how many ways do I have to tell you I didn't touch any girl in that way after the game? Why don't you believe me?"

"Because of these." Niki pulled two eight by ten photographs from her bag. She slid them across the table to Billy.

He picked up the first one. The photograph was crystal clear. They showed the happy coach surrounded by celebrating fans. His left hand thrust into the air. His right hand firmly clasping Flavia Foster's breast, the coach's arm holding the cheerleader tight.

The color drained from Bailey's face, leaving a sickly pale edition of his previous self. He did not attempt to speak, unable to look away from the photograph. Billy grasped it with both hands, still unable to keep the single sheet steady.

Niki glanced at Sara Sue. Billy's wife was fixated by the picture in her husband's hands. A single tear rolled down her cheek and dropped onto her blouse. Sara Sue picked up a napkin, dabbing at her eyes and wiping her nose.

Then Billy laid the photo down and picked up the other one. It was another shot of the happy coach. In this one Bailey was hoisting LaDonne Elgin. He held her off the ground, his face only one or two inches from hers. Both of his hands were under her cheerleader skirt, which was pulled up exposing her buttocks. Each of the coach's hands had a firm grasp on each of the girl's rear cheeks.

By now, there was no color left in his ashen face. Billy

made no attempt to speak, concentrating on the photo with unbelieving eyes.

Sara Sue took one quick glance at the second picture. Her mouth fell open.

"Excuse me." Billy's wife raced toward the restroom, her napkin covering her mouth.

"Honey, wait. I—" Billy did not know how to finish the sentence.

"Let her go," Niki said. "She needs to be alone for a few minutes."

The coach picked up the first picture. Now holding one in each hand, he studied one, then the other, all the time shaking his head.

"I don't know what to say," he began.

"If you were on the stand, you would be charged with perjury. I don't think a jury, whom at least some of them will be female, will believe you don't remember feeling up those girls."

"But I don't." His voice was little above a whisper. "I don't remember it even after seeing these pictures. I can't believe it's me in them."

"Sure looks like you," Niki nodded at the photograph. "Looks like they are the cheerleaders you claim you don't know well."

"I don't. I'm at a loss to explain this."

"You just happened to be groping the areas of their anatomies you talked about in the locker room. You want me to believe that is a coincidence?" Niki's accusatory tone surprised him.

"You're supposed to be on my side."

Her tone did not change. "And you're supposed to be telling me the truth. I can't help you unless I know the truth, whatever it is."

Billy's chin sank to his chest.

"This doesn't look good, doesn't it?"

Niki scoffed. "What do you think?"

Billy sighed. When he spoke, a signal of resignation filled his voice. "No. It doesn't look good. Not at all."

"Do you still maintain you have never been alone in the film room with Flavia?"

He picked up his chin. "I would definitely remember that. No way anybody has my pictures in there with her because it never happened."

"Are you absolutely sure?" Niki pressed him.

"Yes. Absolutely. Never. Never. Never."

Niki pulled out two more sheets from her bag. She slid them across the table. "Then how do you explain this?"

The somber coach silently read the entire two-page report. His eyes widened. Then he read it again.

Niki let him finish, then asked, "How do you explain it?"

"I can't. I wish I could, but I can't."

"What does it say?" Sara Sue appeared back at the table, the tears gone.

"It says—" Billy could not complete the sentence.

Niki did it for him. "It says that one of Flavia's old uniforms has blood on it. There are two sets of DNA in the mixture. One belongs to Flavia. The other belongs to your husband."

"What does that mean?" Sara Sue asked, her mind still garbled by the overload of information.

"According to Miss Foster's statement, it means your husband and she were having rough sex in the film room. Things got out of hand. She alleges that she slapped him, and he bled. Then he slapped her back, causing her blood to drip on top of his on her practice uniform."

"Oh, my God," Sara Sue said as she looked as if she was about to vomit.

Billy did not look much better. He kept staring at the

report, then back at the photographs, then back at the report. Shock spread across his entire countenance.

"There is more," Niki added.

She took another piece of paper from the bag. Billy made no attempt to deny anything at this point. He was a beaten man.

"What else can there be? Is she pregnant with my child?" He asked solemnly.

Sara Sue's hand went directly to her mouth. She again raced toward the restroom.

"Honey, I wasn't serious—" Billy called as his wife disappeared from sight. His shoulders slumped when Sara Sue did not turn around.

He picked up the paper and read it. There was no more emotion, no more disbelief. No more surprises. He dropped the paper on the table and looked up at Niki.

"Her blood was found in the film room. I guess that supports her story about the rough sex."

Niki nodded. "From an initial review, the prosecutor has a tight case. I don't see any holes in it."

Billy pleaded. "There has to be. The only thing I've ever done was to run my mouth in the locker room. I admit that. I'm sorry, but all this other stuff. I don't know where it's coming from."

"Do you still maintain that you aren't guilty?" Niki asked.

"He's innocent," Sara Sue was back at the table, a defiant look on her face.

"I need to hear it from him," Niki said. She nodded in the direction of Bailey. "He needs to tell me all this evidence is fabricated and none of the allegations happened despite the photographs to the contrary."

Billy shrugged. "I definitely never had rough sex or any

other kind of sex with Flavia Foster or anyone else in the film room. It did not happen."

"And the groping of the girls after the game?"

"I don't remember. I know that sounds terrible, but I really don't remember. If I touched them, it wasn't on purpose. I was excited. We were all excited. But I think I would have remembered something like that."

Niki took back the report and the pictures.

"If it is any comfort to you, LaDonne Elgin doesn't remember it either. When they asked her about it, she said she wasn't that close to you during the celebration. She was with your players."

"Then it didn't happen." Hope sprang in his eyes.

"She didn't say that. She said that somebody grabbed her butt during the celebration on the field, but she thought it was a player. Now she thinks it might have been you."

"He's in a lot of trouble, isn't he?" Sara Sue asked.

Niki smiled. "That may qualify the understatement of the year."

Billy frowned. "Niki, you had all these pictures and reports before the hearing. Right?"

The private investigator nodded.

"Then why are you still willing to help me?"

The strawberry blonde hesitated, toying with a coffee cup beside her plate. She answered, "Because I believe you're innocent."

8

CENTRAL HIGH SCHOOL

"Niki, come on in," Jimbo Wax's voice boomed.

"Thanks for seeing me, Coach. I know how busy you are with all that is happening." She took the seat across the desk from the assistant head coach for the Wildcats.

"No problem. How is Billy?"

"Not so good. The charges against him are more serious than he first thought."

Jimbo chuckled. "There's got to be at least a million rumors running around the campus, and none of them are good for Coach."

"That's why I'm here. I want to find the facts. Separate those from the rumors."

"Billy promoted me when he got here this year. I owe him a lot. Now I have a good future in front of me. Whatever I can do to help him and Sara Sue, just let me know."

"How well do you know the two girls who made the allegations against Billy?" Niki asked.

The assistant coach arched his eyebrows. "There are only

two? From what I heard, he was screwing all the cheerleaders and half the dance squad. I didn't know it was only two."

"I thought the judge released their names given the local notoriety, but I guess not. I don't want to expose the girls, so let me rephrase my question."

"Only two?"

"Did the coach show any special attention to any students at Central?""Did the coach show any special attention to any students at Central?"

"Sure. No doubt about it."

"Which ones?"

"The fellows that can run faster, hit harder, and catch a football better than anyone else. He favors the stars of the team, no doubt about it."

Niki did not bother to note that response.

"How about the female students?"

"Pretty much the same. From what I understand, he favors the girls that make good grades in trigonometry. For some reason, it seems more difficult for the girls than the boys."

"Any girls in particular?"

A couple. Sharon Landry and Maddie Cockerham. He likes both of them a lot."

"Do you consider those girls to be attractive?"

Jimbo laughed out loud. "Now you're going to get me in trouble."

"I didn't mean it like that. Let's put it this way. How would you describe these girls to someone who has never met them, but wants to pick them out in a crowd?"

"That's easy," Jimbo chuckled. "For Shannon, I'd tell them to look for the one with the biggest—Wait, you're writing this down—I'd tell them to look for the big-boned girl. Real big bones. For Maddie, I'd tell them to look for the skinniest girl in the crowd with the worst case of acne you'll ever see. Neither of them will win a beauty pageant anytime soon."

"How about the cheerleaders? Did Billy show any favoritism toward any of them?"

Jimbo smiled. "So some of the rumors just might be true? Damn, I was hoping it was all bull."

"Was Billy close to any of the cheerleaders?"

"Not really. Not that I'm aware."

"Did you ever hear the coach make any derogatory comments about the girls?" Niki asked.

"Those sorry—boys. I heard a few of them ratted out Billy."

"What did he say?"

"Nothing that every red-blooded man in the world wouldn't say. That includes me and every other coach on the staff and every player in that locker room."

"Again, what did he say?" Niki persisted.

"Some boys were talking about which girl in school had the biggest tit—mammary glands and which one had the best— butt. They took a vote and talked Billy into voting. Looking back on it, it wasn't the best idea he ever had, but he voted. So did I."

"Who did he vote for?"

Jimbo gave her a look of disdain. "Come on now. It wasn't like he was the only one who voted. The winners got almost all the votes."

"Who were these 'winners', as you so succinctly put it? Was Flavia Foster one?"

Wax winced at the name. "Flavia won the best chest and LaDonne won the best behind. It really wasn't close in either case."

"Did those two girls know about the vote? Did they know they were on the ballot for those categories?"

Jimbo held up his hand. "Hold on. You're making this

sound like sexual harassment or something. It wasn't anything like that. We were only having a little fun, that's all."

"At the expense of the girls. I bet they failed to find the fun in your little game."

"They didn't know, at least not before we did it. They didn't find out until later."

Niki shook her head. "How much later?"

Jimbo's exuberance faded. "The same day. That was last Wednesday."

"What was their reaction?" Niki asked.

"How the hell would I know?" This interview was not going the way he had anticipated.

"It wasn't that long ago that I stood on the very sidelines you now stand on. If you are like every other high school football coach in America, you have a group of players close to you and you're close to them. They would have told you whatever the reaction was from those two girls."

"I guess the best description is they were upset. They didn't take it well."

"Surprise. Surprise. Surprise." Sarcasm dripped off Niki's tongue. "Did anyone, including you coaches, ever think of going to them and apologizing?"

"Why?" Jimbo was amazed anyone would suggest such a preposterous idea. "They're just—"

"Girls. Is that the word you're trying to say? Geez. I don't know why any big macho football player or his coach would think a mere girl is another human being with feelings?"

Jimbo rolled his eyes. "There you go again. You're twisting my words again. We have nothing but respect for those young ladies."

"Sounds to me like y'all respect parts of their anatomy more than you do them."

"Can we move on to important stuff? This is getting old."

Niki laid down her pen. "It's obvious to me, Coach Wax, that you did not consider the impact of your actions on these two girls as worthy of your consideration, but maybe you might consider any possible consequences."

Something clicked within the assistant coach's mind. He leaned forward. "Are you saying these girls made all this up to get back at Billy? Oh, my God. They wouldn't ruin a man's life over a little fun, would they?"

"I don't know," Niki answered. "What you consider a little fun probably made them a target of a lot of unkind comments from other students."

"What? They won. They should have been proud." Jimbo said.

Niki closed her eyes for almost a minute before answering. "You don't get it. But let's consider your view of life. How many girls were on this ballot?"

"There was no ballot. The guys just nominated the girls they like, you know, the ones who qualified in each category."

"So how do you think all the other girls, the losers if you will, how did they feel when they found out? Do you think they were elated?"

Jimbo leaned back. "Hadn't really thought about it much. They weren't supposed to know we did it. I reckon if they found out, then they musta not been real happy."

"You think?" More sarcasm from the private investigator.

He ignored her comment. "Either way, if it was the winners or the losers, then they made up the things they are saying about Billy. He can tell the cops they're lying."

"It will take a lot more than a denial to get Coach Bailey off the hook. He has to overcome some incriminating evidence."

"Like what?" Wax asked.

"I can't you that. But I need some answers that may be of help."

38

"Shoot. Anything for Billy."

"How close were you to him after the win Friday night?"

"During the celebration?"

"Yes."

"I was standing right next to him when the horn went off. He was the first one I congratulated. After that, we kind of drifted apart. Why?"

"Because I need to know who got close to Billy and who didn't."

Jimbo did not look confident. "I wish I could tell you, but I can't. There were three or four guys taking pictures. Maybe you can get a copy of those. I know a lot of the pictures they took were focused on the coach. Plus, everybody has a cell phone these days. Gotta be a bunch of pictures on them."

"Thanks. I thought about the photographers, but I hadn't considered the cell phones. Those may turn up something."

"I'm glad to finally say something that might help. I've got a feeling I haven't done Billy any good so far."

"That helps. I don't have any idea how I will get them, but those pictures might come in handy for our side."

"Or the other side," Jimbo imposed. "What if they show Billy in a bad situation?"

"I don't believe so. Sara Sue would not stay married to a man with low morals."

Jimbo brightened at the mention of the name of Billy's wife. "Hah. She would win both contests. That boy done himself proud, that's for sure."

"I'll be sure to pass that onto her while she is trying to defend her husband of allegations of egregious acts. I'm sure she'll be elated to know you would've voted for her."

"Come on, can you get past that? Let's figure out how to help Billy."

"You're the one that brought it up. Did Billy cut himself after the game, by chance?"

Jimbo looked for answers on the ceiling. "Not that I can recall. It wouldn't have been impossible with everybody jumping on each other, and the players were still wearing their gear."

"What about enemies? Who would like to see Billy in difficulty?"

"How much ink you got in that pen?"

Now it was Niki's turn to be confused.

"I thought he is well–liked. He's been successful in turning the football team around. That used to be all that matters."

"You don't know some of the players or their parents. Some guys think they're a lot better than they really are. Their dads figure a donation to the Wildcat Athletics Fund should guarantee little Johnny a starting position. That's the way it was before Billy got here and started playing the best athletes."

"Any of them stand out in your mind?"

"Maybe the Kings. Steve King is the backup quarterback. He started last year as a junior, but a sophomore replaced him this year. Carl King is his dad. He played for Central back in the day."

"Is he a contributor to the fund?"

Jimbo nodded. "One of the biggest. More than fifty thousand last year. Now he's threatening to sue to get his money back."

"Has Billy talked with Carl?" Niki asked.

Wax chortled. "More like Carl talked to him. Told Billy he didn't know how things really work around here, that he would see to it that Coach wouldn't make the end of the season."

Niki put a star by King's name. "That moves him to the top of the list."

"There are a couple more," Jimbo cautioned.

"All right, tell me.".

"L. J. Wild. I'm not sure what the L or the J stand for. His boy got cut from the team. He's a good kid, but he couldn't tackle a rag doll.

Niki jotted Wild's name on her pad.

"Any friction between him and the coach?"

He paused. "Only if you consider getting knocked on your ass as friction. I guess his ass got a bunch of friction when it hit the ground."

"Wild or Billy?"

"Come on. Billy is an athlete. Wild is a sissy boy. Fights like a girl," he paused. "Didn't mean that. He fights like a sissy. Write that down instead. Anyway, he came to practice one day and mouthed off. Before you know it, he took a swing at the coach. Not his best decision of the day. Coach pummeled him. Hit him so hard, he dang near broke his own hand. I bet L.J. is still feeling that one."

"The players see the altercation?"

"Hah. The whole world saw it. And the ones that weren't there saw it on Huddle later."

"Huddle?"

"That's an outfit we pay to film our practices and games. Good outfit. Crystal clear picture. No more of that grainy crap where we can't see which player is which."

"Are you sure they filmed the fight?"

"Yep. Me and Billy watched it after practice. Then we told them to edit it out before they posted the practice on the net."

"So they post all the games and the practice films on the same site?"

"Yep. They edit out the down time. You know, time out, huddling, halftime, etc. That way the players and us coaches only watch the plays. That's what is important to us."

Niki grinned, her interest expanded. "How would I get access to the footage?"

"Sign on with them. It's thirty dollars a month or you use somebody else's logon ID. Everybody does it."

"Okay, anybody else?"

"You mean parents?" Wax asked.

"For now."

"Paul Nicklaus. His boy, Jimmy, got hurt in practices. He blamed the coaches."

"Why?"

"We run a drill we call '*wildcat*'. One player gets in the middle of a circle of players. Any other players that we point to tries to tackle the guy in the middle."

"And Jimmy got hurt when another player blindsided him? Correct?" Niki asked.

"Yeah. Our all-state linebacker laid a good one on him. Broke two ribs. One of them almost punctured a lung. Out for the year."

"How does this wildcat drill prepare the team for a game? I'm confused."

"It prepares them for life. The kids will get hit from a lot of unexpected directions during their lifetime. They need to know how to bounce back," Wax explained.

"Unless they get two broken ribs. Hard to bounce up from that, isn't it?"

Wax shrugged. "He'll be okay. It's hard for a girl to understand."

"Evidently, it was hard for Jimmy's dad to understand. Did you call him a girl, too?"

Wax shook his head. "He is the kind of guy to get revenge this way, though. He's too much of a wimp to confront Billy directly. This is more his style."

"Anyone else?"

"I probably shouldn't say this, but there is one coach who feels like he got the short end of the stick from Billy."

Niki said nothing, just waited.

"Ricky Delrie, our freshman coach. He believes that he's done well enough with the young guys to get promoted to coaching the varsity. Billy is new here and doesn't know Ricky that well. He told Ricky that he would have to wait and see how he did this year."

"That didn't go over well with Coach Ricky?"

Wax laughed. "Like the proverbial turd in the punch bowl. He thinks he's going to be the next Nick Saban or Urban Meyer."

"Would he try to ruin Billy's career?"

Wax sighed. "In my humble opinion, Ricky wouldn't piss on Coach Bailey if Coach was on fire. He would probably take pictures for his scrapbook instead."

"I'll mark him down as a 'maybe'. Anyone else?"

"I'm sure there is, but I don't know of anyone right offhand."

"This list will keep me busy for a while. By the way, who will coach the team this Friday?"

Jimbo hesitated. "I guess I will. I'm the assistant head coach."

"And first in line for promotion if Coach Bailey doesn't come back."

Wax stuttered. Niki left the office before he formulated a reply.

9

CENTRAL HIGH SCHOOL

THE INVESTIGATOR STEPPED out of the dim reception area of the athletic building into the bright sunlight. She took three steps before a young man approached.

"Are you trying to get that sick coach off? Is that what you're doing here?"

The young man appeared to be one of the students. The calculus booked under his arm confirmed Niki's suspicions.

"I am investigating the case, but I'm afraid I can't discuss it," she replied.

"You're going to discuss it. You aren't going to like the conversation much, but you're going to talk."

The kid dropped his book, and took off his jacket.

"Son, you don't want to do this. You have no idea what you're about to do."

"I ain't your son. I'm going to kick your ass so hard, you won't be able to take a crap for week. You ain't coming back here again."

Niki smiled.

"And just who am I going to get this whipping from?"

"My name is Steve King. If you like, I'll brand it on your ass after I get through kicking it."

"Let's see." Niki recalled the conversation with the Wax. "You're the young man that is no longer the starting quarterback. Is that correct?"

"I'll be the starter now that insane idiot is gone. Everybody knows I should be starting."

"Everybody except Coach Bailey," Niki reminded him.

"Like I said, he's an idiot. But that won't matter unless you stick your nose into it."

"Steve, trust me. I'm looking for the truth. Nothing more. Nothing less. I plan to continue to look until I find it."

"You're done looking."

The football player charged, swinging wildly with both aarms. The detective easily deflected the attempts. When the young athlete swung a roundhouse right, she took a quick step back. An elbow to the back of the quarterback's shoulder, as the blow sailed past her head, aided his momentum. He fell face first in the gravel lane leading to the office.

"I don't want any trouble, Steve. Quit this nonsense before you get hurt."

Steve King raked pebbles from his face, which was now crimson red.

"You got lucky. It won't happen again."

The youngster jumped to his feet and charged at the investigator. Like a linebacker avoiding a blocker, Niki deftly sidestepped the clumsy attack, and tripped Steve on his way by. He again ended up with his face in the gravel.

The student scrambled to his feet. Doubt now clouded his face. But when he looked around, other kids were watching. There was no way he could let them laugh at him because a weak woman was making him look like he played the tuba instead of football. He clenched his fist, getting prepared for another charge.

A firm hand clasped his shoulder. Niki saw a well-built young man maybe a couple years younger than herself holding Steve King back.

"Thank you," she nodded at the adult. "I didn't want to hurt him."

She started to walk away, but the athletic man stepped in her way. "You may like beating up kids, Miss Dupre," he snarled, "but how about trying on a man for size?"

Niki sighed. "Look. I don't want any trouble with any of the students or you, whoever you are."

"I'm Ricky Delrie, and I'm about to teach you a lesson about messing with one of my boys."

"Coach Ricky, trust me. You are in no position to teach me anything. I only want to walk peacefully to my car. Do you understand?"

The freshman coach sneered.

"What I understand is that you're not walking anywhere until I show my boys how a man takes care of business."

"Can we discuss this like adults? We—"

Ricky's swung while Niki was in mid-sentence. She saw his taut muscles tense as the coach prepared for the swing. Like a lot of amateurs, he wound up, lowering his hand behind his back to get more power in the punch.

Niki's instincts took over her body. Before Ricky could unwind, her foot caught him right under his rib cage. To her surprise, the kick did little damage to the rock hard body, but it caused him to miss with the punch.

Instead of connecting solidly, the blow grazed the top of Niki's head. Even with the glancing hit, the powerful punch caused her to stumble backward.

"See, Miss Dupre. It's a little different with a real man instead of a boy. You're about to find out the difference."

Confident now, Ricky bored in. He was a quick learner. Instead of winding up his punches, he threw short hooks and jabs at her head and body. Even when she deflected them, his fists hurt. It was evident the young man pumped a lot of iron instead of wolfing down double cheeseburgers in his spare time.

The primary weakness in his plan of attack was the position of his hands. He held both by his waist, almost creating an uppercut with each punch. This left his upper body and face exposed.

Niki's first effective blow was a straight jab to Ricky's throat. It caught the young man by surprise, causing him to gag. Two quick jabs, one to each eye, made him raise his arms in a defensive posture.

Niki whirled, landing her right foot squarely in Ricky's groin. She spun in the other direction, but stopped. The fight was over. Ricky crumpled over, groaning and moaning.

The private investigator inspected her bruised arms, red welts already apparent from deflecting the blows. But she was satisfied knowing that the young coach would now have to explain his two black eyes to his boys at the hand of a lady.

"You might want to get in your car now."

The voice came from the open doorway behind her. She turned to see Jimbo Wax watching, and the growing crowd of students. She had no idea how long he had been overseeing the event.

She nodded. "Thanks for your help."

"Anytime," he answered, before shutting the door.

Niki walked over to the freshman coach, who still could not stand erect. She grabbed him around the shoulders and helped him to a nearby bench.

"Nothing personal," she said after seating him.

He scowled through gritted teeth.

"That's what you think, bitch."

Niki walked back to the white Ford Explorer, keeping a watchful eye over her shoulder. She wondered how deep of a hole she had dug herself.

10

CENTRAL

"DONNA, how are you doing with the open cases?"

Niki sat her back down, in the townhouse, while addressing her partner.

"Pretty good, Miss Niki," Donna Cross replied. "A couple of them need some attention."

"Which two?"

"Mrs. Slocum's husband is a sneaking scumbag. He's leaving her almost every night again. She wants us to see where he's going this time."

"Keith Stroud wants you to check out a hedge fund manager. He's got a couple million dollars that just cleared from another investment, and this guy is promising him a nine percent return. He wants us to take a look before handing over two million dollars."

"Can't say that I blame him. What does the hedge fund guy invest in?"

"Can't say for sure. Mr. Stroud said hedge funds don't have to tell their clients if they are in stocks, bonds, and options, or blackjack. You just have to trust them."

Niki rolled her eyes.

"With my luck, he would put my two million on blackjack, and bust with twenty-two."

"I'll get as much information about the investment guy as I can. Do you want to tell Mr. Robinson about Mrs. Slocum or do you want me to?"

Niki thought for a few seconds.

"If you don't mind, why don't you ask Drexel to see what John David "Sleazy" Slocum is doing in his spare time. I have no doubt he is earning his nickname once again. The fund manager is more up your alley."

"You're really getting into this thing with the coach and the cheerleaders, aren't you?"

"Despite the evidence, I think Coach Bailey is innocent. Don't ask me why because I don't know, but somebody set him up well."

"Who?" Donna asked.

"I've got three pages of suspects, and not one ounce of proof against any of them. But I will get the answers."

"Why? As far as I can tell, we're not making anything at all on it. It looks like we're down a whole bunch."

Niki shrugged.

"I have a reason. Not one that you or anyone else will understand, but I can't let this happen again."

"Again? When was the first time?"

Niki smiled. "That's a long story."

11

CENTRAL

"THIS IS EARL WASHINGTON." The stockbroker answered.

"Mr. Washington, I am Donna Cross with Wildcat Investigations. Our client is considering investing a sizable sum with you and asked us to vet your services."

"That must be Keith. I don't blame him for being careful with that size of investment."

Donna chuckled.

"Sure is. He said that you are guaranteeing a nine percent return on his investment per annum. Is that correct?"

"Not exactly. What I told Keith is that nine percent is the minimum. We've made a lot more than that every year for the last five years. Our best year, we were up thirty-one percent."

"That's mighty impressive."

"We're proud of our returns. We put a lot of effort and research into our investments"

"What type of investments do you manage?"

Washington hesitated. "You wouldn't understand what we do. None of our clients know what we do technically. We just make money."

Donna replied, "I know a little bit about investing. Tell me what you do."

"We trade derivatives."

"Do you mean options, calls and puts?"

Washington cleared his throat. "Yes. Most people don't know what calls and puts are. You are in rare company."

"Thank you. I had excellent teachers."

Earl chuckled. "You learned about derivatives in school? Well, trust me. They don't teach you to do what we do."

"I didn't learn about them in school. But that's beside the point. How is your investment strategy so successful year after year?"

Donna could hear the pride in Washington's voice. "We write calls and puts instead of buying them. I wish I had time to explain it to you, but it's extremely complicated."

"Really?"

"Yes, it would take months for me to teach you how to write options."

"Hmm. The last place I saw it done, it only took about three seconds to originate a call or put, and list it on the electronic exchange. It took a lot longer to study the stock chart, and determine the trading range, and check for the earnings announcements."

"My, my." Donna heard admiration in the stockbroker's voice. "You really know about writing options. I'm impressed."

"Thank you. Do you buy covering options for protection above the call and below the put?"

"No. That would be costly and hamper our ability to give our clients the excellent returns they have gotten in the past."

"Do you write more puts than calls? Are you bullish on the market?"

Washington whistled. "It sounds like you've been studying our trading log."

"No, Sir. It's a natural inclination. Aside from 1929, black Monday, and the sub-substandard mortgage debacle in 2008, the market generally trends upward. The pandemic was the latest episode where it took a deep dive. Most people are bulls at heart. They expect the market to rise."

"Very perceptive. So you understand what we do, which is a first for me. What questions do you have?"

"What is your percent of deviation on percent returned?"

"Dang, you cut to the chase. The deviation is extremely small. We generally make one percent to two percent per month. When those returns are compounded monthly, it adds up by the end of the year."

"What about the months that yield a loss?"

Washington cleared his throat. "Fortunately, we haven't had but a couple of them. The worst one was about two percent."

"That's amazing. It's also a lie." Donna said.

"Excuse me." There was indignation in Earl's voice. "I can assure you that all our returns have been validated."

"By whom?"

"The financial institution that serves as our clearinghouse. They hold all the funds for our company. That protects my clients from embezzlement."

"No, it doesn't. All the institution does is provide a record of your profits and losses as well as any deposits and withdrawals. It may help in the prosecution against you, but it won't help them recover the money you have lost in the market."

"Young lady," anger filled Washington's voice. "How dare you make these allegations against me without proof?"

"I don't need any proof. I have common sense."

"Excuse me," the broker said.

"There have been several corrections in the market of ten

53

percent or more in the last few years. If you are writing unprotected puts that are leveraged at ten to one or more, then you have several months of double digit losses. With the margin requirements, you would have to liquidate some of those positions before they recovered."

"That's not true. You don't know which stocks we used to write the puts. How could you know what kind of returns we had without that knowledge?"

Donna remained calm. "To get two or three percent returns in a good market, that tells me you're playing with volatile stocks, not utility stocks. That means you took a bath in those down months."

"If you breathe a word of this to anyone, including Keith Stroud, I'll sue you and your firm for slander." The broker did his best to intimidate her, but the young detective could hear the fear underlying his words.

"There is only one way I'm not calling the Louisiana Office of Financial Institutions. That is if you show me the actual P&L statements from the clearing firm for your account."

"I can't do that. This is a private placement. All hedge funds are private."

"Okay, who is the auditor for the funds?"

"We have been an accountant, a third party who is not affiliated with our firm."

Donna laughed. "All that means is he regurgitates whatever numbers you give him to your clients. He does not audit your account."

Washington sighed. "What will it take to convince you we are on the up and up?"

"Give me the login ID and password for your account with the clearing firm. If I can look at the real transactions in your account, every option you bought and sold, then I'll be satisfied.

If I'm wrong, I'll give you a written apology and recommend you to Mr. Stroud."

"I can't—I can't give you my ID and password. That would put my firm in an untenable situation," Washington replied.

"All right, then I'll come by there. You log on and hide the ID and password. But I want to see the trade log. I want to see the actual transactions." Donna was persistent.

Washington hesitated. When he spoke, his voice was barely above a whisper.

"Come by after we close. I don't want my employees or clients know you are questioning the viability of our returns. What about six?"

"Sounds good," Donna replied. "You're right off of Sherwood Forest, aren't you?"

"Yes, and remember, not a word to anyone or I'll file a suit tomorrow."

"Don't worry. I'll be discrete. But there is one thing, Mr. Washington."

"What's that?"

"No tricks. I want to see it all."

"Don't worry, Miss Cross. I plan to show you everything I have."

12

BLACKWATER ROAD

NIKI LEARNED that Flavia Foster's father owned a home inspection service on Blackwater Road. With all the growth in the city, his firm was deluged with requests. Most home buyers wanted to know of any leaks in the roof, broken air and heating units, or malfunctioning appliances.

Flavia had always been the prettiest girl in her class. Or to be honest, she was the prettiest girl in the city, if not the state. She participated in the Miss Teen contest in Louisiana and easily claimed the crown.

Flavia had no single asset that stood out. They all did. Her thick blonde hair accented her perfectly symmetrical face, and baby soft skin. Her figure seemed to have been poured from a mold.

Flavia's full pink lips broke into an infectious smile at the slightest provocation. Her deep blue eyes sparkled gemstones. The curvaceous body was firm, yet graceful.

She was the model of beauty and grace in human form. The cheerleader was living a charmed life. Until—

Donald Foster was rightfully proud of his daughter. She was the oldest of his three children, the other two boys. The youngest was still in junior high, only fourteen years old. The middle child was a sophomore at Central and one of the school's better athletes.

Sean was the starting weak-side linebacker, unseating the incumbent senior who held the position before Billy Bailey became the coach.

Niki figured the overly protective father would object to a one–on–one interview with his daughter. She instead called him first. He was reluctant to talk to the detective, and referred her to the prosecuting attorney. She convinced him some questions would better be answered in private.

The private investigator found the home inspection shop behind the main residence. The four thousand square-foot brick home with a two-acre fishing pond reflected the new wealth of the Foster family. The shop was equally professional and ornate.

"Hello, Mr. Foster," she said when he answered the door.

She saw a strong man in his late forties sitting behind the desk. He looked nothing like his daughter. His dark black hair accented a pair of silver-gray eyes. His smile was not infectious because he didn't have one. A perpetual frown stood on his countenance.

Donald Foster glared at the private investigator as though she represented evil personified. There was no hint of help in his strong expression.

"What do you want?" He demanded without offering the investigator a seat. "I'm busy. I don't have all day."

"I need your permission to talk privately with your daughter. I'm trying to find out the truth."

Niki remained standing.

"No," he was blunt. "No sense in it."

"Mr. Foster, I don't think you understand. A man's life is at stake."

He half rose out of the chair. "What about my daughter's life? What about Flavia after what that scumbag did to her? I would use more appropriate language, but I'm a Christian."

"I can't say that I understand how you feel. I've never had a child, much less one in a situation like Flavia is in."

He exploded, rising to a fully erect position.

"Raped. Is that the situation you're dancing around, Miss Dupre? My daughter was raped by that lunatic of a coach, and now you are trying to get him off the hook."

"No, Sir. If Coach Bailey is guilty of the allegations against him, I'll be the first one to tell the judge. But I don't believe he is guilty, despite the evidence."

Drool formed at the edges of Donald Foster's mouth. "Then you are accusing my daughter of lying. She has already told the cops what he did to her. And it wasn't only one time. I hope you get him off. Then he'll be out here where I can get my hands on him."

"Do you realize that I will get to interview Flavia sooner or later? The defense has the right to question the accuser, even if she is a minor."

"I'll have her attorney with her. She won't have to answer your stupid questions."

Niki shook her head.

"That's not true. Your daughter is the accuser, not the accused. She has no Fifth Amendment rights to decline to answer our questions."

Foster sat back in his chair. "I don't want her to go through that. It's not her fault what happened to her. She doesn't have to say anything else."

Niki again shook her head.

"She has to give us a deposition. During that deposition, we can ask her any question pertinent to her character and her relationships, both with the coach and others."

Foster's eyes grew wide. "You plan to smear her name. That's it. You'll make her look like trash and a slut. I know the game. It won't work."

"We don't want to taint Flavia's reputation. But something happened or she wouldn't be making these accusations. We want to find out what happened."

"She has already told the cops. Why does she need to repeat this to you? This is a heavy burden on all of us." Foster put his hands together.

"Flavia has no choice. Coach Bailey has a right to a vigorous defense. Part of that defense is to hear the accuser's story directly. But if you wish, we can depose Flavia and have her come down to the courthouse rather than in the comfort of your home."

Donald Foster drummed his fingers together. He dropped his forehead until it rested atop his two index fingers.

"Okay. Here's the deal. You can talk to her. Only you. No lawyers. Not Coach Bailey. No one else. It will be only you and Flavia."

Niki paused. "Your daughter is a minor. She has the prerogative of having you or her mother present during questioning."

Foster shook his head. "Flavia is embarrassed by this. She doesn't want to talk about it in front of me. She is afraid of what I might do. It will be better if it's only the two of you."

"When?" Niki asked.

"Tonight at seven thirty. You can have one hour with her, not a minute more."

"I will be as gentle as I can, Mr. Foster."

He pointed both index fingers at the private investigator.

"I would suggest that you do. Otherwise—"

He dropped his thongs on the index fingers, simulating the firing of a pistol.

13

SHERWOOD FOREST

Donna Cross pulled into the parking lot of Washington's business. The building fit in with all the others on the block. Brick exterior. Tiled roofing. Manicured flowerbeds.

Only one vehicle was in the lot, a bright red BMW convertible. The luxury automobile looked as if it had just come off the showroom floor. Not a speck of dust. No dents in the bumper. No cracks in the windshield.

Donna did nnot know whether to go in. She tried the knob. It was unlocked. The young detective opened the door and entered the dark building. Not a single light was on in the reception area.

"Mr. Washington. It's Donna Cross," she yelled.

No answer from within.

"Mr. Washington, are you here?" A little louder.

Still no answer.

Donna opened the door separating the reception area from the rest of the building. She inched down the hallway past closed offices and turned left. She yelled again, but received no response.

The hourglass detective edged down the dark hallway, feeling along the wall. She tried each of the four doors in the first stretch. All were locked. When she turned the corner, Donna saw a light shining from the cracks under the door of the far office.

"Mr. Washington, it's Donna. I knocked, but nobody answered."

She stood in the hallway expecting the office door to open. It remained closed. Trepidation crept through Donna's body. Something was not right. Washington should be able to hear her from this position.

She pulled the Dan Wesson thirty-eight revolver from her bag. Donna slung the bag back over her shoulder and kept the gun pointed in front of her at the door. She eased down the hallway, though her instincts told her to back out and call the police.

But she would feel silly if she alerted the law and Washington was in his office listening to his favorite song or taking a nap. She was now a full-fledged detective, and should be able to take care of herself.

Donna rapped on the office door.

"Mr. Washington, are you in there?"

She twisted the knob. It was unlocked. Donna took a deep breath as the door opened, the revolver level with her chest. Then she stopped, frozen in her tracks.

Earl Washington sat in his plush chair behind the cherry desk. His lips formed a taut smile. The forced nature of his expression puzzled Donna.

"Mr. Washington, are you okay?"

He slowly nodded his head, the forced smile remaining. But he said nothing.

"I'm glad. For a bit there, I was getting worried."

She dropped the revolver to her side and took the three

steps to the edge of the desk. She stuck her hand out toward the broker.

"Nice to meet you," she said.

He did not raise his hand to greet Donna. It was then she saw Washington's hands were tied beneath the desk.

"What—?"

The blow struck the back of her head. The young detective crumpled to the floor. In a semi-comatose state, she heard the broker begging. Pleading.

Then she heard an explosion. The rest of the event slipped past her mind. She imagined holding her revolver in her hand, pointing it at the stockbroker and pulling the trigger. Another explosion. She struggled to open her eyes, but they failed to cooperate.

She heard the door closing, but it was far, far away. Then her world went dark.

14

ZACHARY

Drexel Robinson watched John David 'Sleazy' Slocum backing out of the driveway in the Ford F150 pickup. The dark gray vehicle blended into the black night.

The truck left the Fenwood subdivision in Zachary and turned south on Highway 64 toward Baton Rouge. It passed the ramp to the interstate and went straight.

When Slocum reached Florida Boulevard, he turned right, heading west toward the Mississippi River and downtown Baton Rouge. At the edge of the Mississippi, Slocum turned into the Riverfront Hotel, one of the more upscale establishments in the area.

Drexel tried to close the distance, but two other vehicles squeezed in front of him at the multilevel parking garage. The protective bar across the entrance did not raise until it was his turn to take a time–stamped ticket. He flew up the ramp until he saw Slocum going through the glass doors to the elevator.

Robinson slowed down and watched Slocum hit the *down* button. Then the senior detective searched for a place to park. All the spots next to the elevator access were taken.

He found an empty space one floor above the access doors. Drexel raced down the ramp and banged on the *down* button. He glanced at the stairwell and consider running down the four floors to the bottom.

He punched the *down* button again. The detective heard an elevator stop and soon after, the doors slowly opened. Four other people, two men and two women were already inside the elevator. They were dressed in formal attire, black tuxedos for the men and expensive full-length gowns for the ladies. Diamonds, rubies, and sapphires accented the distinguished women's choices of dresses.

Drexel hopped in and banged on the first floor button. Then he impatiently get the *close door* button.

"She must be cute," one gentleman behind him commented.

"Huh?" Drexel was not paying attention.

"I said the young lady you're meeting must be cute. Or rich. Those are the only reasons to be in that big of a hurry to get down there to see her." All four laughed.

"Yeah. Cute and rich," he responded.

"As long as your wife doesn't find out. If she does, you won't be cute or rich very long."

More laughter from the four.

When the doors inched open in the lobby of the hotel, Drexel leapt out of the elevator, quickly scanning the entire room. Slocum was not at the check-in counter. He was not at the concierge kiosk. He was not waiting at the bank of elevators to the guest rooms.

Drexel double checked, this time more slowly. A thorough examination of the plush lobby revealed no sign of Slocum. Two more possibilities, he thought: the bar and the guest shop.

He took the guest shop first, his logic being that if Slocum went to the bar, the businessman would take longer there than if he stopped to buy a quick gift or some flowers. Drexel walked into the shop and did a quick surveillance. No Slocum.

An aisle by aisle examination confirmed Slocum was not in the store. He walked as fast as he could without attracting attention. In less than two minutes, he entered the posh bar. It took another minute for his eyes to adjust to the diminished lighting.

No immediate sighting of the elusive target. Drexel ambled through the room as though searching for a business associate. He did not spot Slocum.

Drexel went to the bar and sat at the end, giving him a full view of the room and the door. The bartender sat a premium beer on the napkin.

"I'm looking for a friend. About six feet three inches, overweight, black hair with a little gray."

The bartender looked up as if seeing Drexel for the first time.

"Only about two hundred guys a night fitting that description come in here. Sorry."

The bartender turned his back and edged down the bar. Drexel opened his mouth to say something, but changed his mind. He left a twenty and walked back to the hotel atrium.

He stared at the bank of elevators. It was possible Slocum caught one and was now comfortable in a guest room. The slow elevator from the parking garage had afforded the target time to disappear. One way to find out.

Drexel walked over to a plush seat and sat down. He picked up the house phone from the table next to him.

"Can you connect me to John David Slocum's room, please?" He said when the hotel operator picked up.

"Hmm," the operator said while checking the electronic registry. "Sorry, Sir. We don't have a guest by that name registered with us tonight."

"He might be using his nickname. Do you have a fellow named Sleazy Slocum registered?"

More hesitation. "No, Sir. Nobody by that name is registered tonight."

"He must be staying somewhere else."

Drexel hung up the phone wondering how he would explain to Niki he had lost the target in the expensive hotel. That was a conversation he was not looking forward to with eager anticipation.

15

CENTRAL

Niki grabbed a quick bite at the Chinese buffet in Central. Unlike similar establishments across the country, this local restaurant offered delicacies from South Louisiana. Fried frog legs. Fried shrimp. Oysters on the half shell. Fried catfish. Boiled crawfish. Niki found these cultural favorites as well prepared as the twice cooked pork, the Moo Goo Gai pan, and egg rolls.

The investigator tried the fried shrimp dipped in a combination of hot mustard and sweet-and-sour sauce. Then she had to try the boiled crawfish. No self-respecting resident of the southern part of the Pelican state ever passed up the seasonal mudbugs.

She popped a shrimp into her mouth when someone stepped beside her table, towering over the seated investigator. She raised her gaze to find Ricky Delrie, the freshman coach of the football team at Central High.

Niki realized she was at a distinct disadvantage, being two feet below the powerful athlete with both legs trapped beneath the table. The coach stood at the end of the bench, preventing her from getting free without upending the table and making a huge scene. She was friends with the owners and did not want to cause a disturbance within the facility.

"May I help you?" Niki addressed Ricky.

"We have some unfinished business," he grunted, his fists balled up by his sides.

"There is no reason to finish it in here. The owners of this buffet are not part of our disagreement. I'd rather meet you outside."

Niki knew that one–on–one, with her legs and feet unencumbered, the advantage was hers. Despite the extra muscles, Coach Ricky was not an experienced fighter. In a fair setting, he was no match for the investigator trained in martial arts.

"No, I want to settle this right here. Right now." The coach took another half step toward the table.

Niki considered stabbing the coach in his leg with the fork in her left hand. The pain of the puncture would give the detective time to get from under the table, and on her feet. But it would also leave a bloody mess while the other diners tried to enjoy their meals.

The other option was a quick backhand to the big man's groin, which he was leaving unprotected, something an experienced fighter would never do. He might back into a table, but that scenario was better than her original plan of attack. Niki laid the fork on her plate, bought her hand into a fist and tensed her muscles. A split second before she struck, the coach took a quick step sideways and slid into the bench seat on the opposite side of the table.

"Look, I want to apologize for what happened at the school. It was stupid on my part."

Ricky folded his hands in front of him on the table.

Niki took a second to decompress. She saw the

embarrassment across Ricky's face and atonement in the young man's voice.

"Apology accepted." She stuck out a hand.

He accepted it and shook it with vigor.

"Thank you. I would like to explain what drove me to do it."

"Would you like something to eat or drink while you're here? My treat."

"I'll take a Dr Pepper."

They waited until Ricky received the drink before continuing. He drank half the glassful in one long swig.

"You fight really well," he said.

"Do you mean I fight well for a girl?"

He chuckled. "Yeah, that too. It's going to take me a long time to live this down."

He touched his two black guys gingerly, as if an afterthought.

"Sorry, but I couldn't let it go on very long. You're a lot bigger and stronger than I am."

He laughed. "That didn't keep you from horsewhipping my butt in front of the kids. I don't know how I'll ever get the respect back."

"You can start by being a gentleman. This is a good start with you coming here today."

Ricky dropped his gaze to the soda.

"You might not think so when I tell you what I came to say."

"Try me. You never know."

"I want you to quit this silly investigation. Flavia and LaDonne are great young ladies. I've had both in my science class. They are two of the finest girls at Central."

"Because Bailey is also a fine coach and teacher at Central. Doesn't he deserve the truth?"

Ricky sighed. "You already have the truth. Billy molested those two girls. I don't have any doubt about that."

"What brings you to this conclusion?"

"There aren't many secrets in Central. Everybody knows everything."

"And just what does everybody know?" Niki asked.

"That the coach and Flavia had a thing going on in the film room. That he told Flavia if she didn't do as he asked, he would expose her little brother for selling dope at school."

"The one that is a sophomore?"

"Yeah. Sean. I coached him last year as a freshman."

Niki took a notepad from her bag. "Is it true? Is Sean dealing drugs?"

Delrie shrugged. "I don't know. I know that he never failed a drug test as a player. All players have to piss in a bottle at least three times during the season. He was always clean."

"Have you asked Flavia about this?"

"No. But all the kids are talking about it."

Niki scoffed. "Student.com. Twitter, Facebook, cell phones. No rumor goes untold in that network."

"Maybe so. I can't argue that some things I hear are absurd. But that doesn't mean the rest of it isn't true."

"Let me make sure I understand. According to student.com, Coach Bailey was blackmailing Flavia into having sex with him. They supposedly did it in the film room after football practice and cheerleading practice?"

"Correct." The freshman coach nodded.

"Did any of the other students ever witness Flavia going into the film room?"

"None are admitting it. But LaDonne is saying that Flavia told her it happened, and that is one girl I believe. She and Flavia are close. I mean, as close as friends can be."

"Are you saying what I think you're saying?"

He shrugged. "That's been around for a long time. No new news there."

"They don't look like—" Niki protested. "Boy, that's stupid. What do lesbians look like?"

"Not like those two, for sure. That's why I always had trouble believing it. Also, Flavia has a boyfriend. Steve King. He was the starting quarterback before Billy came to Central."

Niki tried to put the pieces of the puzzle together. However, the young coach was adding more pieces that did not fit. Her puzzle was getting bigger and more complicated.

"Let me guess. According to the rumor mill, Coach Bailey threatened to disclose the relationship unless both girls did what he wanted."

Ricky nodded. "That's about the size of it."

"Have you talked directly to either of the girls?"

"That's not my place, but I heard about the contest the varsity took on the girls."

Niki paused.

"Were you there or did you hear about it?"

"I heard about it. Sean told me. He said it was embarrassing to hear about the other guys voting on his sister's boobs. Then when Coach Bailey voted with them, it was too much. He told me."

"What did you do about it? Did you go to the principal? The school board? What?"

Ricky flushed. "I didn't do anything. I work for the man. If word got out that I took something like that to the school board, what do you think my future would look like?"

"So you didn't tell anyone about this egregious act by the head coach?"

He again stared at his soda glass.

"I might have mentioned it to a few of the students in my class."

Niki blew out a long breath. "And you wonder where the rumors on student.com start?"

"That wasn't a rumor. It was the truth. I only wanted—I don't know what I wanted, but I didn't start a rumor. I told the truth."

"And you figured that if enough people knew about it, then it would eventually reach the ears of somebody on the school board, and they would fire Bailey. Am I close?"

Ricky refused to answer. He kept staring at the glass of Dr Pepper.

"Now you want me to forget about searching for the truth and let public opinion carry Bailey straight to Angola. Is that your plan?" Niki's voice rose in the buffet restaurant.

"No. I wanted to apologize to you for what happened at school. I also wanted you to know all the facts, to save you some time before you embarrass yourself and your company."

Niki could feel her temples throb.

"My reputation and my company's reputation will rest on the truth, whatever that is. If Bailey molested those two young girls, I will be the first one to testify for the prosecution. But I don't believe he is guilty."

Ricky half smiled. "You and Sara Sue, huh?"

"What?" Niki's face turned deep red.

"You have to know what is being said after about you and the pretty coach's wife. Do you think we're all stupid?"

"You're making a damn big case for it. For your information, Sara Sue provides temporary workers for my business. We have become friends through that relationship. Nothing more. Nothing less." Her fists clenched involuntarily.

"Right," Ricky replied, the sarcasm in his voice clear. "And you decided, because of this relationship with Sara Sue, to defend that molesting scumbag that you've never met? Who looks stupid now?"

Ricky looked smug, taking a sip on his soda. He even smiled, thinking he had just gotten the upper hand on the girl that had humiliated him in front of the students.

"I have my reasons for taking the case. I see no reason to reveal them to you. But I can tell you, I am in a relationship with someone. I love Dalton Bridgestone, the sitting United States Senator from Louisiana."

Ricky was speechless. He had been so sure he could expose the detective and the coach's wife. Now he was left with an empty hand. Well, not exactly empty. He still had one trump card to play.

"Your friend won't be so smug when the truth about Flavia Foster comes out," he sneered.

Niki shrugged. "Another student.com rumor?"

"Nope. There will be no doubt about this one."

Niki shook her head. "I've got a feeling you will tell me whether or not I want you to."

Ricky had an evil smile as he spoke the words.

"Flavia Foster is pregnant."

The freshman coach left Niki at the table with her mouth wide open. She watched him disappear through the glass doors before she could absorb the full impact. If Flavia Foster was carrying Billy Bailey's child, he was guilty no matter the circumstances.

Donna could see through the fog, but the vision remained a cloudy. She heard the moan emanate from deep within her body. The back of her head pounded, a hammer striking from within every three seconds. The back of her eyes burned like they were on fire.

The young detective felt the not on the crown of her skull. No blood, but sore to the point of unbearable to touch. She rolled over and tried to rise to her knees. The dizziness swallowed her entirely, preventing her body from maintaining its feeble balance. She collapsed to the floor, darkness engulfing her entirely.

Later, and she had no idea how much later, her eyes opened again. The fog subsided and her vision improved greatly. The hammering in the back of her head reduced to a sharp tingling. When she felt for the knot on the top of her head, it was barely noticeable.

Donna rolled up on her knees. The first thing she saw was her thirty-eight Dan Wesson revolver. Grateful that it was not taken, she snatched it up. Holding the weapon with unsteady hands, she rose in the dark room.

The door flew open and lights flooded the room, temporarily blinding the young detective. A scream pierced the air, echoing in her ears. When Donna opened her eyes, she saw the back of an elderly Hispanic lady running away from her down the hallway, still screaming at the top of her lungs.

Donna turned and realized why the cleaning lady panicked. Earl Washington, the stockbroker, was still secured to his chair, his face frozen in fear. Two bullet holes in his chest were highlighted in crimson red. His unseeing eyes stared back.

Donna knew in that instant that she was holding the murder weapon in her hands. The Hispanic cleaning lady saw her pointing it at Washington when the lights came on. The young detective was now a murder suspect.

16

CENTRAL

"Flavia, thank you for talking to me. I know how difficult this must be for you," Niki started.

"I can't believe that," Flavia Foster responded. "Have you ever been raped by someone you trusted?"

"No, I haven't."

"Then don't tell me you know how I feel. Unless you've been there, you have no clue."

Flavia pulled the blanket tighter around her as though it could insulate the teen from an evil world.

"You're right. I don't know exactly how you feel. Your dad said you were willing to answer questions for me."

The teenager's eyes grew hard. "I didn't do anything wrong except trust that bastard. He is the one to blame."

"You're talking about Coach Bailey?"

"Who else would I be talking about?"

"I want to make sure I don't misinterpret anything you say. I need you to know I am seeking the truth, even if that means Coach Bailey is guilty. Understand?"

Flavia wrapped the blanket tighter. "Then you already know he is. Why are you here?"

Niki shrugged.

"I know there is a lot of evidence pointing in that direction. Tell me how it started."

Flavia buried her head. "I don't want to talk about it. It hurts too much."

Niki ignored her plea.

"How did you happen to go in the film room the first time? Did Coach Bailey ask you to come?"

Tears welled in the cheerleader's eyes. Her lips trembled.

"I was looking for Steve. Steve King. He's my boyfriend."

Niki pulled out a pad to take notes.

"Why did you go to the film room to find him?" Niki asked.

"Because he watched them there with the coaches after practice sometimes. He was supposed to meet me at the front of the gym, but he was late. I found out later he was talking to the trainer about getting his helmet adjusted."

Niki watched the young girl, but Flavia did not look up. The blanket almost covered the teenager's mouth.

"Was Coach Bailey in the film room?"

Flavia nodded, but said nothing.

"Was he alone?"

Another nod.

"Did you go inside?"

Another nod.

"What happened after you went inside?"

The blanket dropped an inch or two.

"He told me to come on in. He held a chair for me right next to him."

"So you sat in the chair next to the coach?"

"Yes, Ma'am. He was the coach. I had to do what he told me."

"What happened next?" Niki asked.

"He asked me if I wanted to watch some plays that Steve did in practice. I told him I was supposed to meet Steve in front of the gym."

"Did he accept this?"

"Yes, Ma'am. But then he said something funny. Not *ha ha* funny, but weird sort of funny."

"What did he say?"

"He said that I could help Steve get the starting job back. I asked him how. He said that I would have to come back to find out. He said that I would have to come alone."

"Did you agree to come back?"

"Yes, Ma'am. I'd do anything to help Steve. I love him so much." Flavia paused. "Wait. That didn't come out right. There are some things I won't do even for Steve. You know what I mean?"

Niki nodded. "So you left the film room and nothing happened that day?"

"I could feel the coach staring at me when I left. I don't know how to describe it, but sometimes I know when a guy is watching."

Niki smiled. "I know. I get the same feeling at times, and most of the time, I'm right."

Flavia gave her a brief smile, relieved that the detective was agreeing with her feelings.

"When did you go back?"

"Two days later," Flavia answered.

"I told Steve I had to meet our cheerleading coach to work out some steps in a new routine. Then I went to the film room."

"Who was in the film room?"

"Coach Bailey and Coach Delrie. As soon as I went in, Coach Bailey told Coach Ricky they were through for the day, and he could go home. Coach Ricky almost ran out of the room."

"So that left you and Coach Bailey alone. Is that correct?"

"He motioned for me to sit in the same chair as before. I did. Then I asked him how I could help Steve get the starting job back on the football team."

"Did he answer you?"

Flavia shook her head. "Not at first. He told me Steve's future was entirely in my hands. He, meaning Steve, could be the starting quarterback on a playoff team or he could be a backup for the rest of his high school career."

"What happened then?"

"I cried. I don't know why, but I cried and couldn't stop."

Niki tried to imagine the young teenager sitting in the chair knowing what was coming, but blocking it out of her mind. That would cause any girl to weep.

"And?" Niki prided, although she wasn't sure she wanted to hear the rest of the story.

"He wiped my tears away with a cloth. He was so gentle I thought I might be wrong about his intentions."

Niki knew what was coming next. "But you weren't."

"No, Ma'am. While he was wiping my tears away, he brushed my chin and then dabbed at my sweater."

"I get the picture. What did you do?"

"Nothing at first," Flavia responded. The blanket rose back to her mouth. The words became harder to hear. "I just froze. I mean, I have been in cars with guys trying to feel me up, but never with an adult. A coach."

"What did he do then?"

"He set the towel aside and repeated what he did with his bare hand. But when he dabbed at my sweater, his hand stopped. He squeezed. Then he squeezed harder. Then he grabbed the other one and squeezed it."

Flavia could not hold back the tears. They cascaded down her cheeks, dropping on the blanket. Niki took a tissue from her bag and handed it to the teen. When Flavia reached for it, the blanket opened. Niki saw that the teen still wore her practice uniform.

Niki waited for Flavia to dry her tears and allowed her to continue at her own pace.

The teen's voice was soft. "I guess he took my inaction for approval. I was scared to death, Miss Niki. I hope you believe me."

Niki nodded. "Any lady in that position would be scared. You did nothing wrong."

Flavia shook her head. "That's not true. I should have fought back. I should have scratched his eyes out. But I just sat there."

"Is that when he had sex with you?"

She shook her head. "Not at first. He bit my breast through my sweater. He bit so hard that I screamed. I thought that would stop him, but it did just the opposite. He became an animal."

"Did he leave a mark?"

"Not through my sweater. But later, when I had my clothes almost off, he bit me again. It hurt. Really bad. I slapped him, finally coming to my senses. I bloodied his lips bad. Some of it got on my uniform."

"So that's why both his blood and your blood are on your sweater?"

"Yes, Ma'am. After that, it was a blur. I couldn't believe what was happening, but he was way too strong. He did what he wanted."

Niki began to have doubts about her own feelings. Everything this girl said corroborated the evidence in every way. It was beginning to look like she was wrong to defend Billy Bailey.

"What happened after that?"

"The pig watched me put my clothes back on. He was, I don't know, still ogling at me and smiling, but not in a good way."

"Did he allow you to leave?"

"He did, but he told me that if I breathed a word of it to anyone, then Steve would never play a down, and he would kick my brother off the team."

"Then?" Niki could tell there was more.

"I told him to go to hell. That I planned to tell my dad what he did, and that my dad would kill him."

"How did he react?" Niki asked.

Flavia hesitated for a long minute before answering. She pulled the blanket as tight as she could around her.

"I didn't tell the police this part. I didn't want for it to get out. Will you keep it a secret?"

Niki was caught. If she agreed, then she would not be able to use the information in the defense of her client. On the other hand, if she did not agree, then she would never know what the teenager had withheld from the police. She opted to get the information.

"I agree," she said with some hesitance.

"You can't tell Dad either."

Niki nodded.

"Coach Bailey said he would tell everyone about my relationship with LaDonne if I told anyone and if I didn't cooperate."

Niki stopped writing.

"By *cooperate*, did he mean to have sex with him again?"

Flavia's knuckles turned snow white because she gripped the pillows so hard.

"More than once. It became a usual thing. When he wanted me, he would stop during practice and say *hello, girls*. That was a signal for me to meet him."

"How often did it happen?"

"I don't know. I just closed my eyes and tried to get through it. Maybe six or seven times."

"And LaDonne? What do you know about the relationship between Coach Bailey and LaDonne?"

A single tear rolled down Flavia's cheek.

"Coach said I was getting boring. Not much fun anymore. He told me to get LaDonne to join us. He said that would spice things up."

"Did you talk to LaDonne?"

"Yes, Ma'am. But I told her not to do it. I told her he wouldn't dare expose our relationship as long as he was doing it to me. She agreed."

"What did Coach Bailey say?" Niki asked.

"He said to give her time, and something would happen to change her mind."

"What? What would change her mind?"

Flavia sat quietly for a long time before answering. Her head dropped to the blanket.

"I don't know. He never told me."

For the first time, Niki recognized clear deception on the teenager's face. She wanted to press the issue further, but wasn't sure that particular information was vital to her case. Instead, she changed the subject to the photographs.

"There is a picture of you after the game last Friday night showing Coach Bailey groping your breast. How did that happen?"

Flavia seemed baffled. "I haven't seen it. The lady, the attorney, said someone sent it to her, but didn't say who they were. But they were all jumping around and hugging each other. Then someone grabbed me from the back and squeezed my boob. I thought it was Steve. He does stupid stuff like that. But when I turned around, I saw it was Coach Bailey."

"Did he say anything?"

"No, Ma'am. Just smiled. I tore away from him and ran toward Steve. I cried. When he asked me why, I told him I was happy we won."

"So Steve never knew about your relationship with Coach Bailey?"

Flavia's eyes widened. "Are you kidding? If he had, he would've killed the coach if his dad didn't do it first. They both hated Coach Bailey."

"Okay, just a couple of more questions."

The relief became obvious when the teen's shoulders sagged.

"Good. This is a lot harder than I thought it would be."

"Who else knows you are pregnant?"

Stone silence. The cheerleader seemed to have quit breathing. Her blank eyes stared at the investigator.

"Flavia, who else did you tell?" Niki persisted.

"How—How did you know?"

"It's going around the rumor mill at the school. I wasn't sure it was true until now. After your reaction, I'm positive it's true."

Flavia emitted a loud well. It was so loud that her father opened the door.

"Are you okay, Honey?"

Flavia jumped off the sofa and raced through the open door. Donald Foster glared at Niki.

"What did you say to her?" He demanded.

"Only what I needed to ask to get to the truth. The questions may be a lot harder for Flavia at the trial."

Foster slammed the door shut, leaving the two of them alone in the room. He took a menacing step toward Niki.

"If I ever see you anywhere near my daughter again, I will break you in half with my bare hands." His hot breath blew in the detective's face.

Niki did not back down. "I don't break that easily, Mr. Foster. You won't be the first man to find out if you try."

Foster tensed to throw a blow. Niki prepared to dodge the haymaker from the burly man's right hand and calculated how she would counter punch.

"Don't, Dad. It wasn't her fault."

Flavia stood in the door which was now partially ajar.

"She made you cry, Honey," Foster addressed his daughter.

"She isn't the reason. This is all Coach Bailey's fault. Not hers."

Foster turned to Niki. "Get out, and I meant what I said. Stay away from my daughter."

Niki walked out to the Ford Explorer. When she got in on the driver's side, she did not immediately leave. Instead, the detective reviewed the entire interview with Flavia in her mind. Every piece of the picture seemed to fit perfectly in place. Every bit of evidence supported every word the teenager said. There were no loose ends. The case was open and shut. But—

17

BATON ROUGE

DREXEL ROBINSON WALKED BACK to the parking garage. Slocum's vehicle was still parked in the same slot as before. Robinson checked the engine hood, and it was cool to the touch. The car had not been driven since Slocum left it.

That meant Robinson was still in the hotel somewhere. But he had checked the lobby, the gift shop, and the bar. Slocum would have to have been extremely fortunate to get to the elevator bank, grab one, and get to someone else's room before the senior detective caught up with him.

Then it hit him. The restaurant. Slocum must be meeting someone in the dining room. There were so many eating establishments in Baton Rouge that the hotel restaurant was often overlooked by the locals. But the dining area itself was spread in an oblong pattern almost an entire floor.

Drexel had eaten there several times with clients in a hurry. The food would have been considered outstanding in most cities. In Baton Rouge, it was considered to be good.

Robinson approached the hostess with a smile and a

twenty-dollar bill in his palm. After a brief handshake, he asked about Slocum.

"I don't remember sitting anyone of that description alone," she said.

"How about with the companion? Maybe he was with a lady friend."

"A couple of guys come close to that, but I don't believe either is him."

"Do you mind if I look?" Wendy asked

The hostess did not nod or shake her head. She said nothing until Drexel pulled out another twenty. The hostess pointed at a table about a third of the way through the room.

"One of them is at that table down there. The other is seated with a young lady three more tables down."

Drexel sighed. He wasn't sure how he would show that forty dollars on his expense account. He had not reached the table before ruling out the man seated there. Two old. Too fat.

Drexel continued to the other table. As he neared, his heart beat a little faster. The man faced away from him, but Drexel thought he had found Sleazy Slocum. Same age, same build,

He strode boldly up to the table. Then he smiled to the attractive brunette sitting facing him.

"Hello, I am Pierce Randolph, Madame. May I say that dress goes well with that diamond necklace? Purely exquisite."

"Thank you, Mr. Randolph."

"Hey, but," the man grunted. "Leave my girl alone."

Drexel turned and froze. He was not looking at Sleazy Slocum, but at someone of similar age and body.

"Sorry, my good man. But your daughter reminded me of the stars in heaven, created by our Maker to add sparkling beauty to a dark night."

"She ain't my daughter, Bud."

Drexel turned and walked away, winking at the hostess on his way out.

18

SHERWOOD FOREST

DONNA CROSS HEARD the front door slam. Her instincts were split. Flight or fight. She knew she could escape before the cops got to her. The junior detective also knew the cleaning lady had a clear view of her holding the gun pointed at the dead stockbroker. There was also the distinct possibility Washington had made a notation in the log of his computer or in an appointment book about their scheduled meeting. Then there was the problem with her car parked in the lot. She decided to stay and tell her limited side of the story.

Donna sat on the floor next to the door, wondering about the depth of the pit into which she had fallen. She wished that either Niki or Drexel Robinson was there to help her. She picked herself from the bag just as the sirens came into hearing.

"Niki, thank God. I need help," she yelled.

"Where are you?" Her partner asked.

"At Washington's place, off of Sherwood."

Donna hurriedly gave Niki the address.

"What happened?"

"I shot Mr. Washington. I mean—"

Her sentence was interrupted by the first policeman through the door.

"Drop the phone. Drop the gun. Get your hands in the air," the cop screamed so loud that it shocked Donna into hitting the *end call* button before she finished the sentence.

Instead, the junior investigator dropped both the phone and the gun on the carpeted floor.

"I didn't—"

This time, her sentence was interrupted by the cop's body slamming into hers. Knocking her flat on her stomach. The two hundred forty pounds in uniform forced a knee between her shoulder blades, depressing her petite rib cage as Donna struggled to capture a breath of oxygen with each ragged gasp.

The policeman grabbed her right arm and twisted it behind her back at a sharp angle. The pain caused the young lady to cry out. The cop did the same with her left arm. Only when both hands were securely fastened in the steel handcuffs did he relieve the pressure of his enormous knee.

"Stay down. Don't move." He shouted much too loud to be so close.

His partner pushed past him and went directly to Earl Washington's body, still tied to the chair. One quick check of the corpse's pulse confirmed his suspicions.

"He's dead. Blood is drying up. Looks like he's been dead a while," the second cop stated.

"We'll let the medical examiner figure all that out. At least the detectives won't have to work too hard to solve this one," replied the first.

"Why do you say that?"

"Because we already have a confession."

The second cop pointed at Donna, who remained on her stomach. "You mean her?"

"Sure. Didn't you hear what she said?"

"No. What was it?"

"She's told someone on the phone she just shot Mr. Washington. My guess is the day got tied to the chair is the late Mr. Washington."

"I wonder who she was talking to," the second cop mused out loud.

"It was me. She was talking to me." A feminine voice sounded right outside the door.

Both cops turned and saw the long–legged strawberry blonde addressing them. Niki continued.

"Why is Donna in handcuffs?"

The first cop hooked his thumbs inside his gun belt and smirked. "Because she just admitted killing that chap tied up like a Thanksgiving turkey over there," nodding in the direction of the deceased stockbroker.

The second cop backed up his buddy. "If you were on the phone with her, then you heard her say it."

Niki stepped into the room. She addressed the second cop.

"You admitted you didn't hear her say anything. So don't go making things up. That won't go over with Samson."

At the mention of the head of homicide in East Baton Rouge Parish, the policeman lost his smirk. Then the first cop stepped forward.

"I heard her say she shot Mr. Washington. It doesn't matter who you know, it won't change what I heard."

"What you heard was Donna trying to explain what happened before you pointed your guns at her and barked orders. I heard that over the cell phone."

The first cop displayed his impatience. "I don't know who you are, little Missy, but you're about to be in the same position as your friend there for interfering with a police officer in his line of duty."

Niki gave him a knowing smile.

"I wouldn't try that if I were you."

He scoffed, looking at her lean frame. "Says who?"

"Says me." A deep, baritone voice boomed from the hallway.

Both policemen took an immediate step back from the brute of a man that loomed into the office.

"Sorry, Chief. We were about to teach this little lady a lesson about smarting off to cops."

Chief of Homicide Samson Mayeaux laughed, a rare experience for anyone to ever see the hard man do so.

"The only lesson that was about to be taught was by Miss Dupre. That's Niki Dupre, you numskulls. She would have kicked your ass is so high, you'll be crapping through your ears."

Niki turned to the chief. "Hello, Samson."

Samson grinned and gave the strawberry blonde a big bear hug, forcing Niki to gasp for air.

"Good to see you, Little Girl. Did these idiots give you a hard time?"

"No. They were perfect gentlemen," Niki laughed.

"Who is that?" Mayeaux pointed at Donna.

"Donna Cross," Niki replied. "She works with me."

Mayeaux turned to the two cops. "If you two perfect gentlemen will uncuff and help Miss Cross to her feet, and apologize to her, I might be able to keep Miss Dupre from kicking your asses."

The two cops did not appreciate getting dressed down by the chief in front of civilians.

"Now!" Mayeaux huffed, seeming to grow another six inches in stature.

The first cop hurriedly took off the cuffs and helped Donna to her feet. He started to say something before glancing at Mayeaux. Instead, he mumbled, "Sorry, Ma'am."

His partner followed by muttering under his breath.

Mayeaux called after them as they walked down the hall. "Be careful. Miss Dupre also has very good ears. Now keep everybody but the medical examiner out of here until I can figure out what happened."

The cops trudged outside past yellow police tape. Other squad cars had arrived, along with an ambulance and a fire truck. Both of those were sent away.

Inside, Chief Mayeaux surveyed the situation with keen eyes, leaving no detail of the office, the body, or Donna without scrutiny. After fifteen minutes of silence, the medical examiner came down the hallway. She walked directly to the body.

"In my expert opinion, the cause of death were two gunshot wounds to the deceased chest. I'll have to make a full autopsy to confirm my preliminary findings."

"Meg, you only want to run up a bill. I never took a single course in anatomy, but even I know whoever put their shots in him wasn't trying to give him two more holes to breathe through," Mayeaux said.

Meg Fulton, standing only four feet ten inches tall, paid no mind to the blustering chief.

"Two shots, three inches apart. Both appeared to be fired from about three feet away, according to the GSR." She glanced at Mayeaux. "That's gunshot powder residue for the uneducated."

Mayeaux guffawed at Meg's attempt at humor.

"Yes, Ma'am," Samson replied. "I've seen it a time or two. How long ago was it put on his shirt?"

Fulton ignored the question. She looked carefully at the two entry holes of the bullets. Then she walked behind the chair to find any exit wounds. When she found them, she frowned.

"What is it, Meg?" Samson asked.

"We're looking at two different trajectories. One shot came

from even with the dead man's chest. The other has an upward trajectory, indicating the shooter was on the floor."

"Caliber?"

"I would say it's a thirty-eight or a nine millimeter." Meg Fulton responded.

"It was a thirty-eight. He used my gun to shoot Mr. Washington," Donna pointed at her gun, still laying on the floor next to her cell.

"Don't say anything else until Doctor Fulton finishes," Niki cautioned her young partner.

"But I want to tell my side. I didn't kill Mr. Washington," Donna was almost in tears.

The burly chief took two giant steps to get right next to Donna. "I know you didn't, child. The evidence is all pointing away from you."

Both Niki and Donna were confused by the statement. Donna, because she knew what the cleaning lady saw, and Niki because of what she heard her young friend say over the phone. But neither responded to Mayeaux.

"All right, Doc," Mayeaux turned his attention back to Fulton. "You've had your fun. How long has this gentleman been departed from the earth?"

"I would guess about four, maybe five hours from the amount of rigor mortis in the body and the condition of the blood from the wounds. When I get the temperature of the liver, I should be able to confirm that time frame. That's about as close as I'll get."

The medical examiner finished her examination, and two assistants carefully bagged the body of Earl Washington. The rope that had been tied to the chair was left behind for the detectives that would follow. Niki and Donna remained with Samson Mayeaux in the office.

"What did you mean?" Niki asked. "You said the evidence

pointed to Donna not killing Washington. What are you seeing that I'm not?"

Mayeaux chuckled. "I heard that the janitor lady caught you red-handed pointing a gun at the deceased."

"Yes, Sir. But—?" Donna stopped when Mayeaux gave her a hard look.

"Did she see you get that knot on the back of your head? I saw it when you were still on the floor."

"That happened way before she came in. Mr. Washington was still alive when somebody conked me."

Mayeaux turned to Niki.

"From the looks of the body and the blood, I figured he had been killed for at least three hours before the maid discovered Miss Cross holding her gun on him. I needed the examiner to confirm my observations. If your friend killed Washington, why in the world which she continue pointing her gun at a dead man that long?"

A big sigh of relief escaped Donna's body. Niki put an arm around her attractive partner.

"Tell me exactly what happened," Mayeaux said to Donna. "Don't leave out anything no matter if you think it is important or not."

They went to the office next to the one where Washington was murdered, and Donna told the chief everything. From the phone call, the accusations she made to Washington about rigging the books, her arrival at the office, and seeing him tied to the chair.

"Then a guy knocked me in the head and I went down. I heard a shot but couldn't open my eyes. The guy put the gun in my hand, lifted it up above my body, and pulled the trigger again. Then I woke up, found my revolver and stood up. That's when the lady saw me," Donna finished.

Mayeaux looked up from his writing pad, although he had

taken only sparse notes. Niki knew the mountain of a man could recite Donna's statement without missing a single word. She marveled at the burly chief's intellect.

"You said *the guy* twice, once when he hit you on the head, and once when you said he raised your arm. How do you know it was a *guy*?" Mayeaux asked.

Donna rubbed the sore on her head "I don't know. I guess I assumed it was a guy that hit me, but now that you ask, I'm not sure."

The chief's eyes seemed to turn cold, black staring at Donna. She was glad she was no longer a suspect under the scrutiny of his piercing gaze.

"No, Miss Cross. When you said a guy hit you, the tone of your voice was one of certainty. You know it was the man they hit you. We only need to find out why you know."

Donna closed her eyes, rubbing the lids with the tips of her fingers. Neither Mayeaux nor Niki interrupted her attempt to recall.

Mayeaux gave her a bottle the spring water.

"Don't force it. Let it come to you. It will, if you give it a chance."

Suddenly, Donna grinned. "I've got it. I know it was a man and I know why."

"What is it?" Niki was more eager than Mayeaux.

"He was wearing a jacket. A Central High School coach's jacket. It was maroon and white, our school colors. I saw it when he grabbed my hand." Donna beamed from ear to ear.

Mayeaux's smile was almost as big as Donna's. But when the chief glanced from Donna to Niki, he saw a sullen look.

"What is it, Niki? What's troubling you?" He asked.

"I've got a sinking feeling," her tone a mixture of sullenness and doubt.

"Why?" Donna asked. "I thought you would be happy to know I saw him."

Niki put her hand on Donna's arm. "I'm glad. Mostly, I'm happy you're okay."

"They why the downer? You look like a dog they can't find the bone he buried." Mayeaux stated.

"It's because of the coincidence, and I don't believe in coincidences."

"Me neither," Mayeaux added. "What is the coincidence here?"

"The whole world knows I'm working on the case involving Coach Bailey and the cheerleaders. What they don't know is that Donna is available to help me with my increased workload."

Mayeaux now understood. "And that your firm just happened to catch a case where a Central High School coach murders a wicked stockbroker. You were supposed to be the one who came here tonight."

"That would be the assumption most people would make. I was supposed to die here tonight."

Mayeaux nodded.

"When Miss Cross showed up instead of you, then the guy improvised. He tried to frame Miss Cross, figuring your priorities would change to investigate her case rather than Bailey's."

Niki squeezed her friend's arm. "I would have. I would have dropped everything else to clear Donna."

"So we're looking for someone wearing a Wildcat coach's jacket. That certainly narrows our focus a bit. There can't be more than six or seven coaches at the school."

"One of them is not at the school right now." Niki's mood did not improve.

Mayeaux thought for a second. "Two questions. Could

Coach Billy be the one that wants you dead? Have you found incriminating evidence?"

Niki returned the chief's gaze.

"I'll answer the second question first. Yes, I have uncovered some information that may bury Coach Bailey."

"And the first?" Mayeaux prodded when Niki hesitated before finishing her answer.

"It's possible he could want me out of the way to prevent me from presenting the facts to his attorney. But then, those facts would eventually come out, anyway. They were not hard to find."

Mayeaux smiled. "And I know you. I believe you have taken meticulous notes about every fact you've uncovered."

Niki nodded. "Doesn't make sense, does it?"

Mayeaux rubbed his stubbled chin. "It does if you look at it from a different angle."

"What angle would that be?" Niki asked.

"You said the incriminating evidence has been easy to find?" He asked.

"Yeah," Niki responded. Then she smiled as her conclusions tracked those of Mayeaux's. "Too easy. Somebody wants me to stop here before I find out they're bogus."

Mayeaux nodded. "That would be my bet based on my limited exposure to your case. Now, you only need to find out who wants you to quit. One way or the other."

"That's the part I don't like. The *one way or the other* part."

19

BATON ROUGE

D REXEL R OBINSON SAT in a comfortable chair in the lobby of the Riverfront hotel. He was determined to spot Sleazy Slocum when he returned down the elevator. Maybe his date would accompany him to the lobby, and the entire night would not be a frivolous waste of time.

He reviewed his notes on Slocum's background while he watched and waited. Slocum grew up on the banks of Cane River in Natchitoches, the first settlement in the Louisiana Territory. He constantly was in trouble in high school, and those misfortunes followed him to Northwestern State University.

Though Slocum's intelligence was beyond superb, his grades did not reflect this innate asset. He rarely attended class, but managed to keep his grades high enough to remain in school.

His joy came from the part-time job he attained as a bouncer at the Blue Demon Bar on the outskirts of town. He took great pleasure in booting drunk college students into the parking lot, especially the football players who acted as if they were of a superior mankind. On more than one occasion, a starter on the football team discovered Slocum's other innate talent. He was a born fighter, able to take down much bigger and more powerful students with ease. It happened so often it affected the outcome of some football games. The head coach stopped by the bar to complain, but was told that if his players continued to be unruly, they were responsible.

That's when the idea struck the disgruntled student. He made large bets against the Blue Demons, many times more than the money he had available. Then, when some star players came to the bar, one or two would inevitably get into a brawl, and get thrown out of the establishment. During the process, the football player incurred an injury that affected their play the next day.

The quarterback received a sprained wrist. The speedy running back suffered a twisted knee. The defensive back developed swollen ankles. Never an incapacitating injury, but enough to interfere with their play. The players were afraid to tell the coaches about their injuries and face the wrath for disobeying the ban on the bar.

Then came the day of the Northwestern University game with Louisiana Tech. The Blue Demons, despite their misfortunes, were two-point favorites over the out-manned Bulldogs from Ruston.

Nobody would ever know exactly what took place at the Blue Demon Bar. After the melee was cleaned up, the star quarterback had a broken forearm. The running back's foot was smashed in several places, fractures in most of the tiny bones reaching his toes. Two cornerbacks and one receiver also sustained injuries that kept them out of the game the following day.

Immediately, the point spread changed. By game time, the Bulldogs were favored by three touchdowns. The bettors who took the early spread for Louisiana Tech could not believe their good fortune. Barring a miracle, they were certain winners.

No miracle happened. The Bulldogs blew out the Blue Demons. Louisiana Tech beat Northwestern by six touchdowns. The team from Natchitoches failed to score.

The bookies did okay, except for one odd bet. A student by the name of John David Slocum had placed a bet of eighty thousand dollars in favor of Louisiana Tech, a huge sum on a relatively obscure college football game. But, despite their suspicions, they paid Slocum.

That one game opened a whole new world for the young bully. He became the broker. Instead of kicking drunk students out of the bar, he talked them into making wild bets that had little chance of winning.

In another step on the road to manhood. Slocum discovered how easy it was to get away with murder. One student reneged on a large bet, refusing to pay because of the condition he was in when he placed it.

Slocum knew if he allowed one bettor to squelch on a wager, the word would spread to the other unfortunate gamblers.

One fall tradition in Louisiana's oldest city was the adornment of the cobblestone street on the banks of Cane River with millions of ornate Christmas lights. There was also a hut for Santa Claus to receive the lists from the local kids. It's sat below the cobblestone street, closer to the riverbank.

On a crisp Saturday night, Santa was shocked when he opened the door to the hut. Another Santa Claus sat in the chair. The one in the chair was dead. He turned out to be the student who would not pay the bet he placed was Slocum.

The cops questioned Slocum around the clock, almost certain he was responsible. But they found no evidence to support their suspicions.

Tired of school, Slocum moved to Baton Rouge. More people. More chances to expand his client base. But he ran into a problem. The problem was named Mac Swain.

Swain was the local kingpin of the seedy underworld of Baton Rouge. He had a hand in most of the illicit activity in the capitol city. After a few run-ins with the Irishman's enterprise, Slocum found that butting heads with the Irishman could be bad for his health.

That's when solid information about Slocum disappeared. But the rumors did not. Depending on which versions were popular at the time, Slocum was involved with insurance scams, loansharking, selling protection to local businesses, and a sundry of other activities.

The rumor that most believed was that Slocum had become a mechanic, a solitary hitman who would kill anyone if the price was right. With renewed revenue, Slocum paid cash for a house on Fenwood Drive in Zachary. He also bought a new F250 pickup truck with four-wheel-drive and a diesel engine.

Although the cops listed Slocum as a prime suspect in almost every unsolved homicide, they could never find any evidence linking him to the killings. Forensics discovered that six of his murders were committed with the same gun, a nine millimeter Glock.

They served a search warrant on Slocum for his home and vehicles and came up empty. The task force now in place increased surveillance on Slocum. But he easily gave them the slip, and many times they had no idea where he was.

Two more murders were committed with the same gun. The tax force was pressed to focus their investigation on other suspects.

The only rumored weakness Slocum had was a penchant for young girls, hence he was tagged with the nickname, *Sleazy*. But again, nothing could be proven.

Drexel Robinson was now a witness to Slocum's elusive capabilities. He sat in the lobby of the posh hotel until well past midnight. He stretched his legs and walked back to the parking garage.

When he glanced at the space where Slocum parked, he froze. The F250 was gone. Robinson stared at the empty space until a sedan honked at him to get out of the middle of the ramp. The detective staggered over to the middle of the empty space, his mind unable to accept what his eyes saw.

20

CENTRAL HIGH SCHOOL

LaDonne Elgin was nervous. Beyond nervous. Niki stared across the library table at the attractive teenager with the curvaceous body. She imagined those dark brown eyes had drawn the attention of several Central High School male students.

"Why—Why am I here?" LaDonne's voice unsteady.

"One charge against Coach Bailey is that he inappropriately touched you. It's my job to find out exactly what happened." Niki's tone was calm, as though explaining the job description of a nurse or teacher. She did not want to frighten the timid young lady.

"What do you want to know?" LaDonne asked.

"Tell me what happened after the game last Friday night."

LaDonne looked out the window, then at the door. The private investigator was concerned the teen might bolt at any second.

"Whatever they said happened. That's what happened." LaDonne could not look at Niki.

"I'm afraid you will have to be more specific. I need to know exactly what happened."

"I told you. Whatever they said, it all happened." A tear rolled down LaDonne's brown cheek.

"Who is *they*? Who are you talking about?"

LaDonne's countenance clouded in confusion. "Everybody, I guess. The whole school is talking about it."

Niki sighed.

"There are a lot of rumors floating around. I know some of them are not true. Why don't you tell me what really occurred?"

LaDonne hesitated. Her voice carried a completely different tone when she answered, as though she was reciting a speech from memory.

"We won the game. Coach Bailey lifted me off my feet. His hands were under my skirt. That's what happened."

Niki nodded, even though the girl displayed obvious signs of deception. Inwardly, she smiled, knowing that specific details often revealed rehearsed stories.

"Did he grab you before or after the horn sounded?"

"After," LaDonne replied after pausing.

"How long after?"

"Not long," LaDonne responded.

"Ten seconds? One minute? Three minutes? It's important that we know if Coach Bailey touched you or Flavia first."

"Uh—I can't remember."

"Think about when the game ended. Where were you standing?"

"I guess where we always stand. We have a section in the running track right behind the players' bench. Between the stands and the players."

"I'm familiar with it. I was a cheerleader at Central high not that many years ago. Were all the cheerleaders in that fenced off section when the game ended?"

"Yes, Ma'am. We aren't allowed to leave it except during halftime or when we have to take a bathroom break."

"If I remember, there are twelve girls on the squad."

LaDonne nodded.

"Where did you go right after the game ended? What is the first thing you did?"

"I guess we all jumped around and hugged each other. We were excited."

Niki now knew she was making progress.

"And after that?"

"I guess we all ran onto the field. Everybody else did. At least, all the kids."

"Is the student section still in the east end zone? Is that where the kids came from?"

"Yes, Ma'am."

"Were the other kids already on the field by the time the cheerleaders got there?"

More hesitation from the cheerleader. LaDonne could not decide what the right answer should be.

"I guess so. I don't remember."

"Did you climb the fence or go through the gate?"

"Uh—I don't remember."

Niki gave her a stern look. "Come on. You would remember climbing over the fence."

"I guess we went through the gate. What did Flavia say?"

"It doesn't matter what she said. I want you to tell me what you remember, not what she remembers."

"We—We went through the gate."

"Wasn't it crowded? That's the only gate on that side of the field. I would imagine a lot of fans were trying to get through the same gate."

Niki saw panic in the teen's eyes. She was not prepared for precise questions.

"I told you I don't remember. Maybe we climbed the fence. It was confusing."

"Let's assume you got through the gate. The field must have been crowded by then."

"Yes, Ma'am. Everybody was there."

"Okay. That means students, players, band members, the dance squad, parents, other cheerleaders, the coaching staff. Everybody was on the field."

"Yes, Ma'am."

"Who did you hug first?"

"Gosh. I don't know. I think it was a couple of the players."

"Do you remember which ones? Which players did you hug first?"

"I don't know. I ended up hugging all of them. I'm not sure what order I did it."

"When did you hug the coaches?"

"I didn't—I mean, I don't remember exactly."

"How many of the coaches did you hug?"

"I don't remember. Two or three, I guess."

"Was Coach Bailey the first coach or the last one? When did you celebrate with him?"

LaDonne put both hands together. "He lifted me off my feet. His hands were under my skirt. I was shocked. I didn't know what to do."

"That wasn't the question. Was Coach Bailey the first coach or the last coach?"

"I don't know. He could have been in the middle."

"You don't remember when an adult man reached under your skirt?"

"He lifted me—"

Niki interrupted her. "I've already heard that. What did you do right after Coach Bailey touched you?"

"Uh—I guess I kept on celebrating. I mean, we won the game."

"Did you tell anyone about what happened to you?"

"No, Ma'am. Except Flavia. I told Flavia."

"When did you tell her?"

"Right after it happened. I couldn't believe it."

"What did she tell you?"

"Ma'am?"

"When you told Flavia that Coach Bailey groped you, what did she tell you?"

"I don't remember."

"Where were you on the field when you told her?"

LaDonne squeezed her hands together. "I think we were walking off the field. We were walking together back toward the gym."

"So it was after most of the celebration was over?"

"Yes, Ma'am. We were walking off the field. I remember now." LaDonne's tone was more confident.

"Do you also remember what she said when you told her?"

"She called him a name. I don't want to repeat it. I don't use that kind of language."

"And she never told you what Coach Bailey did to her?"

"Not then. Just called him a name."

"And the two of you went where?"

"We walked to her car. We had to go home and change. We were going to a party at a player's house."

Niki nodded.

"Did you talk about the incident in the car?"

"Just a little. She told me I should report him to the authorities."

"Nothing else? Think hard."

"No, Ma'am. That was it."

"LaDonne, that makes no sense."

"But it's true. Every word of it. I swear I'm telling you the truth."

"That's isn't consistent with what Flavia told me."

"What did she say? Maybe I don't remember exactly right. I might be confused."

"Maybe so. You're telling me that Flavia never mentioned to you that Coach Bailey also groped her?"

"Uh—She did. I forgot."

"You forgot to mention something that supposedly traumatized your best friend. You remembered the name she called him, but you don't remember that."

LaDonne exploded into tears. Then she rose and raced out of the library before Niki could ask her any more questions.

21

NIKI'S TOWNHOME

BACK AT THE townhome that doubled as an office for Wildcat Investigations, the three detectives compared notes with each other. Niki found that it always helped to get a fresh set of eyes on difficult cases.

"I'm telling you," Drexel Robinson said, "that man disappeared like he was a ghost. One minute he was there in the human form, and the next minute he was invisible. I've never seen anything like it."

"Could he have gotten by you while you were in the restroom?" Niki asked.

"I didn't go to the men's room. A good surveillance man learns how to control those sorts of things," he replied.

Niki laughed.

"I'm glad you said surveillance *man*. When I've got to go, I've got to go. Surveillance or dry pants, I'm choosing dry pants."

Donna asked, "Did you go back to the garage after you went to the restaurant? If he made a quick trip to one of the rooms, he may have left why you were flirting with the girl in the restaurant."

Robinson feigned indignity. "Madame, Pierre Randolph is much more of a gentleman than to participate in such barbaric behavior."

Niki laughed again. "But Drexel Robinson isn't past putting his best move on an attractive lady, even if he is using the name *Pierre Randolph* at the time."

"Ah, Madame. You have exposed a foil in my character. I fear that although I have failed to improve, that trait is beyond my control. I can control my bladder, but not the urge to impress an attractive cherie." Then he cleared the tone of his voice. "To answer your question, Donna, that is the only time that I know that he had any chance to leave. Just dumb luck on his part."

Niki did not totally agree.

"He may have spotted you on his tail. He's been shadowed by the task force, the FBI, and lots of undercover detectives. Somehow, he still manages to do this over and over again without being seen."

Robinson ran a hand through his hair. "If he caught me, then he is the best in the business. Either that, or I'm getting too old and slipping up."

Donna piped up. "Did that attractive girl think you are too old?"

"Not if she was comparing me to her sugar daddy. He had a wad of cash that would choke a horse, because he didn't have any other alluring qualities." Drexel sighed.

Niki tapped a pen on her desk. "The only thing we can do is wait until he gets on the move again. Maybe he won't be so lucky next time."

"What did you find out from the interview with Flavia and LaDonne?" Donna asked.

"Unfortunately, Flavia is very believable. If she tells the

jury the same things she told me in the same way, then Coach Bailey is in for a world of hurt."

"That bad?" Donna inquired.

"Worse than bad. She covered every piece of physical evidence and made it sound like her story is the only way it could have taken place. She covered her blood, his blood, the photographs, the motivation, the opportunity. She is a prosecutor's dream."

"But is she believable?" Drexel asked.

"I hate to say this, but I was beginning to believe her myself. She can be a very sympathetic victim. She'll have the judge and the jury eating out of her hand when she testifies."

"If you believed her, then we are in trouble. You're not easy to fool. Is Coach Bailey really guilty?" The junior partner asked.

"I was thinking the same thing last night. After I had time to think about it, I was a bit distracted by your ordeal."

Donna blushed. "Ordeal? It was more like a nightmare. I've never been handcuffed and accused of killing a man before."

"That's not exactly correct. If I remember—"

"You don't have to go there. I remember that. Hey, he was a stockbroker, too." Donna exclaimed.

"Maybe you should stay away from stockbrokers," Niki laughed.

"Or maybe stockbrokers should stay away from you. They don't seem to have much of a future when you show up," Drexel added.

Donna did not see as much humor in this conversation as the other two. She tried to get the subject back to the Bailey case.

"Miss Niki, you said you believed her. Did you change your mind?"

"After I thought about it, I did. She manipulated me like a puppet. She took the conversation where she wanted it to go. Then, when she made her key points, she made sure the conversation was over. I don't see how she did it, but she outfoxed me."

Drexel grunted. "At least I have company. It was getting lonesome being the only one outsmarted last night."

Donna cleared her throat.

"That makes three of us. I walked right into a trap without a clue."

"We all had a bad night, no doubt about it. But if my interview with LaDonne is any indication, we'll have better days ahead." Niki said.

Donna grinned. "Did she spill her guts? Did she tell you they made everything up?"

"Not directly," Niki replied. "But she may as well have. She is not nearly as glib as Flavia. She had one line rehearsed about Coach Bailey groping her. But she was at a loss when I asked her for details. She tried to remember what someone told her to say, but they forgot to cover all the bases."

"So the young ladies made up the story. Why?" Drexel asked.

"That's the sixty-four thousand dollar question."

Donna frowned, a confused expression showing.

Niki answered the un-asked question. "An old game on TV. That's where the sixty-four thousand dollar question comes from."

Drexel laughed. "Not really, but I'm sure that's what you young people think."

"It doesn't matter," Niki said. "But the question was why. We need to find the answer to that before we can prove they're lying."

"Okay, what do you want us to do to help you out?" Drexel asked.

"You both have your hands full with your own cases. I can't take you off those."

Both detectives nodded.

Donna spoke first. "I may need some help on mine. I don't have a clue where to begin."

Niki's cell rang. The other two detectives heard very little of the conversation. Niki listened a lot more than she talked, her face growing more grim as the minutes passed.

"Okay, Samson. Thanks for calling."

She turned to the other investigators. "Samson. At least we now have a clue."

Robinson shook his head. "I don't like the sound of that. You don't look like you're pleased."

"You're right. They found some evidence. It won't help us defend Coach Bailey."

"What did they find?" Donna asked.

"He found a photo in Washington's desk. It's Billy Bailey being serviced by a young girl. He didn't recognize the girl, but that really doesn't matter. It will go to his character and his propensity to abuse underage girls."

"Wow," Drexel said. "So the theory goes that Coach Bailey went there to get the picture back one way or the other and finds out that Washington has an appointment later. Bingo. A new, better plan. Kill Washington and blame it on Donna."

Niki nodded. "That's what they're thinking."

"But isn't that a stretch?" Donna asked. "That's theory requires a lot of supposition and coincidences. How would Coach Bailey know that I would be carrying a gun?"

"That's what I was thinking until he told me they had more evidence. They found a weightlifting glove, the leather kind. It had the initials *B B* marked on it in permanent ink."

"Somebody could have put those initials on it and dropped it there. That doesn't prove anything," Donna said.

"But it will when they run the DNA test on it. I've got a feeling they will find Coach Bailey's DNA on the glove."

Donna hesitated. "That means the two cases are linked to each other. At least we can work together. If we can figure out one, we can solve both."

"They are definitely linked. But now we'll have to prove Bailey is innocent in two cases instead of one."

Robinson smiled. "Looks like I hit the jackpot. I've got the easy case, and it isn't linked to child abuse or murder."

Niki shook her strawberry blonde mane. "I wouldn't bet on that."

22

WILDCAT INVESTIGATIONS

Niki sent Donna to track down the film of the game. Huddle, the firm that produced and edited all the films in the area, had an office not far from her own. She sent Drexel home to get some rest. She wasn't sure when Slocum would be on the move again, but wanted Drexel ready to go on short notice.

The long–legged private investigator wanted to interview Ricky Delrie. He was the most demonstrative of all the coaches, and she felt like he had more to say than he did in the restaurant.

She walked outside the townhome, and toward the door of her Ford Explorer. That's when the egg splattered against the window of the vehicle. Without realizing immediately what the projectile was, the investigator dropped and rolled, coming up on one knee with the thirty-eight Daniel & Wesson in her hand.

The three boys froze, two of them with eggs still in their cocked hands. The one that had thrown the egg cursed out loud. This escapade had suddenly turned more serious than he had planned.

"Drop those eggs, boys," Niki said, now recognizing the scope of the incident.

The other two boys dropped the eggs. Niki watched the white ovals splatter on the hard surface. All three boys raised their hands above their heads.

The three young men wore leather jackets that signified they were athletes at Central High School. All three had football emblems, and one also had to figure of a basketball. The one with the basketball was in the middle. He had tossed the first egg.

"All right, guys. Go over there and wipe that egg off my vehicle," she instructed while holstering the revolver.

The two boys on the outside moved forward. The leader held out his hands.

"Hold on, guys." He turned to Niki. "We don't have any towels. How are we supposed to wipe up the egg?"

"You should've thought about that before you threw the egg. I don't care if you have to lick it off, but you will get it off." She answered, her body posture telling them she was not kidding.

Again the two outside boys took a step forward. Again, the middle boy stopped them.

"Wait, guys. She ain't gonna shoot us. We ain't armed, and she knows it. If she shoots us, they're going to put her in jail."

The want to his right nodded. The one to his left was not so sure. He took a step back.

"Come on, guys. Let's get her," the middle boy reached into the pocket of the letter jacket and more eggs appeared in their hands. All three hurled eggs at Niki and charged.

Niki deflected the first one. She caught the second and the third. Immediately, she returned fire at the two outside boys. The first egg got the kid on the right of the leader on his forehead. He jerked back. The second hit the other outside boy in his neck, yellow pigment oozing down the front of his shirt.

The middle kid charge of full speed, his head down like a bull focused on the red blanket of the Matador. Niki easily sidestepped the athlete and chopped his neck as he passed by. The tall young man fell hard on the parking lot surface. The boy on the right came in swinging. Niki caught his right hand and use the momentum of the blow to flip him over. The kid landed on his back, air in his lungs gushing out of his body.

The third kid, the unsure one, looked at his buddies on the ground and sprinted away. He did not bother to look over his shoulder until he was well out of sight.

The largest boy struggled to get off the ground. He turned to face Niki, an evil snarl on his lips.

Niki chuckled. "I'll give you this much. You're braver than you look. Not very bright, but brave. Are you sure you want more this?"

The kid spat blood out of his mouth.

"Ain't no girl going to get away with this. You're gonna pay."

He charged again. The results were similar to his first attempt. Niki watched him sprawl on the parking lot surface. She turned her attention to the other boy and took a step toward him.

The kid's eyes grew wide. He blubbered and wet his pants. After looking down at his soaked trousers, he turned and walked away. She refocused on the leader.

"You're all by yourself now. Why are you doing this nonsense?"

The boy rolled over, and managed to get to one knee. Niki had trouble understanding his words.

"Because you're trying to hurt Flavia. She's our friend, and we ain't gonna let you do that," he mumbled.

"I'm not trying to hurt Flavia. I'm searching for the facts, not the rumors and stories that are floating around the school."

117

"No, you ain't," the boy retorted. "That ain't what we heard. We heard you gonna get that pervert off."

"I don't know what will happen," Niki said calmly. "But I know at least part of the story is fabricated. It wasn't true last Friday, and it isn't true today."

"You got any proof?" The boy was now on his feet.

Niki considered the question. "I don't. But I will get some. If part of the story is proven false, and the whole lie will fall apart."

"How you gonna get the so-called proof?"

"We're working on it. Somebody will eventually tell the truth. I'm sure of that."

"We'll see. Ain't nobody at school gonna help you. Flavia is one of us. Always has been. Coach Bailey is new. He ain't one of us yet."

The boy spat more blood.

Niki saw no matter what she said, she had no chance of convincing this young man. In his mind, Flavia was as pure as an angel and Coach Bailey was as guilty as sin.

She briefly wondered how many others felt the same. She was facing an uphill battle. She needed to prove Billy Bailey's innocence. A simple not guilty verdict would fail to keep the wolves from his door.

The boy brushed off his clothes, and spat once more, this time directly at Niki.

"This ain't over. Me and my friends will be back, and we won't be so nice the next time."

He turned and walked away, his shoulders slumped.

23

CENTRAL

Niki changed plans.

"How are you holding up?" The strawberry blonde nests coach Bill Billy Bailey at his home in Honey Oaks subdivision.

The home was neat and orderly, a reflection of Billy and Sara Sue's personalities. The neighborhood was middle-class, mostly homes ranging from eighteen hundred to three thousand square feet. The Bailey's brick home was right in the middle, three bedrooms and two baths, on a large country lot.

The furniture was fairly new, but not expensive. The walls had more photographs and memorabilia than artwork. A bright purple and gold Afghan covered the back of the sofa with the words *Geaux Tigers* emblazoned across the park she could see. A signed LSU football helmet took up all of a short shelf.

"I'm doing okay. It's tough to sit inside here all day while I know somebody at the school is talking about me," Bailey replied.

He said in the over sized recliner, the TV remote resting on the table next to the chair. Old and fresh newspapers filled the magazine rack on the other side of the recliner.

"We're doing everything we can. We made some progress, but we've had some setbacks." Niki replied, looking around to make sure Sara Sue was not home.

Billy seemed to read her mind. "She's not here. She's at the shop. One of us has to work or we would both go crazy."

Niki smiled. "Good. There are a couple of things I need to discuss with you. And it might be better if Sara Sue didn't hear us."

Bailey let out a long breath. "What could she hear that could be any worse than what she has already heard?"

"This, for one." Niki pulled out a copy of the photograph Samson Mayeaux gave her in Earl Washington's office.

When she handed the picture to Bailey, he blanched. His mouth moved, but no words were forthcoming. The coach could not take his eyes off the images on the paper.

"When did this happen?" Niki asked.

"I—I don't know. Who took this? Where did you get it from?" Billy was flustered.

"Who is the girl?" Niki pressed.

"I don't know. I've never seen her in my life. I have no idea who she is. Where did you get this?"

"The police send it to me." She answered truthfully. "I'm sure they also sent a copy to the prosecutor. This won't look good at your trial."

"But that's not me," his voice shrill.

"It sure as hell looks like you. Do you have a twin out there that Sara Sue doesn't know about?" "No. No. No twins. But they can't be me. I've never seen that girl. I don't know who she is. You gotta believe me. Somebody is making this stuff up."

The look on Bailey's face was pure dread and trepidation.

"Disinterested know that you have a penchant for little girls?" Niki tested him. "No. She doesn't. Wait, that's not right.

She doesn't know because I don't. It's not me." Desperation replaced dread.

"When did it start?" Niki asked. "Or has it always been that way?"

"I don't have to say it more plainly. I don't have young girls doing that sort of thing to me. Not now. Not ever." His gaze still glued to the photograph.

Niki knew the prosecutor was preparing to grill Bailey mercilessly while showing this photograph to the jury. It was better to push the coach now rather than wait for the trial with the rest of his life was on the line.

"You know, there are several studies that have found most male teachers, including coaches, take those positions so they can be in contact with school-age girls as often as possible. Most fantasize about being with the girls. Many don't act now their dreams, but some do. It appears that you fall in the latter category."

Bailey's eyes were wide and unblinking.

"I'm telling you. This isn't me. I know it looks like me, but it isn't. I would remember something like this. It didn't happen."

"Okay, let's leave that for a minute."

"But you don't believe me. I can tell. You still think I did it." An accusatory tone filled his voice.

"It doesn't matter what I think. What matters is what the jury will think. If you have any skeletons in the closet, it's better to tell me now rather than wait until it's too late for me to do anything about it."

Bailey silently handed the copy of the photograph back to Niki.

"Do you know a man by the name of Earl Washington?" She asked.

"Sure," Billy replied without hesitation.

"How do you know him?"

"We put our IRAs with him. He is our financial planner. So far, he's done a good job."

"When was the last time you talk him?" The private investigator hoped it had been more than a year.

"Yesterday. He called me on the phone."

"Why?"

"He said I needed to sign some papers. He said he was moving our accounts over to a more aggressive portfolio. He tell me that as young as we were, we should take more risks so we can get a better return."

Niki groaned. "Please don't tell me you went to his office yesterday."

"Why? Why is it important? Yes, I didn't have enough to keep me busy around here. I already seen that episode of Gilligan three times. So I went down there and signed the papers. Then I left."

"Billy, I told you to stay inside this house. Not to go to the store. Not to go out to eat. Not to get gas. Nowhere."

"But I needed to sign the papers. Why is it important? Did Washington report me to the cops?"

"You really don't know, do you? Have you watched any of the local news today?"

He shook his head.

"The only news I watch is Fox News, mostly politics. I'm afraid local news will have something about my case, and I don't want to hear that garbage."

"Earl Washington was killed yesterday, not long after you say you left his office. Is that a coincidence? The police don't think so."

Bailey held up both palms toward Niki. "He was alive when I left. Whatever happened to him, it took place after I was gone."

Niki ignored his protest. "What were you wearing when you went to his office?"

"Hmm. What I already had on. Some sweatpants and a T-shirt. I put on a jacket because it was a little chilly outside."

The private investigator did not want to single out the coat, so she asked about the sweats first.

He replied. "Just regular sweats. Maroon, like our school colors." Niki did not like where she anticipated the description of the close going, but she had no choice but to ask about the shirt. Bailey pointed to the one he had on. Across the front it said, *Property of Central High School athletic department.*

"Like this one. I've got a bunch of them."

"In the jacket?" She asked.

"My coach's jacket. It has become my favorite since I began coaching here. Why all these questions about my clothes? I've already told you I was there. What difference does it make if someone saw me?"

Niki again ignored the question.

"Were you wearing gloves?"

Billy looked confused. "It wasn't that cold here yesterday. I didn't need gloves."

"I need to be clear. Did you have any gloves with you when you went to Washington's office?"

"Not that I recall," the coach answered.

Niki's time became more firm. "I don't need that kind of answer. That sounds like your dodging the question. Did you have any gloves with you, in your pockets, on your hands, anywhere?"

"No. I seldom wear them. I wouldn't have taken them with me yesterday."

"When do you wear them?"

"Only when I'm sitting outside in the cold. Like at a football game or deer hunting. If I move around, I don't need them. My hands stay warm."

"Are you positive? You never wear gloves at any other time?"

"Yes. I believe so. I can't remember wearing them any other time."

"I want you to think hard. Has there ever been an occasion where you work gloves except at an outdoor event are when you go hunting? I don't need a maybe answer. I need a yes or no answer."

"If you put it that way, the answer is no."

"So you don't work last when you lift weights?"

Bailey's eyebrows arched. "That's not the same. I was thinking of close. Those I wear weightlifting onto plus. They are—They are different." "What you call them?"

Bailey closed his eyes before answering. "Gloves."

"So what you tell me before wasn't true."

"It was. I wasn't lying. I just wasn't thinking of that type of glove."

"Where you keep that type of glove?"

"In my office in the gym. There's no reason to bring them home. I keep them in a locker in my office." He avoided eye contact with Niki.

"Are they still there?"

"Why wouldn't they be? Sometimes, I'd let one of the kids bore them, but I always get them back."

"When was the last time you saw them?"

"In—When I lifted weights last Thursday before I watched film. I try to get a few reps in every day, except game days."

Niki glanced at her previous notes.

"Were they marked in any way? Was your name on them?"

"I wrote my initials on them. B.B.. That way, I'm sure I'll get them back."

Niki's chin dropped an inch or two.

"What's wrong?" Billy asked. "Why all these questions about my weightlifting gloves?"

"Because he dropped one of them in Washington's office." She paused. "And you were wearing your coach's jacket when you went there."

"Hold on. I didn't drop my gloves and Earl's office. I couldn't have. I didn't have them with me."

"Then how do you want to get close end up on the floor next to a dead man who had a photograph of you in a compromising situation in his desk? Is it all just one big coincidence?" "Earl had that picture? Why? I've already told you it's not me."

"It sure looks like you to me."

"Why would I have a will weightlifting glove with me to visit my financial planner? It makes no sense."

Niki sighed. "It does of you believe the scenario that the police are considering. They think you went there with the intention of beating Washington to a pulp because he threatened to blackmail you with a photograph. When you find out that Donna was coming, you had a change of plans. That's when you decided to kill Earl."

"Donna? It was Donna?"

"My partner. She is the one that saw your jacket right before you hit her on the head, then used her gun to kill Washington." "I never met her. Why would the mention of her name make me change my plans, though I didn't have any. Not the kind you're talking about."

Niki mulled that's over for a minute. She looked directly at Bailey when she spoke.

"That's the first thing you've said that I'm positive you're telling the truth. There is no way for you to know Donna was working with me."

More confusion in Bailey's eyes. "What difference does that make?"

"Because whoever set this up expecting me to go see Washington. They weren't expecting Donna to show up. They wanted the police to think Washington had mention my name to you, and that was the reason you changed your plans."

"But I never had any plans. I only went to sign some papers."

"Was this the first time he ever ask you to come by to sign those kinds of papers?"

"Yeah. He told me the only reason was because of the change in the goal of the IRAs."

"Did he ask for Sara Sue to go with you?"

"No. He said that I could sign for both of us since Louisiana is a community property state."

"Just so you'll know it in the future, you can never sign for your wife on investment document unless she has given you the power of attorney for her financial matters."

"Oh." A sad expression from the coach. "I didn't know. I'm a football coach, not a financial planner."

Niki smiled. "At least I know the situation we're in. One more question. Have you made a substantial withdrawal of cash recently from your accounts?"

Billy laughed out loud. "That question seems I have substantial sums in my two accounts, one savings and one checking. I can assure you I don't. Sara Sue and I are just getting started."

"Good. That's one thing in our favor. Although maybe not. The courts may think without any money, the only way to prevent Washington from exposing that photograph was for you to eliminate him."

"I didn't know he had it. Heck, I didn't know there was a

photograph out there like that want anywhere because they can't be me."

Niki sat back in the chair, pretending to read through her notes, but in reality taking time to put all the pieces of the puzzle together in her mind.

When she spoke, she was clear and concise.

"Somebody is going to a lot of trouble to frame you for rape and molestation of minors. And now with murder. Who has something to gain with your demise?"

Shock filled Billy's face. "Are you saying that someone set me up for financial gain? That is ludicrous."

"Do you have a better explanation? Are you guilty?"

"No."

She nodded. "For a little while, I doubted you. But they made a mistake. The best way for their scenario to fit was if I went to Washington's office. Instead, Donna went and you have never met Donna."

"And now you believe me?"

"I do, but they've done a helluva job setting you up. You couldn't have done a much better job even if you tried."

"What now?"

"We find out why somebody wants you out of your job. Wants you out bad."

Daily rubbed both hands on his thigh. "I know of no one that hates me that much."

"Let's start with the basics. Who will replace you? Who will become the head coach?"

Bailey thought for a second. "It's up to the principal and the school board. The principal will make a recommendation, and the board will either approve it or reject it."

"Who is he likely to recommend?"

"Jimbo Wax. He's the assistant head coach, so it would be a natural promotion for him."

"Anyone else?" Niki asked.

"He's the logical choice. The others would probably move up. Somebody would have to replace Jimbo, and then that creates another opening."

She nodded.

"So, almost everyone on the coaching staff would get a promotion. How about the freshman coach, Ricky Delrie? How would he fit in?"

Billy's face clouded. "I made a mistake with Ricky. I should have moved him to the varsity, but I didn't know enough about him. But he's good. I should have seen it earlier."

"So he has something to gain if you're convicted?"

Billy gave a slight nod. "He will almost definitely move up to the varsity. I have no doubt about that."

"Who else?" Niki asked.

"That pretty well covers the coaches. Like I told you before, Steve King's dad is fit to be tied. Carl envisioned Steve playing for LSU or some other D1 program next year and now he can't win the starting job in high school."

"Jimbo also mentioned others." Niki checked her notes. "Jimmy Nicklaus was hurt in some sort of drill at practice, and Richard Wild's dad had a confrontation with you."

Billy chuckled. "LJ, that is Richard's dad. He was all hot and bothered because I cut Richard from the team. He was drinking one day and had a little too much."

"Did you hit him?"

"Yes, but only after he took a few swings at me. Luckily, LJ isn't any better athlete than his son."

Niki imagined the scene.

"So you busted him in the head and knocked him down? Am I close?"

Billy chuckled a little more. "That's pretty much it. Wasn't really much to it. He has never said anything else about it to me. I just figured he forgot about it."

"Would you? Would you forget getting knocked on your keister in front of your son and all his friends? Tell me you would forget it."

Billy was no longer chuckling. "That's not fair. There's a big difference between me and LJ Wild."

"And what is that?" Niki asked.

"I—I'm a man."

Niki scoffed. "And what is LJ Wild? Is he a woman dressed up like a man? Is that why you enjoyed hitting him so much?"

Billy grimaced. "You're twisting my words. That's not what I meant. He's not a—"

"Real man like you? Is that what you meant? One who takes pictures of himself with little girls?"

Billy stammered, trying to make a comeback. He slammed the recliner back to a sitting position and jumped out of it. He closed the distance between them, his fists clenched.

The coach stood glowering at the strawberry blonde for several seconds. Then his hands relaxed, and he returned to the recliner.

"Sorry. I've never hit a female."

"Don't worry about it. You weren't going to hit me either, but I'm glad I didn't have to prove it to you. I've never had a client before."

"All right, tell me about Carl King."

"He's a big donor to our athletic program. He figures that should buy him some favors. When I benched his son, he vowed to pay me back."

"Did he ever threaten you physically?"

"Nope. That's not his style," Billy replied.

"What is his style? What would he do?"

"Find a reason to sue me. Talk to the principal or the school board. More administrative stuff than physical stuff."

Niki kept looking at Billy until he became uncomfortable.

"What?" He asked.

"Don't you realize what you just said? You told me Carl King is just the sort of person to set all this up."

Billy wiped his forehead.

"I don't get it. Flavia and LaDonne are the ones that have to be lying. How does Carl fit in?"

"You said, or somebody did, that Steve King is Flavia's boyfriend. I'll have to look at my notes to remember who said it."

"You don't have to look. Steve and Flavia have been dating for a while."

"I ran into Steve King outside your office. He was not real pleased with you."

"That's an understatement. Kinda like not being pleased with a rattlesnake after he bites you."

"Does Carl King, Steve's dad, have the kind of wherewithal to put something like this together?"

Billy nodded. "I see where it could happen. He could talk to Steve. Then Steve could talk to Flavia. Then Flavia could talk to LaDonne. I see where it might have happened like that."

"Is Carl a photographer?"

Billy considered the question for a few seconds. "I don't know. Why do you ask?"

"Because, if you are innocent, then someone went to a lot of trouble to fabricate those photographs showing you with the girls. Those are a good bit more sophisticated than kids playing with Photoshop or a program like that."

"How do we prove it?" Billy asked.

"We have to find the weak think. I need to visit Carl King."

Niki's automobile alarm blared from the driveway. Without

saying anything, she raced to the front door. A pickup truck disappeared around the corner at the first cross street. She turned her attention to the Ford Explorer. All four tires were flat, having been slashed with a knife. Across the windshield were the words, *stop or die.*

"What is it?" Billy arrived around at the door, peeking over Niki's shoulder.

"Somebody wanted to send me a message. They just delivered it."

24

AMBER LAKES SUBDIVISION

Niki fumed while driving to Amber Lakes subdivision in Central. The new community was built just a stone's throw from the high school. The upscale homes were recently erected and most backed up to the man-made lakes formed when the contractor use the dirt to raise the building lots.

Carl King onto one of the higher valued homes in the exclusive neighborhood. Most of the homes consisted of fifteen hundred square feet to two thousand and sat on half-acre lots.

King's house, or more aptly estate, more than doubled the others and occupied over three acres. The Tudor mansion sat a few hundred feet off the street in the back corner of the development. The other homes shared the lakes with their neighbors, but Carl King had a private lake in his backyard.

A triple garage rested to one side with an enclosed walkway connecting it to the house. Niki could not see inside to find out if any cars were parked.

When she rang the doorbell, she half expected she would not get an answer. Thus, the investigator was pleasantly surprised when the door swung open. A neat lady in her early forties looked at her with a curious expression.

"May I help you?" The slim lady with jet black hair asked.

"I'm Niki Dupre. I have a few questions I need to ask Carl. Is he in?"

"What kind of questions?" The lady did not invite her in.

"I'm working on the case for Coach Bailey at the high school. I think Mr. King may be able to fill in some blanks if I can get a minute with him."

"He's not in." The lady shoved the door a little shut.

"Are you Mrs. King?" Niki stepped forward into the opening.

"I don't see where that is any of your business, young lady. Now, if you will excuse me—"

"Please. It's important. A man's life is at stake. Just a couple of questions."

The lady stalled, her eyes somewhat blank. She, from Niki's perspective, seemed torn between letting the private investigator in and closing the door.

"Please," Niki begged. "Three questions. No more."

The lady opened the door. "I'm Carla King. Please come in."

Carla walked stiffly to a large sitting room with a raised ceiling. Brown wooden beams crossed the area, giving it an outdoor feeling. Most of the art was photographs of exotic animals; elephants, tigers, lions, leopards, giraffes, bison, water buffalo, zebras, wildebeests. Most, except for the bison, could be found in Africa.

"Did y'all go on a safari?" Niki asked.

"Yes. You have two more questions," Carla King answered without expression.

"Did your husband take those photographs?" Niki pointed at the ones near them.

Carla turned slightly red. "No."

Niki had expected to get a lot more information from Carl King's wife. She carefully considered her last question, phrasing it to get a more expansive answer.

"Tell me about the problems between your husband and Coach Bailey."

"That's not a question?" Carla stated.

"Consider it asked in question form. What would you say?"

"I'd say it's none of your business. Now that you've asked your three questions, I need to get back to my business. I will tell Carl he missed you."

"Will you ask him to call me?" Niki held out a business card.

"That's an extra question," Carla did not accept the card.

"I'll put it here," Niki said as she walked over to an end table. "Just in case you get a chance to mention I dropped by."

While placing her card on the table, the private investigator glanced up at the nearest photograph. It was a magnificent image of a charging zebra stallion, it's mouth flared open and its ears flattened along the striped neck. Then her gaze fell to the autograph at the bottom.

C. King. And the date the photograph was taken.

Carla King had lied. Carl took those pictures that ordained the wall. They were of professional quality. Mrs. King knew a lot more than she had told Niki.

25

CENTRAL HIGH SCHOOL

Niki's new four tires purred along this short stretch between the subdivision and the high school. When she pulled into the athletic department parking lot, she saw several students in a cluster. Each of them stared at her vehicle.

Among the students were Flavia Foster and LaDonne Elgin. When they saw Niki looking at them, both girls hurried to the nearest class building, disappearing behind double doors.

The slim detective entered the gym to find Jimbo Wax and Ricky Delrie in a heated discussion. They were so involved in the intense conversation neither man noticed Niki until she was right next to them.

Ricky turned to her and flushed.

"What do you want? You ain't welcome around here. Did you get the message?"

"What message would that be?" Niki feigned ignorance.

"I know you received the message this morning. You must not be too bright. Next time, they may make it more obvious so you will understand it."

She walked within two feet of the football coach. "Next

time, why don't you send it yourself instead of using a bunch of innocent kids and possibly ruining their futures."

"I might just do that. Except I won't to be as nice as they were."

"Good. I would love to give you a personal reply, one that you won't have any trouble comprehending."

Niki turned from Ricky to Jimbo.

"Maybe we talk in your office?" She asked.

"I'm fine right here. Unlike Billy, I don't have any secrets to hide from the other coaches." He remained standing by Ricky.

"But I do. Unless you want to ruin every chance you will ever have of becoming a head coach, I'd suggest we talk in your office.."

The stern tone of the statement caught both men's attention. Delrie promptly walked away and yelled at some kids in gym shorts.

"Morning," Wax said, his posture tense as he walked toward his office before getting a reply.

Niki followed him into the small room and shut the door. She stood on the other side of the desk rather than taking a seat.

"You'd better quit prodding these kids unless you want one of them to get hurt," the investigator blurted.

"Wait. Wait just one minute. How can you come in here and accuse me of talking any of the students into vandalizing your vehicle?" He glared at Niki and rose from his chair.

"How did you know they vandalized my vehicle? It only happened a couple of hours ago and you supposedly have been in school all day. I said nothing about my Explorer getting vandalized."

"I—I must've heard the kids talking about it when they got back." The hesitancy of his words and the deep red color along the lines of his face told Niki the assistant head coach was not telling the truth.

"Jimbo, we both know you're lying. Now, I have two choices. I can go to the school board and let them know you are contributing to the delinquency of minors. Or—"

The assistant coach was beaten, and he knew it.

"Or what?" He sat back down in his chair.

"You can quit fighting me on this and cooperate. If not, you will get the students seriously hurt, if not killed. Do you really want that on your conscience?" Before saying the last sentence, Niki leaned over, placing her hands on his desk.

"It wasn't meant to be serious. A few of the kids wanted to leave you a message on your windshield. I didn't see any harm in that."

Niki leaned further over the desk. "You're leaving out the part where they slashed all four tires. Don't you think that is *harm*, or is it just more innocent kids sending me a message?"

Jimbo leaned back in his chair, putting as much distance between himself and the angry private investigator as he could.

"I didn't tell them to do that. I didn't know about it until they got back. I'll pay for your tires. I didn't mean for that to happen."

"R–I–G–H–T. Next time, send me a letter. That way, you won't be putting any of those kids in danger."

"Did you recognize them?" He asked.

"Nope. Didn't even get a good look at the vehicle they were driving."

Niki received a confused look.

"Then how did you know it was kids?"

She smiled. "I didn't until you just confessed. I knew somebody put them up to it, and it was the sort of thing kids would do. I figured I'd start with you and work my way down the list. Now, I don't have to."

She turned and walked out of the coach's office, leaving him with an open mouth and wide eyes.

26

CENTRAL HIGH SCHOOL

"I DON'T LIKE her being here," LaDonne said, while watching Niki enter the gym.

Flavia responded. "Relax. She knows nothing or she would be over here talking to us instead of the coaches."

LaDonne let the slat in the blind drop. "But you should've been there this morning. She asked me all sorts of questions. I didn't know how to answer a lot of them."

Flavia put her hand on her friend's shoulder. "Of course you didn't. You're in a state of shock. You're traumatized by being molested by someone you trusted. Someone you thought of as a father figure. That would confuse anyone."

"But you weren't there. You don't know how bad it was."

Flavia stayed calm. "She came by my house last night. There is no way she didn't believe me. When she got into things I didn't want to talk about, I cried and ran out. Then she had to deal with my dad."

"What if she wants to talk to me again?" LaDonne picked the slat back up, peering at the gym.

"Just cry and run out. Nobody can blame you for not

wanting to talk about what happened to us. Remember, we're the victims in this thing. Coach Bailey is the one who has to worry."

LaDonne turned and hugged her friend.

"I guess you're right. But I don't know how long I can keep doing this. I didn't know it would be this hard."

Flavia pushed her back at arm's length.

"Look, girl. We're in this together. I can't afford for you to get weak now. We'll both be in a boatload of trouble if you do."

"I'm just scared," LaDonne cried, tears running down both cheeks. "I didn't want anyone to get into trouble, including Coach Bailey."

"Me, either," Flavia replied. "But it's too late for that now. He's in a lot of trouble, and unless you want us to be in just as much, you had better keep your mouth shut."

"I know. But it's gonna be hard."

Flavia watched her friend walk out of the empty classroom. She picked up a slat and saw Niki walk out of the gym and glance in her direction.

The cheerleader hit a speed dial button on her cell. When the other party answered, she glanced around the room to make sure she was still alone.

"We may have a problem," she whispered.

27

WILDCAT INVESTIGATIONS

"Any luck?" Donna asked as Niki entered the office.

"Some," the strawberry blonde answered. "At least, I now have four new tires courtesy of Jimbo."

"Huh?" Donna stopped what she was doing.

"It's a long story. I'll tell you about it when we're all three together. I don't want to have to repeat it to Drexel. How about you?"

"I think so," Donna answered.

"What do you mean? That was as noncommittal as you can be if you ask me."

Donna let out a breath. "It's more of what I didn't find than what I found. But it is good news."

Niki plopped down in her chair, her mind exhausted from the day's interactions.

"I speak three languages; English, French, and Spanish. But your talking in one I'm having trouble interpreting. Can you tell me in one of those three what is so good about not finding anything?"

"Si, Señorita," Donna laughed, and even got a small chuckle from Niki.

Then she continued. "I got access to Huddle. You know, the outfit that films all the games. I logged onto the website and downloaded the game from last Friday night against Zachary."

"Yeah, we won. That's good, but I don't see how it helps us."

Donna nodded. "Me neither at first. They cut out all the time between plays, between quarters, and the halftime when they edit the film we can download."

"Okay," Niki said, unsure where the conversation was leading.

"That version did me no good, so I call the guy up at Huddle. He does the editing on all the film. He told me that was the only version allowed with your new subscription."

"My new subscription?" Niki did not know she had one.

"Yep. You are now a customer of Huddle. Anyway, that version didn't help, so I asked him if he could get me the unedited version."

"And he agreed?" Niki asked.

"Nope. He said he couldn't do it without the owner's permission. He just works there. You know how these computer geeks are. Not very radical, to say the least."

Niki nodded, secretly hoping to get to the conclusion of the story.

"Anyway, I could tell he was a geek, so I asked him if I could treat him to lunch. He agreed, and we met at Linda's. I didn't have any trouble spotting him, and I made sure he had no trouble spotting me."

"Huh?" Niki blurted.

"I wore a blouse from a couple of years ago before these grew out," Donna pointed at her chest. "That's all Norman, that's the computer guy, looked at the whole time. He didn't even eat his catfish."

"I bet," Niki said. "So now I'm out a subscription to Huddle and a lunch for two at Linda's for something you didn't see."

"Yes, Ma'am. But I got the full version of what they filmed. The cameraman kept rolling after the game, and they sold some of the celebration footage to a local TV station. You know, with everybody jumping up and down and running onto the field."

"Okay,"Niki said, still not sure why Donna was so excited.

"Here," the young partner said. "Sit at my computer and watch. Their software lets me highlight anyone I want. Just put the spotlight on them and they stay in a spotlight until you turn it off."

Niki changed positions with her partner and saw that Donna had keyed the film to the spot where the game ended. She had also highlighted Billy Bailey on the sidelines.

Donna reached over and moved the arrow key to the *play* button and clicked on it. The figures on the field jumped into action. The circle of light around Bailey followed him onto the field where he celebrated with his players. Then it followed him across the field when he went over to shake the hands of the opposing coaches.

After that, the film showed the coach returned to the celebration. By now, the fans, parents, and cheerleaders had joined the joyous affair. The cameraman kept filming until the elation died down and the field cleared.

It showed the coach walking to the locker room midst his players, slapping each one within reach on his shoulder pads.

When he got to the sidelines, the film showed his wife, Sara Sue, jumping into his arms for a long embrace that lasted almost two minutes. Many players walked by, grinning at the young couple in each other's arms.

When Bailey set Sara Sue back on the ground, he gave her one final kiss, and jogged out of sight to the locker room. A few seconds later, the film shut off.

Niki was tempted to run it again. "I didn't see anything."

Donna beamed. "Me either."

Niki shook her head. "How does that help us?"

Donna pointed at the monitor. "If Coach Bailey molested those two cheerleaders after the game last Friday night, we should have seen it on the film. It wasn't there."

Niki frowned.

"But there were times when he was in the crowd, and we can't see who he was hugging or where his hands were."

"True. That's when I went back and highlighted each of the cheerleaders during the celebration. Watch this."

Donna hit the button again, the focus highlighted on Flavia Foster. The third run of the celebration, she had a circle of light around LaDonne Elgin. When the third run finished, she sat back in her chair and grinned at Niki.

"They never got close to Coach Bailey, not one time," Niki exclaimed.

"Nope." Donna continued to grin. "And there's more."

"What more could there be? This is amazing."

Donna ran the film to the last part where Billy and Sara Sue were in an embrace. She stopped on one picture.

"See anything familiar?" She asked.

"No—Hey, it can't be."

"It is," Donna shoved the photograph of Billy with his hands on LaDonne Elgin's buttocks over to Niki.

"It's the same exact shot of Bailey as in the file. Same expression and everything. The only difference is that the butt belongs to his wife, not LaDonne Elgin."

"They photo-shopped it. This proves it. But the result was phenomenal. How about the photo with Flavia?"

Donna shook her head. "I haven't been able to find it yet, but this film is from a different angle than the photographs. My guess is that someone was taking pictures from the stands."

"That makes sense. Now we know how they did it. Next we have to figure out who did it." Niki stated.

"One thing is for sure. Both Flavia and LaDonne are in this up to their pretty little necks. We can probably put enough pressure on them to make them help us."

Niki went back to her desk.

"LaDonne, yes. I thought she was about to break when I talked to her, but now if I show her this film, she'll cave. I don't think Flavia will. She had me going in circles when I talked to her. Very believable. Plus, we don't have an exact image to confront her. She can always claim he did it while in the crowd of students and fans."

"But she didn't get that close to him. He was never close enough to her to grope her boob."

"It doesn't look that way from the film. I'd rather go after LaDonne. She's the weaker of the two."

"Want me to go with you? I'm free tonight."

"No," Niki answered. "I think I'll call her and set up a time to see her tomorrow at school. That will give her all night to worry about what we found. She'll be a nervous wreck by tomorrow."

Donna laughed. "That's evil."

Niki smiled. "No more evil than what those two girls had done to Billy Bailey and Sara Sue."

28

CENTRAL

"HELLO, LADONNE. THIS IS NIKI DUPRE," the private investigator said into her cell.

"Hi." A timid reply from the teenager.

"Hey, we found some new evidence in the case. I need to show it to you before I take it to the police."

"Police?" LaDonne barely whispered. "What evidence?"

"I'd rather show it to you than tell you about it. Once you see it, then we can talk."

"I'm busy. I don't have time. I've got a ton of homework tonight."

Niki chuckled.

"No problem. What time is your study hour tomorrow? I can come by the school then."

"Uh—Tomorrow is not a good day. I have a lot of studying to do. I have three big tests next week."

"Okay, I'll come by at lunch. I don't mind having the other kids around if you don't. But I have to warn you. You may want to be alone with me when you see what I have."

Niki heard a deep intake of breath on the other end.

"Come on by during study hour. I can meet with you in the library again. My study hour is the second class period."

"Great. I'll see you then."

"Wait," LaDonne yelled. "Can you at least tell me what you found. If you're gonna show me tomorrow, you might as well tell me tonight."

"I'll wait," Niki replied. "After you see it, I'll have a few questions for you. Those will better be asked face–to–face. See you tomorrow."

Niki hung up, leaving a worried teenager on the other end of the call.

29

CENTRAL

"WHAT DO YOU THINK IT IS?" LaDonne asked.

"There is no telling," Flavia replied into the cell.

"I'm scared. What if she knows?"

"She will have to prove it. There is no way she has proof or she would have already gone to the cops."

LaDonne blubbered. "Why is she coming to see me? Why not you?"

"I don't know. Maybe Niki thinks you're a lot easier to scare than me. Maybe this is just one big hoax to get you to admit something."

LaDonne continued to cry. "I don't think so. She sounded too sure of herself, like she had some kind of evidence. What could she have?"

Flavia was getting frustrated with her friend and concerned at the same time.

"You've got to keep it together. If we fall apart now, we'll both be in hot water, maybe with an appointment at the juvenile center or jail for a long time. Is that what you want?"

The sobs increased.

"Jail? I can't go to jail. I wouldn't last a week in there. Do you know what they do to new girls in jail?"

Flavia's tone was much more harsh. "Listen, you don't have a choice. We've already done what we've done. We can't go back and undo it."

"We've got to do something," the desperation in LaDonne's voice overrode all other emotions. "I can't talk to her tomorrow. Is there anything we can do to keep me from doing that?"

"We may do something. Here's what I want you to do. But you have to promise not to tell anyone. This has to stay between us."

30

CENTRAL

"Coach Bailey, this is LaDonne Elgin."

"LaDonne? Why are you calling me? I'm not supposed to be in contact with you or Flavia or I can go to jail."

The feminine teenager replied, "Don't worry. You didn't contact me. I contacted you. You can't control who I talk to. You won't to get in any trouble."

Bailey paused for a few seconds. He was debating whether to hang up and report the incident to Niki, or to listen to the teenager. While he was trying to make a decision, she continued.

"Please, Coach. I've done some terrible things to you, and I want to tell you about them."

"Okay, tell me," Billy made his choice.

"No. I want to tell you in person, not over the phone. You might be recording this."

Bailey shook his head even though LaDonne could not see him. "I'm not recording anything."

"Can you meet me tonight?" The teen asked.

"Sure. I'll need to let Niki know. She may want to come with me."

"You can't do that," LaDonne pleaded. "This is hard enough admitting what I've done to you. I don't want to have to explain it to her."

Another longer pause.

"How do I know you're telling the truth? How do I know this isn't a trick that will get me in more trouble?"

A soft chuckle. "How much more trouble can you get in, Coach? It looks to me as if you're at the bottom of the barrel now."

Bailey sighed. "Tell me something that makes me believe you. I need to know something before I agree to meet with you."

This time, LaDonne was the one that paused.

"Okay." She finally said. "I know they've shown you the photographs of you groping me and Flavia."

"I saw them." The images had not left the young coached since Niki showed them to him.

"They're fake. They're not real," she said.

"Jesus. I knew it. I knew I would remember doing something like that even under those circumstances. How did you two do it?"

"Well," LaDonne began. "That's what I want to talk to you about. That's why I want to meet you."

"Can't you just tell me over the phone?" He asked.

"No, Sir. It involves someone else besides me and Flavia. I'm not going to tell you who that is that's over the phone. I will tell you if you meet with me."

Adrenaline flowed through Billy Bailey's body like flavoring through a sno-cone. The cloud that had been hanging over him for the last few days now had a ray of light piercing through. While his curiosity was strong, his elation was even higher.

"Where do you want to meet?" He asked.

"On the football field. By the bench on the home side of the fifty yard line. Come through the fan's entrance at the end of the field on the other side. That way, I can see you for a long time and I'll be able to tell if you're alone."

"What time?" He asked.

"Midnight. If I see anyone with you, I'll leave and you'll never know what I have to tell you."

Bailey let out a deep breath. It was not the best situation he could imagine, but it was a lot better than the one he was in before the phone call.

"I'll be there. But I have to warn you. No tricks."

He spoke as sternly as he could under the circumstances, though he knew his words held little threat to the teenager.

"Don't worry. You'll be impressed and surprised at what I have waiting for you." LaDonne hung up.

Bailey put the phone down and then picked it up again. He wanted to hit the speed dial button for Niki Dupre. But if he did, he knew she would not allow him to meet with an alleged victim alone in the middle of the night. He placed the phone back on the table.

31

BATON ROUGE

Drexel Robinson watched Sleazy Slocum pull out of his driveway around nine o'clock. He followed the vehicle until he was sure it turned east on Florida Boulevard toward the posh hotel on the banks of the Mississippi River.

Robinson passed Slocum's car on the four-lane highway without glancing over at the target of his investigation. He sped past the remaining dozen blocks and pulled into the hotel parking lot minutes ahead of Slocum's car.

Drexel ran to catch the elevator to the lobby of the hotel. He wanted to get there before Slocum to determine where the elusive man was heading, and how he could get there. The senior detective took a seat facing the parking garage entrance where he could see the bank of elevators to the guestrooms.

He picked up a copy of the *Morning Advocate*, the daily newspaper in Baton Rouge. While the paper distribution was suffering like most other hard-copy papers in the country, the *Advocate* maintained an avid customer base with its online edition. Drexel rarely missed a day browsing through the website to catch up on the LSU sports teams.

The baseball team traditionally led the nation in home-field attendance among all colleges. Tiger Stadium, nicknamed Death Valley, was rated as one of the toughest places in the country for an opponent to play. The basketball team showed signs of becoming more than competitive in the Southeastern Conference arenas. The girls' softball and basketball teams had national aspirations in most years.

But the purpose of the paper tonight was to camouflage the detective's presence. He did not yet want Slocum to know he was being shadowed. At least not until he knew what the sly man might be planning.

With the newspaper held at eye level, Robinson kept a steady surveillance on the parking garage entrance. Three minutes passed with no sign of Slocum. Drexel squirmed in his chair.

Five minutes passed. Still not a glimpse of his target. Drexel worried. A crowd of people suddenly appeared in the entrance. More than a dozen people moved as one toward the bar. Drexel laid the paper aside, studying the faces and bodies among the new contingent.

Slocum was not among them. A dreadful feeling overcame the investigator. With his pulse pounding, Drexel walked to the parking garage passageway and rode the elevator to the third floor, where the enclosed span reached across from the hotel to the garage.

He almost ran across the short enclosure and searched for Sleazy Slocum's F150. It was not in the same spot as the night before. A Honda Civic occupied that space.

Drexel ran down the ramp to the ground floor. He did not spot the vehicle. His shoulders sagged, and he walked back up the ramp. There were seven stories in the garage above the span across the hotel. Robinson walked up every one of them, carefully scanning each car and truck on both sides. Sleazy Slocum's vehicle was not among them.

Dejected, the detective returned to his car. He sat for several long minutes replaying the episode in his mind over and over again. Why had he left the tail to get ahead of his target? Does Slocum know he is being followed? Did he purposely lead Robinson on a wild goose chase? How could he have been outsmarted two nights in a row? The one thing bothering Drexel the most was the report he had to give Niki.

32

CENTRAL HIGH SCHOOL

BILLY BAILEY PARKED in the small lot next to the main entrance gate to Wildcats Stadium. When he was first named the head football coach at the high school, he was not comfortable with the field.

In the past, the field was adjacent to the high school, as most facilities are located. But a new high school was built on a different road, more than two miles from the old campus. The football field remained behind.

The old high school was converted to a junior high school, and the varsity practiced by their new school, but played the home games on the old field.

Then a new junior high and elementary school were built, and most of the buildings at the original site were torn down.

No lights of any kind were available to break through the darkness when Billy shut off his headlights, his visibility limited to a few feet. No other cars were in the lot, making the coach wonder if LaDonne Elgin had changed her mind about meeting.

The gate was unlocked, and Bailey slipped through it and

onto the oval track surrounding the playing surface. He could see nothing, but was familiar enough with the layout to find his way past the cinderblock concession stand.

Still, there was no sign of the cheerleader. Bailey continued to probe through the darkness to the edge of the stands. The red clay on the track separated the bleachers from the football field. A chain-link fence on the inside of the oval track prevented intrusion by the fans. The access gate for players and coaches was just before the fenced off section the cheerleaders occupied during the games. In this confined area, they were in back of the players and in front of the ardent fan base.

The coach groped along the fence until he reached the access gate. He called out.

"LaDonne. It's Coach Bailey. Are you there?"

He received no response.

The coach edged forward, feeling his way in the darkness. In less than a minute, he found the end of the bench. Using the structure as his guide, he walked toward the fifty yard line.

Bailey tripped and almost fell. He reached out for something to stabilize his balance. His hand fell on LaDonne Elgin's body.

"I'm sorry. I didn't see you in the—"

He froze, realizing that his hand was wet. Without thinking, he wiped it on his sweatpants. Then he extended his hand and touched the girl again. Her arms were warm to his touch, but he knew she was dead.

The coach placed two fingers on LaDonne's neck. No pulse. Pulling his hand back, his fingers bumped into a hard object. Bailey grabbed it and instantly knew he had made a mistake. He was holding the knife that killed LaDonne Elgin.

Without warning, flashing lights and sirens exploded through the darkness from the other side of the field. Three squad cars raced toward the stunned coach, still holding the murder weapon in his bloody hand.

Billy ran. He stared at the police cars flying toward him. There was nowhere for him to go. He could not outdistance the cars, their spotlights already highlighting the coach running from the dead girl. He stopped and held up his hands, holding the knife in the right one.

Two officers in the first car leapt from their vehicle with their guns drawn.

"Dropped the knife. Do it. Drop the knife now."

The stunned coach did not react. His brain sent out messages that his body could not react to. Somewhere along the transmission, comprehension disconnected.

"Sir, put the knife on the ground," one cop yelled.

Billy stared blankly into the spotlight unable to see the officers through the blinding glare. He looked at the blood dripping down the knife onto his clothes, his ability to understand its meaning lost when the synapses in his brain failed to click.

The coach heard the two probes from the taser hit him in the chest rather than seeing them. The electrical shock that followed paralyzed his whole body, a charge of ten thousand volts streaking through his muscles.

The coach collapsed at the feet of the officers. Instantly, the first policeman charged while the second on his finger on the trigger of the taser. The deputy kicked the knife away and placed handcuffs on the coach's wrists.

In the bright beam of the spotlight, Billy could see the limp body of LaDonne Elgin, red streaks of blood staining the light blouse. The other two squad cars arrived and officers jumped out of the vehicles, their full attention on the coach and the dead teenager.

They did not see the figure sneaking through the gate

behind the stands. It crossed the open field behind the stadium and entered the remains of the historical buildings left when they tore down the junior high.

An ambulance passed only fifty feet from the killer's vehicle with lights and sirens piercing through the quiet black night. The killers smiled, got in the car, and drove away from the commotion back on the football field. The killer smiled, knowing there would not be a soul left in the Central community that would no longer doubt the guilt of Coach Billy Bailey.

33

CENTRAL

"Niki, this is Billy. I need your help."

The investigator tried to clear the cobwebs from her mind. She had fallen into a deep, peaceful slumber until her cell buzzed. Glancing at the bold numbers on the clock beside her bed, she saw it was a little past two in the morning.

"This had better be good," she grumbled.

"It's not," the coach replied. "I'm in jail again."

Niki became alert with a jolt.

"What do you mean *in jail again*? We posted your bond. You're supposed to be free until the hearing." Her thoughts began to assemble.

"It's not that. I've been charged with murder."

Niki exhaled. "They have no evidence tying you to Earl Washington's death. Unless they found something they haven't shared with me."

"It's not Washington."

"I hope you're kidding. Who did you kill?"

The coach's voice broke. "I didn't kill anyone. You have to believe me."

Niki was losing the little patience she had left. "Who do they say you killed?"

"LaDonne Elgin, the cheerleader."

"When?"

"Around midnight."

"It shouldn't be a problem, Coach. Sara Sue can vouch for you being at home. You can't be two places at once."

Bailey taking a deep breath before replying. "I wasn't exactly home."

Niki moaned. "Where were you? I told you to stay put. After the deal with Washington—"

"I was at the football field."

"Is that where LaDonne was killed?"

"Yes," Bailey's voice barely above a whisper.

"What else?" Niki asked, although she dreaded the answer.

"They found me there next to her body holding the knife that killed her."

The breath gushed out of Niki's body. "Holy Mother of God. Are you serious?"

"Niki, I'm in a lot of trouble. Can you help me?"

"I'll be down there in a few minutes. First, I need to take a shower. You aren't going anywhere."

34

SHERIFF'S SUBSTATION

CENTRAL

"WHAT IN THE world were you thinking?" Niki blasted across the table at Billy. They were at the small East Baton Rouge Parish Sheriff's substation in Central on Gurney Road.

"I wanted to find out who was behind this."

The strawberry blonde did not let up. "I can tell you who looks guilty, no doubt about it. You just gift wrapped an open and shut case for the prosecution."

"I didn't mean to. I thought I could get all the answers we're trying to find." The coach was almost in tears.

"From now on, leave the investigation to me. That's why you're paying me. You have to let me do my job."

"I'm not."

"What?" Niki was thoroughly exasperated.

"I'm not paying you. That's one reason I wanted to help. I feel like I'm accepting charity by leaving you to do all the work and not paying you."

"That doesn't mean you have to act like you're stupid. I was already working on LaDonne. She was the weakest link in this whole mess. Now we don't have her available."

The coach dropped his head. "I'm sorry. I wasn't thinking. I was so glad to get a break I didn't realize what could happen."

"Now you know. I gave you explicit instructions to stay at home. The judge gave you an explicit order to stay away from Flavia Foster and LaDonne Elgin. You ignored both of us."

Bailey did not raise his head.

"She sounded so good on the phone. I didn't even tell Sara Sue where I was going. I told her I needed some time to think. I needed to take a ride to clear my head."

Niki pointed a finger at him. "You lied to your wife. You ignored me. You ignored the judge. You went alone to meet with one of your alleged victims at midnight on a deserted football field. Do you have any idea how guilty this makes you look?"

Bailey slowly nodded his head. "Can you help me?"

"I don't know. You certainly aren't making my job easy. I should walk away and try to help people who actually are trying to help me defend them. You aren't doing that."

"I'm trying," he cried. "You've got to believe me. I was only trying to help."

"Any more of your kind of help and Sara Sue will be watching them stick a needle in your arm at Angola. Is that what you want?"

Shock spread across the coach's face. "My God, I haven't called her yet. They only let me have one phone call, and I used it for you."

Niki softened.

"I'll go by your house and tell Sara Sue where you are. I've got plenty of time before she opens the office."

Bailey's eyes were still wide. "She's gonna be pissed off. She was already upset with me about all this, and what happened tonight might send her over the edge."

"Why didn't you think of that before you lied to her?" Niki asked.

"I don't know. I didn't want her to get involved with meeting LaDonne. She has her business to run."

"*H–E–L–L–O*. Earth to Billy Bailey. She is involved in this, though not by her own choosing. She is married to you. Your actions, no matter how stupid they are, affect both of you."

"I realize that now. I don't know how I'll ever be able to make it up to her."

"Start by doing what I tell you and don't circumvent the investigation."

Bailey sighed. "What do we do now?"

Niki stared at the coach. "My plan is to get you out of this mess. I'll try to get bail for you again, but I'm not sure why. If you're in here, you can't get in much trouble."

Dread was apparent in Bailey's face and his voice.

"I can't stay in here. I don't belong in jail. I won't survive with these people."

35

CENTRAL

"Oh, my goodness. Please tell me you're kidding."

Sara Sue could not believe what Niki was telling her. They sat in a tiny office at the temporary agency. Two assistants were busy on the phones trying to match applicants with job openings.

"I wish I were kidding. Unfortunately, your husband is in jail, and I'm not sure the judge will let him out on bail this time," Niki replied.

"He told me he was going for a drive. He said he needed to clear his head. When he wasn't home when I got up, I tried to call, but it went to his voicemail."

The private investigator nodded. "The police have it. I'm sure the call log will show he spoke to LaDonne Elgin to set up a meeting."

"Why is this happening? We're good people. Billy is a good man. Why is this happening to us?" Tears streamed down Sara Sue's cheeks.

"I'm trying to find out. I believe we were close to getting

some answers from LaDonne, but somebody got to her before we did."

Sara Sue buried her head. "He's in a lot of trouble, isn't he?"

"I won't lie to you. He is in a ton of trouble. He still has the rape and molestation charges filed against him. Now, he will face murder charges for LaDonne, and may be charged in the death of Earl Washington."

"Lord. Will he ever get out?"

"We can get the molestation charges dropped against him for LaDonne. We have the video proof the event never occurred."

A brief smile came across Sara Sue's lips.

"At least that's a start."

"Not a very good one. Unfortunately, we didn't tell Billy until we had a chance to sit down with LaDonne. The prosecutor will assume your husband was eliminating one of his accusers."

"But if he was innocent—"

"He didn't know we had the proof. It won't help him."

Sara Sue sobbed while Niki was quiet. There was nothing the private investigator could say to ease her pain. Finally, the agency owner regained a bit of composure.

"What do we do?"

"I'll get Kemp to try to get the judge to set a new bail. I'm not optimistic."

Sara Sue shrugged. "It really doesn't matter. We have no money, and I can't let you spend any more of yours."

"I don't mind," Niki replied. "If the roles were reversed, I'm sure you would help out one of your friends."

Sara Sue continued to shake her head.

"It's too much. I heard what you said about getting the bail money back, but I don't think you'll ever get your money back from the attorney no matter how this turns out."

Niki let out a breath. "You're right. But Durwin is earning his money if he can get your husband out of jail until the trial starts, you guys will have some time together. I know it's tough, but you need to enjoy every minute."

"Why are you doing this? We're friends, but you don't know me that well. You don't know Billy at all. There has to be a reason."

Niki sat quietly for a long time. A single tear rolled down her cheek.

"It's because of something that happened when I was a little girl."

"What? What could affect you this much?"

More hesitation from the private investigator. She dug a tissue from her bag and dabbed at the corner of her eye.

"My uncle was a high school football coach. Uncle Otis. He was my dad's brother, and my favorite uncle. I loved him. We used to go to his ranch and ride his horses and play with his goats."

The strawberry blonde paused to dab more at her eye. Sara Sue remained silent.

"One day a girl at the school made some allegations against him. The school board didn't wait. They fired him immediately. He and Aunt Nancy were devastated. It was one of those *he said–she said* things."

"What happened?" Sara Sue asked.

"Uncle Otis was broken, literally. His heart failed him less than a week later. They couldn't save him. Aunt Robbie couldn't live without him. She took her own life the day after the funeral."

Sara Sue gasped. "That's horrible."

Niki wiped both eyes. "That's not the worst part. After the death of Aunt Robbie, the girl admitted she had lied. Uncle

Otis never did anything to her, except she failed a test in his class."

"That's horrible. What happened to the girl?"

"Nothing. Everyone still saw her as the victim, even though she lied. They said there was too much pressure on her to maintain good grades, and she took the only avenue she could."

"Now I understand," Sara Sue said.

"I couldn't let that happen to someone else. You told me Billy was innocent and I believed you."

Sara Sue cried again. "I'm glad you believe in him. I'm having my doubts."

36

WILDCAT INVESTIGATIONS
CENTRAL

"I SWEAR, Niki. That man is a ghost. I've never lost a target two nights in a row in my life," Drexel Robinson held his palms up, showing his frustration at his inability to keep up with Sleazy Slocum.

"He's had a ton of experience from what I understand," Niki replied.

"Besides that, you're getting too old to keep up," Donna added, laughing at the senior detective.

Drexel ran his hand through his hair before taking a sip of the steaming dark brew before him.

"I'm beginning to believe that myself, girl. Believe me, that thought has crossed my mind several times."

"Hush that kind of talk. You still know more about this business than I'll ever know. I just hope I squeeze some of that knowledge out of you." Niki put her arm around her friend.

"I was only kidding. You're not that old. I'll get you a cane so you can walk faster," Donna giggled at the expression Robinson emitted.

"You—" He started.

"Don't get too upset. That old heart of yours may not be able to handle the excitement. Then I'll have to go see you in some nursing home and wipe the drool off your face."

Even Niki smiled at Donna's humor.

"You little whippersnapper. I'll—" He began.

"Hold on. Don't get excited. I don't change diapers for you old guys either," Donna retorted.

"Let's get back on focus. We've got a man's life in her hands," Niki admonished.

"You two do. I don't know what I've got in my hands, not my client's husband for sure." Drexel replied.

"Isn't that funny?" Niki asked.

"I didn't think she was that funny," Drexel nodded at the hourglass blonde.

"I don't mean her, and I don't mean that kind of funny. I was talking about Slocum."

"What's funny about him except I can't keep up with him?" Drexel asked.

"Maybe I could," Donna said. "I can still see out of both eyes."

She playfully pinched Drexel on his shoulder.

"Let's not get on that again. No, I was talking about the coincidences," Niki said.

"I'm not following you," Donna stated.

"What she is saying, for those too young to understand adult conversations, is it is mighty strange we catch the Slocum's case when two murders are committed on consecutive nights when we're supposed to be watching him." Drexel smiled at the junior private investigator.

"You're right. I don't believe in coincidences, and this is a mighty big one, to say the least." The long–legged detective confirmed.

"The phone call came from Mrs. Slocum. How would she be involved with Flavia Foster?" Donna asked.

"Did you talk directly to her?" Niki asked.

"Yes, Ma'am. She told me who she was and said she had used this before. She asked me if we could do it again."

"Hold on," Niki said.

Niki picked up her cell and scrolled through the phone list. When she got to Josie Slocum's name, she punched the button.

Drexel and Donna could only hear Niki's side of the conversation.

"Hey, Josie. This is Niki Dupre."

"Yes, I'm doing fine."

"I know it's been a long time. I've been meaning to call you, but we've been awfully busy."

"I know. There never seems to be enough time, anymore."

"No. Not yet. Can I ask you a question?"

"Thanks. Did you call our office this week and speak to my partner?"

"Aha. Then we misunderstood. It must have been another case. I'll try someone different."

"Yes, Ma'am. Those things happen. Please tell John David *hello* for me."

"Thanks. Bye."

Niki hit the *end* button, a peculiar expression in her eyes.

"That's odd. She isn't the one who called us and asked us to track down her husband."

Drexel rolled his eyes. "Then it's been a game all along. He knew I was back there even if he couldn't see me."

"Yep. Somebody is playing an awful game, and we're being played like fools." Niki sighed when she said the last part.

"But why?" Donna asked. "It makes no sense."

"I have no answers to that. But it makes me wonder," Niki replied.

Niki dialed the number for Keith Stroud. When the wealthy investor answered, she conducted a conversation similar to that she had with Josie Slocum.

When she hung up, a serious frowned appeared.

"Keith didn't call us. He is happy with his current investments. Said he is making twelve percent a year."

Drexel whistled. "Twelve percent. I need to get in on that gravy train."

"I would too," Niki said. "But right now, I have most of my investment capital tied up in bail money. If we're lucky, I'll have a lot more to invest with Keith's advisor."

Donna looked the verge of tears. "I'm so sorry, Miss Niki. But the guy on the phone made me think he was Mr. Stroud. I—"

Robinson poked her playfully. "It's all right, child. Even us old folks with one foot in the grave were young once and made stupid mistakes."

Donna turned on a torrent of tears.

Niki frowned at Drexel. The senior investigator had nothing to say in his defense, a rare occurrence. She walked to the other side of the desk and put her arm around the young lady.

"Don't worry about it. We know now we were being played all along. The real question is why someone was willing to go to this extreme." She continued to embrace Donna.

Drexel rose, pacing up and down. Niki remained by Donna's side, consoling her new friend.

"I've got it," Ricky said loud enough to get the attention of the other detectives.

"What is it?" Niki asked.

"The phone calls came in while you were talking to Bailey at the jail, if I'm not mistaken," he said.

"It was while I talked to Billy and Sara Sue, but it wasn't at the jail. We were at Frank's. Then I dropped by the high school," Niki replied.

"That fits my theory even better. Who was at the bail hearing?"

"The other coaches. A lot of parents. I didn't recognize most of them, but I met with a couple of them since."

"Where were you sitting?" He asked.

"Next to Sara Sue. She was having a hard time coping with everything happening."

"And those parents and coaches saw you sitting with the coach's wife?"

"The courtroom isn't that big. They had to see me sitting there."

"They had plenty of time to get a plan together that would distract us and take your attention away from finding the truth about Bailey." Drexel grinned as he revealed his theory.

"But how did they know that Keith and Josie were my clients? Nobody could've found out about them in such a short time," Niki retorted.

"Unless—" Drexel shifted his focus to Donna. "Did anyone come by the office that morning? Phone repairman? Electrical guy?"

Another stream of tears.

"I forgot with everything happening. I absolutely forgot. A guy came by to make sure our computers were virus free. He said he came as part of the warranty. I didn't think anything of it."

"What did he look like?" Niki asked.

"It was hard to tell. He kept looking at the floor, but he was tall. Taller than Drexel." Donna replied.

"My guess is he was about six feet three inches, a little overweight, and some gray in his black hair," Wendy stated.

"That's close, but I wasn't paying that much attention. Do you know someone who looks like that?"

Niki answered for him.

"Sleazy Slocum. I don't believe it. He came into my office and looked at my case files on my computer."

"Doesn't take a genius to figure out why. The one case with his wife wasn't enough. Another case at the same time would take time away from the Bailey case."

Niki rose neared Robinson. "It makes sense. Only whoever hired him didn't know that Donna was also an investigator. That put a cramp in their plans."

"But how did they get Mr. Washington to go along?" Donna asked.

"They didn't. Washington didn't know about the potential investment until you told him," Niki replied.

"Who hired Mr. Slocum?" Donna asked.

"That's what we need to find out. First, we can find out the *why*, then the *who* will be obvious."

"Do you think Slocum killed Washington and the girl?" Drexel asked.

"Sure. What better alibi could he have? You were watching him at the hotel while the murderers were being committed. That's pretty solid."

"But I wasn't watching him. I was giving it my best shot, but he was a step ahead of me." Drexel said, though it was hard for him.

"But you saw him arrive at the hotel, and you didn't see his truck missing until after the murders were committed. Sounds like an airtight alibi to me," Niki sat in her chair.

"How will we find out who is paying him?" Donna asked, wiping the tears away.

"He'll make a mistake," Niki pause. "Or his client will. But it's also a blessing."

"How so?" Donna asked.

"We only have one case, not three."

Drexel scoffed. "That only means you have three cases that aren't paying you. You still have to pay us even though you're gonna lose a lot of money on this thing, no matter the outcome."

"There's more to life than money," Niki declared.

"That's a good theory. But when you run out of one, you hope you don't have much left of the other." Ricky replied.

37

CENTRAL HIGH SCHOOL

Jɪᴍʙᴏ Wᴀx ᴀᴅᴍɪᴛᴛᴇᴅ Flavia Foster into his office. The student looked like she would rather be taking a final exam than sitting with the assistant coach.

"Come in. Take a seat."

Flavia did as she was told. There cheerleader could not look Wax in his eyes, but became suddenly interested in her feet.

Jimbo waited for her to say something. She did not.

"You wanted to see me," he said. "I can't help you if you don't tell me how."

Flavia looked up, her lips quivering. "Coach Bailey got me pregnant."

"Are you sure?" Jimbo blurted before realizing how his question would sound.

"If you mean if I'm sure that I'm pregnant, then the answer is *yes*. I took three of those home tests, and all three were positive."

Wax was not sure how to phrase the next question. He decided on the direct approach.

"How do you know Coach Bailey is the father? Why not Steve? You guys have been dating."

"I'm not a slut." Fire erupted from Flavia's eyes. Then she buried her head again.

"I didn't say that you were, but you and Steve have been dating for years. It's only natural—"

Flavia picked up her head. "That doesn't mean that we do what everybody else does. We wanted to wait until we were married before we took the next step."

"I commend both of you. That had to be a hard decision."

The teen said nothing.

"How long have you known?" Jimbo asked.

"I found out last week. I took the test three days in a row to be sure," Flavia replied.

"What do you want to do?"

"I want to kill him. I hope he rots in hell for what he did to me," she answered.

"Okay. So why tell me?"

"Because I'm thinking about getting an abortion, and I don't want anyone to know. I went to the clinic, and they said I had to have an adult sign off on it."

"Wouldn't that be your father or mother? I'm sure they are in a better position than me to approve this," Jimbo said.

"I don't want them to find out. It would kill my mom if she knew. If I tell my dad, he would tell Mom," Flavia replied.

"But wouldn't that be illegal?" Jimbo asked.

"The lady at the clinic said it wasn't. She said I'd be surprised at how many teenagers get abortions without their parents' knowledge. That's why they accept any adult signature."

"Why me?" Wax asked.

"Because I trust you. You won't tell anyone about it. There aren't many adults I can trust."

Jimbo was happy that the cheerleader trusted him with her secret. The truth was the freshman coach, Ricky Delrie, had already told him. The revelation was no secret.

38

BATON ROUGE

DREXEL ROBINSON once again followed the Ford F150 belonging to John David "Sleazy" Slocum from Zachary to the hotel. This time, he made no attempt to be discreet. He stayed no more than two car lengths behind his target at all times.

When Slocum pulled into a space in the parking garage access next to the hotel, Drexel watched him exit the vehicle and walk to the other side. The detective followed him across to the elevator. Drexel waited for Slocum to take the down elevator and then took the next one. When he entered the lobby, Drexel searched the entire opening without seeing Slocum. Not finding him, he caught the eye of Donna Cross sitting in a chair facing the elevators.

"Where did he go?" Drexel asked after rushing over next to Donna.

"I never saw him," Donna replied.

"You had to see him. He came down that elevator not more than two minutes ago." Drexel was losing his patience.

"I swear. I've been watching that door for the last thirty

minutes, ever since you called and told me Slocum was on the move. Nobody close to his description came out."

"Are you sure? Did you go to the restroom or the gift shop?"

Donna turned red. "I told you already. Nobody looking like Mr. Slocum came out of that elevator. I've been watching it from that chair the whole time. I may be young, but I can still see."

Drexel softened his voice. "Calm down. I'm just frustrated. I trust you."

"Thanks. I needed that," Donna said as she hugged the older man.

39

BATON ROUGE

Niki watched the white Ford sedan exit the parking garage. She slid down behind the steering will, but not before recognizing Sleazy Slocum as the driver. The sedan passed her and turned back west on Florida Boulevard, away from the Mississippi River.

When the vehicle was out of sight, Niki made a quick U-turn, and fell in three or four cars behind Slocum. Her Ford Explorer did not stand out on the busy highway.

She maintained surveillance until Slocum reached a major intersection and took a right turn. She followed, although he was some distance ahead. The two vehicles stayed on a weaving path until they reached College Drive leading to the LSU campus.

Niki thought about going past Slocum and picking him up again before he reached the maze of streets surrounding the University campus. But as she was considering that, Slocum turned left on Corporate Boulevard.

She quickly switched lanes and barely made it through the intersection before the light turned red. She lost his car for a moment. Then she spotted it pulling into a parking lot of one of the better restaurants in Baton Rouge, Mansur's on the Boulevard.

Niki and her fiancé, Senator Dalton Bridgestone, dined there several times a month when he was in town. It was one of their favorite places to eat, if not their most favorable.

She pulled in the parking lot and found a space on the side of the restaurant next to Home Suites Hotel. The lot was almost full, even at this early hour. The private investigator was confident her vehicle would not be easily noticed.

While she was waiting, she called Drexel's cell and told him about Slocum changing cars at the hotel. After listening to the senior investigator groan for a minute, she instructed him and Donna to meet her at the restaurant. She did not want to lose Slocum again.

Twenty minutes later, two cars pulled into the lot, but had to park in the Home Suites area because the restaurant lot was completely full. Drexel and Donna walked across the few feet of grassy area and climbed into the SUV. Donna got the honor of sitting in the front seat.

"I guess this explains why I missed him in the hotel. He never went inside." Drexel said.

"You've got to hand it to him. That's a slick move. I wonder who he is meeting with in there," Niki responded.

"You haven't been in?" Donna asked.

"No. He knows what I look like from the previous cases. He also knows what you look like because he saw you at the office."

"I reckon that means I volunteer to go inside and try to spot the elusive Mr. Slocum," Drexel said from the back seat.

"Heckuva deduction, Sherlock. You might make it as a detective after all," Niki laughed.

Robinson went back to his car and added a tie and snug hat to his wardrobe. He winked at the ladies when he again passed by the SUV. When he got to the door, he gave one last tug on his tie and entered.

The attractive hostess could not have been more than twenty years old, but she had all the assets required of the job. Thick flowing hair. Curves in all the right places. Unblemished skin. An infectious smile. Drexel wondered if there might be an opening at Wildcat Investigations that required those skill sets. If not, he thought, there should be. He would have to mention that to Niki if this case did not cause her to go bankrupt and lose the firm.

The alluring young lady flashed a becoming smile as soon as Drexel stepped inside.

"How may I help you?"

Robinson thought of a number of ways, but most of them he dared not verbalize. At least not in this setting.

"Is it possible that you have a table available?" He asked.

"Sorry, we have a lot of people ahead of you with reservations. One of our sous chefs called in sick. We're running about forty minutes behind. Would you like a seat at the bar?"

He nodded.

"That will be great. First, I have to visit the restroom."

She flashed the engaging smile again and pointed through the entrance to the main dining area.

"Right that way."

Robinson walked past the hostess, inhaling the seductive lure of her perfume. He moved with his head facing forward, but could visualize every table.

Back in the far corner, Drexel spotted Sleazy Slocum sitting at a table along, the menu covering most of his face. The detective remained focused on the hallway to the restrooms, bringing no notice to himself.

On his way back, he confirmed Slocum was still at the table

with no other diners. When he reached the hostess station he stopped.

"My apologies, Madame. I received a call moments ago that requires my immediate attention. Perhaps on another occasion."

He made a slight bow, soaked up the tantalizing scent emanating from the pleasant hostess, and exited the restaurant. When he arrived at Niki's Ford Explorer, he was still grinning like a boy after a successful raid of the cookie jar.

Niki laughed. "I can tell you met Lisa."

"Who?" Drexel feigned. "My attention was entirely on our target tonight."

"Why do I get the feeling your target changed when you saw Lisa?"

"Do you mean that innocent lass with the girlish figure? I barely noticed."

"So why are you drooling all over your tie?"

Donna giggled. "She's way too young for an old fart like you. You wouldn't have a chance."

Drexel straightened his tie. "Never underestimate the advantages of experience over the trappings of youth. Lisa might need some personal tutoring."

"Did you take your eyes off of her long enough to find Slocum?" Niki asked.

"I believe that was my charge. He is seated alone in the main dining area. Mr. Slocum was already scanning a menu. I do not expect he is awaiting company."

"Did he see you?" Niki inquired.

"Not a chance. I used my vast experience to elude any possibility of detection," He responded.

"Let's wait him out and see what happens. He didn't dodge you at the hotel for no reason. He's got something up his sleeve."

All three investigators leaned back in their seats, each occupied by their own thoughts. They waited in silence for another fifteen minutes.

"Movement at the ten o'clock," Drexel announced.

A young man dressed in all white stepped out of the rear door. He quickly lit a cigarette while looking around. He seemed to pay no attention to the three detectives in the Ford Explorer.

When he finished the smoke, the young man went back inside. They waited for another twenty minutes, watching diners come and go with no sign of Sleazy Slocum.

Then the same young man who had taken a smoke break came through the front door. He carried a large bag with both hands. The youngster walked directly to Niki's SUV to the driver's side.

The strawberry blonde put the window down.

"May I help you?" She asked.

"Miss Dupre?" He questioned.

"Yes. How did you know?"

"Mr. Slocum asked me to bring this out to you. He said the three of you might be hungry by now."

Confusion and surprise could not be hidden by Niki. "He said that?"

"Yes, Ma'am. He said that he wanted to treat you guys for making it a fun night."

Niki accepted the bag from the youngster and watched him hurry back to the restaurant. She sat for a few seconds trying to put it all together.

"What did he send?" Donna asked. "I'm hungry."

Niki handed her the bag, which the young investigator immediately tore open. Donna pulled out three to-go boxes and examined each.

"We've got choices," she announced. "Would you like

Redfish on a Plank, Veal Marcella or Shrimp Scampi? Hey, he sent house salads and bread. We've got some bread pudding, too."

Niki did not immediately respond, her gaze fixed on the front door of the restaurant.

"I'll take the veal," Drexel said from the backseat.

"Miss Niki, would you like to redfish or the shrimp?"

"I'm not hungry," the detective responded. "You two split those."

"What got your goat?" Donna asked.

"Something went wrong. Really wrong. I can't figure out how he spotted us."

Donna grinned. "That's easy. The advantage of experience still can't keep up with the vitality of youth."

Drexel groaned behind the ladies, but Niki kept staring at the door.

40

BLACKWATER ROAD

"Mr. Elgin, I'm Niki Dupre."

LaDonne Elgin's father was hesitant. Niki had driven to the ranch-style home on Blackwater Road hoping to find some evidence of a conspiracy between his daughter, Flavia Foster, and an unknown person.

"May I come in? I need to ask you a few questions." She took a step closer to Adam Elgin. He was not an old man. His hair was jet black, his body trim, but not sculptured. His eyes were dark as night.

"You killed my daughter." His tone was as dark as his eyes.

"I'm sorry," Niki replied.

"If it wasn't for you, my daughter would still be alive." His voice did not vary.

"Mr. Elgin, I had nothing to do with LaDonne's death. I'm attempting to find out who killed her."

"They already know who did it. That Bailey guy. He was the one who killed my little girl."

"I don't think we should discuss this on your front porch.

Maybe we should go inside where we can find a little more privacy."

"If you didn't pay his bond, he wouldn't be out on the streets killing little girls. Are you proud that because of you LaDonne is dead?"

Niki had not even considered that line of thought. She believed in Billy Bailey's innocence and did not imagine the consequences of her actions if that assumption proved to be untrue.

"Mr. Elgin, we have proof that LaDonne's allegations against Coach Bailey are false. He had no reason to cause any harm to your daughter."

"He killed her. I know it. You know it. Now I guess you want to smear LaDonne's name. Drag her through the mud. I won't allow it."

"I'm not trying to hurt LaDonne's reputation, but I know that she wasn't telling the truth about Coach Bailey. I'm trying to find out why."

Adam Elgin's countenance turned from dark to pure evil. "If you don't leave my property in the next five seconds, I will kill you."

The somber father pulled out a Glock from his back pocket. He raised the pistol and pointed it straight at Niki's head.

"Five, four—" He counted.

Niki turned and walked back to her SUV. She was surprised by Adam Elgin's reaction, only because she had not considered Billy Bailey's guilt. Now, she must include a completely different point of view before attempting to interview other friends and family of LaDonne Elgin and Flavia Foster.

41

CENTRAL HIGH SCHOOL

"I'm sorry, Flavia. I can't do what you're asking me to do." Jimbo Wax told the teenager, "I don't believe in taking a child's life no matter how it is conceived. Believe me, I wish I could help you. If you don't want the baby, my wife and I will be happy to I adopt it."

"You won't sign the papers at the clinic?" Flavia could not believe her ears.

"No. I can't. I couldn't live with myself if I participated in killing your baby."

"But it's not my baby yet. If I don't do something soon, it will be."

Jimbo nodded. "That's the exact reason I can't help you. I'm sorry."

When Flavia said nothing, Jimbo pulled a few sheets of paper from his desk.

"My brother wrote this. It reflects how I feel."

MOMMY, MOMMY

From that moment I was first conceived
My world was only you
Only you and I could have believed
The secret we both knew
A little life grew inside of you
Those little eyes so blue
Oh, What joy I had planned for you
My world was only you
What lay ahead I could not wait to know
When I would smile at you
And touch your face
Hug you tight
And call out your name
Mommy
Mommy
If you could only hear my first cry
And nurse me into life
Before you must decide
And If you chose a name to call me by
My growth you would not hide
But the cost of bearing me was high
you did not count the joy
All that time I never made a cry
Did you know I was a boy
A little life grew inside of you
And I reached out for you
If I could only touch your face
And smile at you
Oh, what joy I had planned for you
My world was only you
One day I would smile at you
Touch your face
And hug you tight

And Call out your name
Mommy
Mommy
I know you struggled with just what to do
I know you loved me too
My love for you just grew and grew
My only world was you
But you decided not to know
The joy I had planned for you
You would never see my smile
Or Touch my face
Or Hug me tight
And Never call my name
But all I wanted was
to reach out to you
And touch your face
And smile at you
Bring joy to you
And Hug you tight
And Call out your name
Before He formed me in your womb
He knew my name
Had plans for me
Gave me a future and much hope
That tragic day marked the end you thought
But God would change my fate
The life in me is what he sought
He met me at the Gate
He saw my smile
He touched my face
He hugged me tight
and called out my name
He Saved me by his Grace

Mommy, I see you now
I love you now
And I wait for you here
Every day I walk these streets of gold
And worship at the throne
My love for you I've so often told
All tears and pain are gone
The saints up here all love you too
Ma and pa are still the same
Aunt Gene is the same as we all knew
The Angels all know your name
I see you now
I love you now
I wait for you here
One day soon I will touch your face
And I will smile at you
I'll Bring joy to you
Hug you tight
And call out your name
Mommy, I Love you

Mommy, I can see you now
I love you now
I wait for you here
One day soon I will touch your face
And I will smile at you
Bring joy to you
And Hug you tight
And call out your name
Mommy
Mommy
I Love You

Jeremiah 1:4-5

Then the word of the Lord came to me, saying:
5 "Before I formed you in the womb I knew you;
Before you were born I sanctified you;
I ordained you a prophet to the nations

When she finished reading, the teen wadded up the paper and threw it towards the trash can. It fell two feet short.

Flavia snarled. "I thought you were my friend. I looked up to you. Now you want me to have that bastard's child. You aren't any better than he is."

"I'm sorry you feel that way, but I have to live with myself. Killing your baby isn't going to solve any problem. It will create a lot more." A deep furrow crossed Jimbo's brow. His hands found no easy place to rest.

Flavia's eyes became daggers through the small confines of the coach's office.

"I hope you rot in hell with your friend." She slammed the door on her way out.

Jimbo was left in his office alone wishing he had better answers than he had given the cheerleader, but he could think of none.

42

GREENWELL SPRINGS ROAD

NIKI DECIDED to try to get with Steve King's father at his place of business. She didn't know exactly what he did for a living, but he made a lot of money. The address she had gotten from Donna's research showed an office on Greenwell Springs Road, between the Magnolia bridge over the Amite River and Joor Road.

She found it without a lot of trouble. The name on the sign out front simply said *King*. She parked in the sparse lot along with only two other cars.

She walked inside the brick office building to find an ornate reception area. Pictures of exotic wildlife, similar to those he found in Carl King's home, lined the white pine walls.

A middle-aged lady appeared from the hallway leading to the back of the office. She was neither attractive nor ugly, neither tall nor short, neither obese nor lean. If there was ever a case for an average-looking woman, Niki was looking at her.

"May I help you?" The woman asked, though not eagerly.

"I'd like to speak to Mr. King. Is he in?"

"What is the nature of your call?"

Obviously this lady was a buffer between King in any salesman attempting to make a cold call.

"I'd like to speak to him about Steve," Niki said, seeing no reason to go into detail when brevity might serve her purpose.

"Your name?"

"Niki Dupre."

"I'll see if he has time to fit you into his schedule." Her tone was much like her, neither enthusiastic nor defensive.

Niki took a few minutes to glance at the photographs on the walls. Every one depicted wildlife in one form or another. Two cat squirrels chasing each other in the top of a massive live oak. An alligator sunning on an embankment in the marsh. A close-up shot of a crawfish, its claws extended. A water moccasin coiled in a strike position.

"How do you like them?" A strong masculine voice asked.

Niki had not heard the man enter the room. She turned to find an almost exact replica of Steve King, only twenty-five years older. He has a pleasant smile, though a bit reserved.

"They are beautiful," she replied. "Did you take all of them yourself?"

"You're a detective, aren't you? Can't wait until we officially meet each other until you start asking questions."

Niki blushed. "I'm sorry. I'm Niki Dupre. I'm working—"

"I know who you are, Niki. I'm Carl, but you already know that or you wouldn't be here. Come on back to my office and we can talk. I like to be more comfortable when I'm getting grilled by a pretty lady."

The detective followed Carl King down the short hallway to a small office. The hallway in the office was lined with more wildlife photographs. A bald eagle. A brown pelican. A bullfrog. A school of speckled trout.

The chairs were not very ornate, but comfortable. The desk ordinary. Everything in the office except for the photographs was designed not to draw attention. All could be overlooked by the casual observer.

"What can I do for you, Miss Dupre?" Carl asked.

"Tell me about your relationship with Coach Bailey. How would you describe it?"

"Nonexistent," King answered in one word.

"You have had discussions with him?"

King nodded. "Of course. I support the Central Wildcats Athletic Association. I believe that is a worthy organization."

"Can you describe the nature of those discussions?"

"They were not productive."

"Did they center on the status of your son on the football team?" Niki asked.

"Some did. Most involved the future development of the facilities."

Niki paused, wanting to phrase the next question properly. "Are the two subjects connected?"

"That's not for me to say."

"Did you threaten to withhold funds from the football team if Steve was not the starting quarterback?"

"I'm not in a position to make a threat of that nature. You have some bad information."

Niki looked at her notes from the interview with Jimbo Wax. "Is it not true that you are the major contributor to the Association and also hold a leadership position with it?"

"That is true," Carl acknowledged.

"Doesn't that put you in a good position to determine how the Association spends its money?"

Carl shook his head. "We have a truly democratic group of leaders. One person—one vote. You can't get any more democratic than that."

"Who puts together the list of prospective projects that require funding?"

"I do," he answered.

"It is my understanding that the projects for the football team fell off the list after one of your discussions with Coach Bailey."

He nodded. "According to our records, the football program had received a disproportionate share of the funding in the past. We simply needed to balance the expenditures."

"I want to make sure I understand. Not funding the biggest revenue generator for the high school is the best way to balance the expenditures? Is that really what you're saying?"

King smiled. "We believe every athlete at Central High is equally deserving of appropriate facilities, whether it is the boys' basketball team or girls' softball. All of them need upgrades in the facilities and equipment."

Niki realized Carl King was well prepared for this line of questioning, although she did not believe a single word. She knew that at almost all high schools in South Louisiana, the football team received the lion's share of the donations from the respective athletic associations.

She pursued a different subject.

"Do you know John David Slocum?"

Carl's jaws tensed, and he squirmed uneasily in his chair. His once steady gaze flickered. All the symptoms told Niki the man had not prepared to answer this question and also revealed the answer before he spoke.

"Yes. He and I are acquaintances."

"How do you know him?"

"He sometimes does some investigative work for me. He is very good. A little more low-key than your firm, but just as effective."

Carl coughed in his hand, knowing he had said more than he should.

"What kind of investigations?" Niki asked.

"I'm sorry. I can't reveal the nature of those assignments. I can't break the confidentiality." More squirming and more flitting of the eyelids.

"Is that because of the confidentiality or is it because of the questionable legality?"

Niki was not surprised when Carl's mouth involuntarily opened, and his eyes widened. Again, the question was answered without King saying a word, but she was not surprised by his verbal denial.

"My business is on the up and up. I do not get involved in illegal activities."

Niki placed her fingers of her left hand on her temple. "What exactly is your business, Carl? How do you make money here?"

He coughed again in his hand. "I don't believe my business model is pertinent to this discussion. However, I am extremely busy, so if you don't mind, I need to get back to it."

"One more question before I go."

"Make it quick." He rose from his chair.

"Is Slocum currently working on any investigations on your behalf?"

He held his hand toward the door. "That is none of your business. Thank you for dropping by."

Niki walked by herself back to the reception area. The ordinary lady was seated behind the desk.

"Mr. King forgot to give me a business card. Can I get one from you?" Niki asked.

"He doesn't have any," the lady replied.

43

STATE COURTHOUSE

"Your Honor, the defendant willingly disobeyed your specific order, and contacted a victim in this case. Something went wrong, and he killed her. We do not believe the defendant should be on the streets. He is a menace and danger to society. We recommend his bail be revoked and he remain in custody until trial." The prosecutor laid out her best scenario against Billy Bailey.

The judge turned to Durwin Kemp.

"Does the defense have any comments?"

Kemp rose slowly. "Your Honor, my client acknowledges his mistakes in meeting with Miss Elgin. But we're confident that when the facts are revealed, they will prove his innocence against all the allegations against him."

A shout rose from the benches behind the side of the prosecution.

"You killed my daughter. You deserve to die."

The judge nodded at the East Baton Rouge Parish trooper stationed by the door. The officer immediately strode forward, grabbed Adam Elgin by the arm and escorted him out of the room.

The judge turned his attention back to the prosecutor. "This is not the trial. Can you give me a feel for the conclusiveness of the evidence against the defendant?"

Kemp leapt to his feet. "Your Honor. You are asking for only one side of the case, and we have not yet had time to prepare to address the integrity of the evidence."

The judge turned to Kemp. "You will have your opportunity at the appropriate time, Counselor. It is my duty to ascertain if the defendant poses a threat to our community. Objection overruled."

"But, Your Honor. I—"

"Sit down before I hold you in contempt of court." The man in the black robe did more than glance at Kemp.

The prosecutor could barely contain her smile. This hearing could not be going any better for her side.

"Your Honor, the defendant was discovered around midnight on the high school football field holding the murder weapon over the victim. When he made a call from the police station, he admitted he killed Miss Elgin. We have recordings of that conversation."

Kemp jumped to his feet again. "Your Honor, that is preposterous. This is the first the defense has heard about an alleged phone call."

"According to the discovery rules, we are not yet required to turn evidence we have gathered until we have finished," the prosecutor injected.

"Both of you will address the court and not each other. This is a court of law and not a tennis match." The judge rapped his gavel to reinforce his words.

"Your Honor, may I have one minute to confer with my client?" Kemp asked.

"One minute. No more."

Kemp turned and Niki handed him a note she had quickly scribbled. Kemp read it and showed it to Bailey, who nodded.

"Thank you, Your Honor." Kemp turned back to the judge. "As the prosecution is aware, these words were stated by my client."

The prosecutor emitted a huge smile.

"But," Kemp continued. "The prosecution is also aware that these words are being taken out of context in an attempt to prejudice this hearing. These words are part of a denial of the allegations against my client, and are in no way an admission of guilt."

The smile from the other side faded.

The judge addressed the District Attorney. "Madam Prosecutor, I hope this is not true. Is it?"

"—Your Honor, I have only had time to review snippets of the conversation. I do not know the entire context." Sweat dripped from her forehead.

"Madam Prosecutor, please provide the entire recording to the court and to the defense by the end of the business day. For your sake, I truly hope this is not an attempt to unfairly bias this hearing."

The prosecutor shifted her weight, realizing her entire career may have taken a fatal blow. She nodded, but said nothing out loud.

"Madam Prosecutor, you among all people, know that an answer must be verbalized to be recorded by the court reporter. Do you understand my instructions?"

See again nodded meekly. "Yes, Your Honor. We will submit the entire conversation without edits."

He continued to glare at her.

"I was prepared to revoke the bail and remand the defendant into custody. However, because I do not appreciate shenanigans of any sort, I will release the defendant for seven days."

He then addressed Coach Bailey directly.

"I will personally review the outline of the case against you including the phone call. If I think it is sufficient to find you are a threat to our community, I will put you into custody."

The judge then addressed both sides.

"You will both be in my court at this time one week from today. I will give you my decision then. In the meantime, the defendant is released on the standing bail. I suggest that he prepare himself for a lengthy incarceration."

The prosecutor frowned. Durwin Kemp frowned. Billy Bailey grinned from ear to ear. Niki did not know whether to frown or grin. She was happy for the short-term victory, but feared the implication for the period after the following week.

44

CENTRAL HIGH SCHOOL

JIMBO WAX WAS ELATED. He prepared to act as head coach of the Central Wildcats against the Denham Springs Yellow Jackets on his home field. The game presented the first opportunity for the assistant coach to lead a team he could call his own on the battleground. The game prompted more excitement because it was against one of Central's most hated rivals.

The team finished the pregame meal consisting of peanut butter and jelly sandwiches along with bags of potato chips. The meal was a long-standing tradition for the Wildcats football team.

Jimbo could not relax. He went from player to player, imparting encouragement and reminding each of his part in the overall game plan. Before long, he had visited with every player and assistant coach.

He moved to the coach's office to reflect and regain the composer required to coach the Wildcats in such an important game.

Jim walked into Billy's office and sat behind his boss's desk.

He did not bother to turn on the light, preferring the darkness. The vacuum allowed him to concentrate on the task ahead.

Jimbo reviewed the first five scripted plays on offense in his mind when the phone rang. At first, the assistant coach did not know whether or not to answer it. It was the line of the head coach. He opted to pick it up.

"Hello," he tried to sound confident.

"Coach?"

"Yes, this is Coach Wax. Who is this?"

"It doesn't matter. You need to listen."

"I'm listening," Wax turned red with anger.

"I don't need an attitude, Coach. You are in this up to your neck."

"Up to what?" Wax asked.

"You know what. I want you to know you will not go unscathed. You will pay for your involvement in this," the voice said.

"I have no idea what you're talking about." Wax was now more than angry.

"Of course you do. Think about it," the voice on the other end was quiet after saying that.

"Hello. Hello." Jimbo yelled into the phone. His mind was no longer on the football game.

CENTRAL HIGH SCHOOL

NIKI AND SARA SUE attended the football game. Sara Sue went because Billy insisted she go. He wanted a first-hand account of the event, not from a second view. In spite of all his troubles, the coach still cared about his team.

Niki had a different agenda. She wanted to keep an eye on the major participants in the investigation. To her surprise, Carl King and LJ Wild sat together. Carl's son, Steve, had been the starting quarterback before Billy arrived at Central.

LJ Wild's son was cut from the team, a move by Billy Bailey to allow the most athletic players to get the reps in practice. An argument ensued, followed by a brief physical altercation. LJ was knocked to the ground after taking a swing at the coach.

Niki found it suspicious those two parents happened to sit next to one another. She saw Wild point to one of the players warming up on the field. She saw the number on the jersey and referred to the game program. She placed a quarter–page advertisement for her company in it weekly, not that the ad would generate much business. It was her way of giving back to the school.

The players that LJ pointed to was listed as Bert Wild. To her astonishment, it was apparent that Jimbo had reinstated LJ's son to the team, despite his proclamation that Bert was not a good player.

Niki watched Flavia Foster during the pregame activities. The athletic cheerleader acted as she did not have a care in the world. She jumped, pranced, and performed somersaults the investigator would have been proud to accomplish when she was cheering on the same sideline during her high school years.

Jimbo looked distracted. He ambled among the Wildcats team without much encouragement. Several times, Niki saw him scanning the bleachers, searching for someone. His eyes briefly settled on Niki and Sara Sue, but the acting coach quickly averted his gaze.

Ricky Delrie was helping the varsity. Niki wondered why Jimbo would promote Delrie with the case against Billy still pending. This was another move that Bailey would not have made.

Steve King walked over to Flavia and gave her a quick peck on her cheek. He was all smiles and full of energy. He ran through the warm–ups with the first string players.

Before the game started, the announcer asked for a moment of silence for LaDonne Elgin. Her father, Adam walked to the center of the field. After a few seconds, he addressed the crowd with a handheld microphone.

"My daughter loved this school. She loved this field. She loved her classmates. LaDonne was happy until someone came to the school and dishonored her. Then he killed her. I ask you to support her memory by supporting justice. There can be no closure, no peace, until there is justice."

He walked off, staring at Sara Sue Bailey during the entire trip to the sidelines. Billy's wife maintained her outward composure, but Niki could see her hands trembling. The private investigator had her arm around the coach's wife.

The game began. The Central Wildcats accepted the kickoff and returned it to the thirty-one yard line. On the first offensive play from scrimmage, Steve King attempted a short sideline pass to a wide receiver.

A Yellow Jacket cornerback cut in front of the wideout and snatched the ball out of the air. The only things separating him from the end zone were green grass and yard markers. Central was down by touchdown before the Denham Springs offense ran a play.

Groans erupted from the fans. Niki glanced at Carl King to see his reaction. Her gaze froze, not from King's reaction, but because of the occupant in the seat next to him on the other side of LJ Wild.

A big man, around six foot three inches and a little less than two hundred fifty pounds, was idly watching. The other spectator was not fazed by the interception and return. Niki gazed at the elusive Sleazy Slocum.

Then another person sat next to Slocum. It was none other than Adam Elgin, the father of the slain cheerleader. He spoke briefly to Slocum and patted him on the shoulder.

Niki's mind went into overdrive considering the full gamut of possibilities. All three parents were at least familiar with Slocum. All three had reasons to encourage Billy's downfall. It seemed difficult to believe that the elusive Slocum was there simply to root for the Wildcats.

The game itself did not go well for the home team. Steve King threw four interceptions and fumbled twice during the rout by the Yellow Jackets. Most of the fans left during the third quarter. When Niki glanced again at Slocum, he had once again disappeared.

After the game, Niki and Sara Sue walked to the Ford SUV among whispering and pouting from the few remaining fans. They did not speak to each other on the way to the parking lot. Niki hit the open button on the keypad and then sucked in her breath.

"Good evening," Sleazy said, as he stepped from behind her vehicle.

Niki's hand instinctively went to the small of her back, but then remembered leaving the thirty-eight revolver under the seat of the Explorer. She quickly scanned the big man for weapons.

A bulge on his right hip suggested he was carrying. She also saw a protrusion from his right ankle suggesting a backup weapon. Her advantage was that both guns were holstered, and she could close the small distance between them before he could draw and fire. To be sure, she advanced another step forward toward the big man.

He took a step toward her, leaving only two feet of separation. Niki smiled, now confident.

"Easy, Miss Dupre. I am here to talk. Nothing else." Slocum's hands came up, his palms out.

Niki relaxed. "Talk."

"Call your dogs off. You're wasting your time and mine. Besides that, you're hindering my activities." He dropped his hands.

"If your activities involve killing young girls, then I hope I continue to hamper them."

Her muscles again tensed when Slocum's hand neared the gun on his hip.

"You are making a mistake. If I wanted to kill someone, I could've taken out your detective during his poor attempt to track me. You might tell him not to leave his vehicle unattended. You never know when someone might leave a parcel in it that would make it go *boom*. That would be most unfortunate."

"Is that a threat, Slocum?"

"No. Just an observation."

"Let me tell you something." There was steel in Niki's voice. "If something happens to Drexel Robinson, there isn't a snake hole on this earth where you will be safe. I will find you."

Slocum smiled and disappeared behind the SUV. Then Niki realized the amount of tension in her body. She wanted to hit something. Someone. She wanted to hit Sleazy Slocum.

46

CENTRAL

"THAT'S ABOUT IT," Niki finished telling Billy Bailey about her observations at the ballgame.

"He actually started Steve? What in the world was he thinking?" Billy set a cup of coffee on the table.

Niki leaned back in her chair. "Of all the things I've told you, that is what got your attention? Not the fathers sitting together? Not Flavia? Not Slocum? You focused on the starting quarterback?"

"Sorry, but that is a poor decision by any stretch of the imagination. It's not Steve's fault. He just isn't ready to start." Billy shook his head in wonderment.

"Hello. Do you understand that if I don't come up with something before a week from today, the judge is sending you to jail? Can we focus on that instead of who is reaching under the center's butt?"

The coach picked up the cup again. "I'm sorry, but I think first as a coach. The rest of the stuff will take care of itself. I've got the best detective in Louisiana on my side."

Niki looked at him with unbelieving eyes.

"I wish I shared your confidence. Somebody doesn't want you coaching."

Billy smiled. He put the cup down and picked up a saucer loaded with a piece of pecan pie. "See, you've already figured out the *why*. Now you've just got to figure out the *who*."

"It seems like we've got a pretty large list of people."

Bailey savored a bite of the succulent dessert.

"Not really. From what you told me, it seems fairly obvious you've narrowed the list to three parents and two coaches."

"And one thug that may be better than me," Niki retorted.

Another bite from the delicacy.

"Slocum? He's not the driver in the plot. He's only the tool."

"A high-powered tool. Somebody is paying him a lot of money. He doesn't come cheap."

Bailey laughed.

"Then I would concentrate on the dad's. Coaches, especially assistant coaches, don't make a lot of money in high school. We can barely afford cable TV, much less hire a man like Slocum."

Sara Sue placed another piece of pecan pie on Billy's saucer.

"Do you really think someone hired the Slocum guy to do all this dirty work?" She asked.

Niki let out a long sigh. "I don't know any other way to read it. I'm not sold on the idea, but it's the one that makes the most sense with the little bit of evidence we have."

"Why would he do it? We don't even know him, and he doesn't know us."

"Money," Niki answered. "A guy like Sleazy Slocum will do anything for money. It takes a hardhearted man to take the life of an innocent teenage girl."

Billy pause between bites.

"She wasn't innocent. I didn't grope her, and she said I did."

Niki nodded. "Point taken, but she was still a teenager. I suspect her good friend, Flavia, talked her into doing this, and she wasn't comfortable with it. That is why she had to be eliminated."

"Speaking of that, you left out Miss Foster and Steve King as suspects," Billy said.

"True. I'm not sure they have the wherewithal to hire Slocum."

Billy set the saucer down. "If he is hired? If not, those two kids could have set all this up."

"I don't think so. Those photographs were done by a professional," Niki said.

Bailey agreed. "You're describing Steve King. He learned from the best. Carla is one of the premier photographers in Baton Rouge."

"Carla?" Then Niki understood. "C. King. I assumed it stood for Carl, not Carla. So she wasn't lying after all."

"Huh?" Billy Bailey and Sara Sue were stumped.

"Oh, nothing. I asked Carla if her husband took those wildlife pictures at their house. She told me he didn't and I assumed she wasn't telling the truth."

Billy sat forward. "Steve is perfectly capable. I remember he took a picture of the cheerleaders, then inserted the coaches' heads in place of the girls. Everyone got a big kick out of it."

Niki's eyes widened. "Why didn't you tell me this before now?"

Billy frowned. "Why? Is it important?"

47

CENTRAL HIGH SCHOOL

JIMBO WAX FINISHED WATCHING the unedited film of the game. He knew he had screwed up. He should not have started Steve King. He should not have called the pass plays that required a stronger arm than Steve possessed.

Jimbo let the bus carrying the players leave without him. Because the field was adjacent to the old junior high school, and not the high school, the bus was required even though it was only an eight-minute ride. The acting coach addressed the team in the locker room, but did not mention the misgivings he had about the game plan.

Now, he sat alone in the quiet locker room. The disgruntled fans had departed like rats on a sinking ship. Wax had to admit that his ship was taking on water, if not sinking.

He thought about the upcoming game a week ahead against the Live Oak Eagles. The Wildcats possessed superior athletes, giving him the advantage of speed, power, and quickness. Thinking about it, he smiled. He could imagine no scenario resulting in a second loss.

Then the assistant coach heard the door creaked open to the old facility.

"Did y'all forget something?" He hollered, expecting a response from another coach or a trainer. They were always leaving a piece of equipment behind.

The shot grazed the back of his head only because he turned at the last second. Wax heard the lead slam into the locker behind him. The coach went through a momentary stage of shock before the realization hit him like an ice-cold shower. Someone was trying to kill him.

The second shot tore through his jacket and ripped the fleshy part of his upper arm. Wax yelled out, not so much from the pain, but from the severity of the situation.

He turned and sprinted forward toward the old showers, cinderblock units no longer used by the team. The pipe and shower heads were brown with rust. Green mold covered each stall.

Thinking quickly, Jimbo climbed up on top of the third shower and pushed his body tight against the outer wall, giving him limited cover. He heard the heavy footsteps entering the locker room. He cringed, knowing there would be no escape if he was discovered.

The shooter fumbled around in the dark, unfamiliar with the old facilities. Jimbo heard the clanking and clanging as benches and lockers were bumped. He twisted, trying to figure a way out of the trap. If the shooter turned on the lights, his position would be quickly uncovered.

The shooter reached the small hallway leading to the showers. Jimbo heard a scrape of a shoe or boot on the concrete floor only ten feet away. Wax thought of the things he would never get to do in life. Kids. Vacations. Better coaching opportunities. Leading the LSU Tigers to another national championship. That was his ultimate dream.

Then he heard the sweetest sound he had ever heard in his lifetime. A police siren pierced through the night air, penetrating the tranquil peace over Wildcat stadium.

The shooter bolted for the door, knocking over the benches and chairs between the showers and the exit. A broad grin crossed Jimbo's countenance despite the burning pain in his shoulder.

Wax struggled down and stumbled to the open door, where he stepped outside. He saw the fleeting shadow of a figure disappear into the woods at the east end of the stadium. He knew the thin strip of trees contained a fishing pond with a road leading to the highway. The shooter probably had a vehicle stowed away.

He looked toward the road only to see the police car speed right on by, paying no attention to the dark athletic facility. It was not responding to the shots fired within the locker room. Jimbo did not care at this point. The siren had saved his life.

Now he tried to figure out who wanted to kill him.

48

CENTRAL

"Somebody tried to kill me," Jimbo told Niki, his arm bandaged in a sling.

Niki took one of the unattractive chairs in the small hospital room.

"So why call me?" The private investigator asked.

"Come on. You have to see the connection between this and the case against Billy. The two have to be connected." Jimbo winced when he accidentally moved his arm.

"I'm not so sure. Is there something going on in your life that would offend someone else?"

Jimbo did not smile.

"If you're asking me if I'm screwing someone else's wife, I'm not. I am faithful to my wife and she is faithful to me. There is no jealous spouse out there gunning for me."

"I had to ask. I don't want to follow any little bunny trails only to end up where I started."

Niki sat her bag on the floor beside her chair.

"Are you willing to help me?" Jimbo asks with facial lines drawn. "I really need your help."

"Why didn't you think of that when I tried to get you to help me? You were, shall we say, less than sincere in your answers to my questions."

"I'm sorry. I guess I never really believed Billy did all the stuff to those girls. That is so out of character of who he is. It would be impossible for him to take advantage of anyone, much less a female student."

Jimbo grunted again as pangs shot through his arm despite the strong pain medicine fed through the IV tubes.

"Do you know who is behind this charade?" Niki took no notes, but leaned forward on the edge of the chair, anticipating an immediate denial from the coach.

"Yes," he answered, surprising the investigator.

"You do?" Niki could not believe her ears.

"I'm ninety percent certain. It was dark in the locker room, but I'm almost positive I recognized the shooter."

Jimbo groaned out loud.

A nurse opened the door to the small room. She took one look at the equipment spitting out readings of the coach's vital signs. She turned to Niki.

"You'll have to leave. The patient needs his rest."

"Can you give us just one minute? He is about to tell me some critical information," Niki protested.

The nurse ignored her requests, adjusting the amount of sedative being fed through the IV to Jimbo. After fiddling with the various adjustment needles, she smiled at the investigator.

"You may have thirty seconds before he is dead asleep, but I wouldn't trust anything he says in the state he is in." She walked out of the door, leaving a frustrated private investigator sitting on the edge of her uncomfortable chair.

She put her hand on Jimbo's good arm. "I'll be here first thing in the morning. Don't forget you promised to tell me the whole truth."

Jimbo half nodded, his eyelids already beginning to insulate him from the outside world and the egregious events that resulted in his hospitalization.

Niki waited until he closed his eyes without trying to reopen them. A soft snore originated from within his chest. She considered staying in the room so she would be there whenever he awakened.

"The nurse said he'll be out for several hours," a soft feminine voice came from the doorway.

Niki looked up to see Pattie Grace Wax. Although they had never met, Niki has seen her at the ballgames and in Walmart.

Pattie Grace still looked like a teenager, a cute button nose highlighting a dark complected face. Her figure bordered on the lean side, no hint of any extra flab anywhere. The only things giving Niki a clue of her anxiety were the deep wrinkles in the corners of her eyes.

"Hey, Pattie Grace. I don't believe we've ever formally been introduced. I'm Niki Dupre."

The coach's wife tried to smile. "I know who you are. Everybody in Louisiana knows who you are."

Niki flushed. "I doubt that. People in my profession aren't the topic around the water coolers and coffee pots."

"But you are. Ever since you solved that thing on Spirit Island, we all know you. I mean, we know who you are and what you look like."

"Can I buy you a cup of coffee? It's not that great, but at least it's hot."

Pattie Grace looked down at her husband lying in the hospital bed. A tear rolled down her face. "Who are these idiots around here who think football is more important than Jimbo's life?"

Niki was taken aback.

"Do you think this happened because Central lost the football game?"

"What else could it be?" The dam broke and tears cascaded down Pattie Grace's face.

"I think we need to talk," Niki said before rising to guide the stricken wife from the room. They found a visitor's room complete with vending machines and free coffee. The pot was empty, but as soon as Niki got Pattie Grace situated on a sofa, she found the coffee packets in a cabinet. Less than five minutes later, she had a fresh pot of community coffee ready to go.

"How do you take yours?" Niki asked Pattie Grace.

"Three sugars and three creams," Pattie Grace responded.

Niki shook her head at the unusual concoction, but put the condiments in the potent brew and carried it to Pattie Grace. Niki waited for Pattie Grace to take a couple of sips before trying to engage her in a conversation.

"You said you think someone tried to kill Jimbo because we lost the game?"

Pattie Grace nodded. "That has to be the reason. Everybody loves Jimbo. I don't know anyone who doesn't love him."

"Is there anyone that would have a reason to harm your husband? Jealousy? Envy? Anything?"

Pattie Grace coughed out a laugh. "We don't have anything for anyone to be jealous of or envious about. We're just starting out."

"I know this is awkward, but are you seeing anyone outside of your marriage?"

The tears shut off as though someone suddenly turned the tap. Pattie Grace's eyes grew wide.

"Heavens, no. I've never even considered it. I'm so lucky to have Jimbo. I never considered jeopardizing our relationship."

She paused. "You don't think she is seeing another woman, do you?"

Niki shook her head.

"I have no reason to believe so. In fact, I'm certain he is completely satisfied with his marriage to you."

"Why did you ask?"

"I had to see your reaction. Now that I've seen it, I don't need to go there again."

"This has to be about the football game? If you rule out everything else, there is nothing left except that stupid game. I hope Jimbo never coaches again." The tears returned.

"There are some other things going on that may have a hand in what happened tonight. I'm not certain how they fit in exactly, but he spoke to me for a second before the sedatives took effect."

"What did he say?" Pattie Grace's demeanor softened.

"I don't know how much you know about the allegations surrounding Coach Bailey."

"If you mean he diddled a cheerleader and killed another one, I know all about that. He should be ashamed of himself."

Pattie Grace made those observations without reservation..

"Okay." Niki did not want to anger the wife in this situation, but could not allow the accusations to go uncontested. "First, I don't believe Coach Bailey is guilty of the allegations. Second, I believe your husband has some information relevant to Billy's innocence."

"What do you mean? What information?" Pattie Grace asked.

"That is what I don't know yet. The sedatives hit him before he could tell me. I plan to be here first thing in the morning to find out."

"Are you saying that someone tried to kill Jimbo because he

has some information?" Pattie Grace had difficulty absorbing the full meaning.

"Yes, I do. Tomorrow morning, I intend to find out what that information is."

Pattie Grace shook her head.

"But if that is the case. Then why is it information that will clear Coach Bailey? Could it be information that will confirm his guilt with those two girls?"

Niki had not even considered this possibility. She assumed, based on the holes in the evidence, Billy Bailey was innocent. But what if Pattie Grace was correct? What if Jimbo had information confirming Billy's guilt? Where was Billy after the football game? Niki hoped he was home with Sara Sue, but in the back of her mind, she had a sinking feeling.

Niki did not vocalize her doubts to Jimbo's wife. "Billy has been more than forthcoming with all the information about himself and those girls. He has no reason to kill your husband."

"What would Jimbo know that could put him in danger then? He's already told me he didn't see Billy with any of the cheerleaders or anyone else."

The strawberry blonde had the same question. "Has he talked to anyone in the last couple of days about the case?"

"Of course. The whole school is talking about it. Heck, the whole town is talking about it. When I go to church and the grocery store, everybody asks me if I know anything. Everybody assumes that Jimbo knows something since he took over as head coach."

"Does he?" Niki asked.

"Not as far as I know. But Jimbo keeps a lot of things to himself, especially if it concerns one of the kids."

"I hope that doesn't kill him." Niki rose and left.

49

LANE MEMORIAL HOSPITAL

ZACHARY

"IF YOU NEED ANYTHING ELSE, Coach Wax, just punch that button, and we'll be right here." The nurse in the white uniform gave a final tuck on the covers and left the hospital room.

Jimbo tried to relax. The massive dose of pain killers through the IV tubes helped. The bullet to the upper arm struck no bones, but did damage to several veins extending from his neck.

A series of closures and rerouting would make him as good as new in a few months. At least that was the prognosis from the lead doctor. Flashes of pain shot through the full length of his arm, reminding the coach that the healing process would be no picnic.

Of more concern was the wound in the side of Jimbo's head, much deeper than he first thought. The path of the projectile resulted in a minor fracture in his skull. The doctor expressed amazement he had not lost consciousness when the bullet plowed through thin skin and thick bone.

Pattie Grace, his wife, had briefly visited him after he checked in. When informed that neither injury was life-threatening, she left the room to meet with Niki. Jimbo did not want to meet with the investigator again. He wanted to make sure he had all his faculties in working order before talking to Niki. That was one reason he feigned going to sleep after the nurse came in to warn her.

Now he was awake again. His mind transferred into overdrive. Why did someone attempt to kill him? He was fairly certain it was because of the allegations against Billy Bailey. He was sure of it.

Jimbo had time to think after meeting with Flavia Foster when she had come to him about getting an abortion. However, things did not add up when he tried to put all the pieces of the puzzle together.

That's when he approached Flavia Friday afternoon. He had told her they needed to talk. He did not believe her story and told her so. The look on the cheerleader's face at that moment should have been a huge warning sign. He never dreamed the end result would be an attempt on his life.

He heard the door open, expecting to see the nice nurse coming in to check on him. His mouth dropped when Billy Bailey entered. The head coach looked worn and haggard, his appearance having aged at least ten years over the past five days.

"Hey, Billy," Jimbo managed, his voice weak.

"Jimbo, you're alive—I was so worried."

Wax flashed a hint of a smile. "They can't keep a good man down. Even if he blows a game he should have won."

Billy edged to the side of the bed. He placed a hand on Wax's good arm.

"Don't worry about the game. It's not important right now. We need you to get healthy again so you can take your place on the sidelines."

Another faint smile from the patient.

"My place is standing right next to you. I realize that now."

A huge sigh of relief escaped Bailey. "You can't imagine how nice that is to hear. I was scared you would blame me for all this mess."

A slight shake of Jimbo's head. "I know better now. In fact, I know you are entirely innocent. I figured it all out."

The jolt of surprise exploded throughout Billy's body. "What do you mean? What did you figure out?"

Jimbo tried to shift in the bed, his bad arm firing streaks of pain because of the effort. He moaned. Billy's focus changed to the health of his friend.

"Do you need me to call the doctor?"

Jimbo pointed at the panic button. Billy grabbed it and punched much harder than necessary.

"Yes, may I help you?" The voice came through the speaker at the head of the bed.

"This is room three twelve. Coach Wax is in a whole lot of pain," Billy replied.

"I'll send someone right down."

Less than one minute later, a uniformed nurse burst through the door. She took one distracted look at Billy, then went directly to Jimbo's side. She quickly checked the bandage on his head and then inspected the wrapping around his shoulder. The nurse bore a frown when she discovered the back of the bandage covered with blood.

She hit the panic button again. When a voice came over the speaker, she asked for immediate help. Two more nurses, one male and one female, flew into the room less than thirty seconds later. The original nurse yelled something at them that Billy did not understand.

The two new nurses repacked the whole bandage over Jimbo's shoulder. They applied a thick gel under new sterile cloths. The first nurse took a vial out of the medicine cabinet and added it to the IV. After the entire amount dripped into the IV, the nurse turned to Billy.

"Are you family?" She asked.

"No, Ma'am. I coach on the same team as Jimbo. At least I used to." Bailey amended his answer.

"Then you're—You're Coach Bailey," she accused.

"Yes, Ma'am."

"What are you doing here? You're the last person in the world the patient needs to see right now." She stepped away from the bed.

"I just wanted to see him. We're still friends, despite what has happened."

The nurse pointed a finger at Billy. "I don't know what happened, but I know what you did. You're not welcome in this hospital. We don't cater to the likes of you."

"I didn't—"

"Never mind. I'm not the judge or you would already be in jail. Now you're going to get out of here before I call the police." She pointed at the door.

Billy slunk out of the room, his confidence and his outlook shaken.

The nurse turned back to Jimbo. Between the efforts of all three, they blocked the flow of blood from the veins that had reopened. After inspecting their work, they left the assistant head coach asleep on the hospital bed. The large amount of sedatives finally took effect.

A few minutes later, the door opened again. A figure dressed in green hospital scrubs slid into the room. The figure withdrew a large needle from the front pocket and drove the point into the IV tube. The killer smiled at the coach lying beside him and patted Jimbo's arm. Wax flinched, but did not open his eyes. It was too late for him to do anything at this point.

50

CENTRAL

"WHERE IS HE?" Niki demanded of the startled Sara Sue.

Billy's wife dressed in a night robe, but it was obvious to the detective she had not been asleep when Niki banged on the door.

"He said he was going for a ride." Sara Sue knew Niki was asking about Billy. "He didn't tell me where he was going. He just left."

"Does he have a cell with him?"

Sara Sue nodded. "I think so. I begged him to stay here tonight. We don't need any more trouble, and it seems to come up when he goes out at night."

"No kidding," Niki picked up her phone and hit a couple of buttons.

"Where are you?" She yelled into the phone.

"I'm almost home," Billy answered.

"I'm here waiting for you." Niki disconnected.

Eight minutes later, Billy Bailey pulled into the driveway. Niki met him outside his home and approached him before he got out of the vehicle.

"Where have you been?"

"Can we go inside? I don't want to wake the whole neighborhood. We've already been enough of a distraction to them." Billy responded.

They trudged into the house.

As soon as they got inside, Niki turned on the coach. "So where did you go?"

Billy groaned. "I went to see my friend. He's still my friend no matter what."

Niki exhaled. "Please tell me you're kidding. Please tell me you did not go to the hospital."

Billy stiffened. "I did. Look, I appreciate everything you've done for me and everything you will do for me, but you're not my boss. You can't tell me where I can go and who I can see."

Niki erupted. "You don't get it. I'm trying real hard to keep your butt out of jail, and you're doing everything imaginable to get stuck back in there."

"I only went to visit Jimbo. I see no harm in doing that. He was about to tell me something, but he passed out before he had a chance."

Niki ran both hands through her long strawberry blonde hair.

"Billy, I'm trying to keep my patience, but you are making it difficult. Didn't we agree that you would stay home and leave the investigation to me?"

The coach slouched in his recliner. "That was before Jimbo was shot. I can't stand around playing house husband while somebody is trying to kill my friends. I'm not built that way."

Niki stared at him. She remained standing.

"Do you remember that first night in jail? Do you remember what you told me?"

The coach slowly nodded, but said nothing.

Niki continued. "Do you remember how scared you were about what might happen to you?"

Another slow nod. No words.

"Think about twenty or thirty years of that. Think about worrying every minute of every day and every second of every night who might pay a visit to your jail cell."

Billy issued a weak reply. "I just wanted to see Jimbo. Nothing happened."

"Did anyone see you there? Did anyone see you go into Jimbo's room?"

Billy could no longer look at Niki, the fight having left his body.

"The nurse. Actually, three nurses. They came into the room while I was there. Jimbo started bleeding again."

Niki squeezed her eyes tight. "So you were in the room alone with him when he had a setback and began to bleed."

Billy face jerked up. "It's not like that. I only happened to be there. I didn't cause Jimbo to start bleeding. You're twisting things again."

"What do you think the prosecutor will do to you? Do you think she will only ask the questions that make you look innocent? Do you think she will take you at your word you had nothing to do with your friend's setback?"

"But you make it sound like I'm guilty."

Niki threw up both hands. "Duh. If you think I'm trying to make you look guilty, wait until you get in the stand in front of a judge and twelve of your peers. That's when you'll look guilty."

Billy sank back in the chair. "I know you're mad at me, but my visit almost paid off. Jimbo was about to tell me who he thought was behind all this when his wound opened. I think he knows who is trying to frame me."

Niki nodded, her voice softening a bit, but still firm. "I

talked to him before you did. I believe he can break this case wide open. I'm going back in the morning to talk to him."

"What time? I want to go with you."

Niki blew out a long breath. "What will it take to get through to you?"

Billy stood.

"It's my butt on the line here. I have a right to find out what's going on."

"You don't have a right to tamper with any potential witness. The court will frown on your visit tonight if they find out. You can't afford to piss off the judge again."

"But I want to go."

"Listen, I'll call you as soon as Jimbo tells me what he knows. That's the best we can do."

"But—"

A knock on the door interrupted Billy. Both he and Niki stepped back when he opened the door.

"Mr. Bailey," the policeman said. "I'm Kenneth Aiken. I work in homicide at the Sheriff's office. We need to ask you about your visit to Lane Memorial Hospital tonight."

51

CENTRAL

N<small>IKI GAVE</small> Billy a '*I told you so*' look.

"Officer, I'm Niki Dupre. Mr. Bailey is my client. What is the nature of your questions?"

"Are you his attorney?" The homicide cop asked.

"I'm a private investigator working for the attorney representing Mr. Bailey."

"How long have you been here?"

"About twenty minutes. I came to talk with my client about some new developments in the case." Niki stepped in between Billy and the officer.

"Dupre? Dupre? You're on our list. We have a report you visited Jimbo tonight."

"Yes, I did. Then I spoke with Pattie Grace Wax, his wife, in the visitor area in the hospital. Why are you asking?" Niki did not feel comfortable with the direction of the questioning.

The cop ignored her question. "What time did you leave?"

Niki shrugged. "I'm not sure. Maybe an hour ago. Maybe a little longer. You can ask Jimbo. He might remember the time."

The officer frowned. "We would like to, Miss Dupre. But that isn't possible. Mr. Wax is dead."

Niki's hand went instinctively to her mouth. Then an imposing figure loomed in the doorway. Chief of Homicide Samson Mayeaux entered without being asked.

"I'll take it from here." He told the two policemen, nodding toward the door.

They gave him a slight nod of their heads and left without saying anything further. The chief turned back to Niki, Billy, and Sara Sue, who seemed to be in a state of shock.

Samson stood shifting from one foot to the other until Billy settled into his recliner. Mayeaux sat on one end of the sofa and Niki occupied the other. Sara Sue, as though in a trance, remained standing in the entrance to the hallway leading to the bedrooms.

For at least sixty seconds, Samson said nothing, staring intently at Billy. Niki glanced at the coach, trying to determine what held the Chief's attention. Billy's complexion morphed into the hue of a boiled egg, no color apparent in his cheeks or his temples.

Mayeaux took out a small pad that looked even smaller in his huge paw. Niki could not have written one complete sentence on one of its pages. But Samson eyed the tiny pad as though it contained the entire works of William Shakespeare.

"Tell me about it." He motioned toward Billy, his instructions intentionally vague.

"About—About what?" Billy stuttered.

"What happened tonight?" Samson asked, his eyes now focused on the small tablet.

Billy gave him a brief recap of his two minutes alone with Jimbo, including the conversation with the lead nurse. He also told the chief about Jimbo's intention to tell him more about the situation with the cheerleaders.

"He was alive when I left. The nurses, as far as I could tell, had stopped the bleeding. I don't know what could've happened after I left to make him start bleeding again." Billy finished the summary.

"Who told you he started bleeding again?"

"Uh—I assumed—What else could it have been to cause his death?" Billy squirmed in the recliner which had become uncomfortable since Samson's started talking.

"He was poisoned." Mayeaux was terse.

"My God." Sara gasped from her position.

Mayeaux did not look at her or Niki. His gaze remained focused on Billy. The private investigator said nothing, waiting for the coach to speak. Niki now understood that Samson was searching for signs of a *tell*, a facial spasm or involuntary movement that would indicate the coach was lying. She shifted her attention to Billy to see if she could pick up any hint of deception.

"I didn't know. Who would want to kill Jimbo? Everybody loved him." Billy's chin sunk into his chest, but his mind raced. His eyes continued to go from one object to another, unable to stay focused on any particular spot.

"You tell me." Again, terse words from Samson.

Instead of answering the chief, Billy turned to Sara Sue. "Do you mind making a pot of coffee? I think it might help right now."

Sara Sue almost ran to the kitchen, thankful for having a concrete task to achieve. The other three could hear her going through the pantry, having forgotten where she kept the coffee grounds.

"So, now that your wife isn't here, who do you think killed Jimbo Wax?" Samson asked.

"I've been thinking about it since you told me he was dead. I'm not sure." Bailey replied, his voice now firm.

"What are your thoughts? You have obviously come up with at least one suspect." Mayeaux pressed.

"I'm thinking of two different possibilities. Maybe just one. I don't know. I guess both of them would fit together."

"I'm listening," Mayeaux still had written nothing on the small tablet.

"It goes back to somebody setting me up. Now somebody has killed Jimbo. Also, LaDonne was killed in order to either frame me or to keep her quiet."

Mayeaux said nothing but gave a slight nod.

Billy continued. "It seems now the head coaching job is wide open. The way things work, there is only one person who can fill the position for the rest of the season, including the playoffs."

"Who is that?" Mayeaux asked.

"Ricky Delrie, the freshman coach. At least he was. I understand he helped coach the varsity tonight." Billy buried his head in his hands.

"Why is he the only one? Aren't there are several assistant coaches?"

"The school has a requirement that the head coach must have a Masters degree. I have one. Jimbo had one. The only other person on the staff that has one is Ricky Delrie."

"Why can't the school hire someone from another school? Why does the replacement have to come from the current staff?" Mayeaux jotted something down on the small pad.

"Our policy is if the position becomes vacant during the active season, then the school is required to offer the position to a member of the coaching staff. They figured it would be easier to transition."

"That leaves Delrie in the catbird's seat to replace you. Is he the kind of fella that would kill two people to get your job?" Mayeaux returned to staring at the coach.

Sara Sue returned with three cups of hot coffee. She handed one to each of them and went back to the sanctuary of the kitchen. All three took a sip of the dark brew, each in private thoughts.

Finally, Billy answered the question. "I didn't think so. But then, I never dreamed anybody I know would be capable of killing people for personal gain. It never dawned on me."

"Why have you changed your mind?" Samson asked between sips.

"Because it has to be somebody close to the school. Flavia and LaDonne are involved. At least LaDonne was involved. Flavia still is."

"Why does that narrow it down to Delrie?"

Billy blew out a breath between quivering lips. "He's the only one I know who has enough to gain and has enough of a friendship with the kids to pull it off."

"Do you think he did himself?"

Billy shook his head. "No. I don't see that in Ricky's makeup. But then, until now, I didn't think having two people killed was in his makeup either."

"Who would he get to help him? Any ideas?"

Billy threw one palm up. "No. None. I don't know those kinds of people."

"Maybe I do," Niki interjected.

Mayeaux shifted his gaze to the private investigator.

"We think Sleazy Slocum is tied to this case one way or the other. We've had a tail on him for the past few days."Niki said.

Mayeaux smiled for the first time. "That's good. Then you can tell me where Mr. Slocum was when the young lady and the coach were killed."

Niki turned beet red. "I can't. We lost him every time we put a surveillance on him. I wish I could tell you where he was, but the truth is, I don't have a clue."

That was the first time Niki mentioned to Billy about their unsuccessful attempts to monitor Slocum's whereabouts. She glanced at him for a reaction, but the coach was absorbed with his own demons.

Mayeaux caught her glance and winked at Niki. "Don't worry about it. I've lost Sleazy on more than one occasion myself. He's one of the best in the business."

Niki ran a hand alongside her face. "I don't like being made a fool. I have to admit that Mr. Slocum has gotten under my skin. He knows how to push my buttons."

Mayeaux smiled. "Sleazy makes a living by irritating his foes. He figures if you are pissed off at him, you will more likely make mistakes. Looks like he might be right."

"Maybe so," Niki replied. "But doesn't it look like two separate killers? LaDonne was killed with a knife and Jimbo was poisoned. Two different methods. That suggests two different killers to me."

Mayeaux looked at his tablet, but he was not reading any of the information it contained.

"Normally, I would agree with you. I was considering the possibility myself. The knife and the stark nature of the attack on LaDonne suggests her murder was committed by a man. The poisoning of Coach Wax is gender-neutral, but if it was the same guy, then why didn't he use a knife like he did with LaDonne? It took longer to inject the poison in the IV tube then it would have taken to slit his throat."

Billy recovered his focus. "So we're talking about two different people being involved? A man and a woman?"

Mayeaux nodded. "That's the way I'm considering it now. I don't know where it will lead, and I don't know how Mr. Slocum fits with any of this."

Niki stared at her coffee cup. "If you are correct, then Slocum killed LaDonne, and a woman killed Jimbo."

Mayeaux nodded. "Slocum could have poisoned Wax as well. Putting the poison in the IV tube gave him time to get out of the hospital before the coach reacted and died. That might explain the two different techniques."

"Do you know if Slocum has used either in the past?" Niki asked.

"We haven't been able to directly tie Slocum to any of our open cases. If we could, I would be the first one to arrest him." Mayeaux sighed at the admission.

"I understand. Maybe I'm not the only one who has been fooled by him. How about the cases where he is a suspect?"

Mayeaux closed his eyes, as if mentally sorting through every open case in East Baton Rouge Parish that might remotely tie to Slocum.

"We suspect Sleazy has used a variety of methods to eliminate his targets. Some were shot from a distance. Some were shot up close. Some were stabbed to death. At least one was strangled. Three people were blown up with a car bomb."

"You didn't mention poisoning. Do you suspect him of ever using poisons to kill someone?"

"Not so far. But we could be wrong."

"But even if we find out he killed Washington, LaDonne, and Coach Wax, we still will have to find out who hired him."

"My best guess right now is Delrie. He's the kind of weasel that would hire somebody else to do his dirty work."

Mayeaux stood, indicating that he was through speculating.

52

CENTRAL

"So you're now the acting head coach," Niki used an accusatory tone.

"Looks that way." Ricky Delrie could not help but suppress a smile.

"Where were you this morning?"

"Huh?" A noticeable tic at the corner of Delrie's eye.

"Where were you when Coach Wax was killed?" Niki expanded the question.

Shock spread across the young coach's face. "Are you serious?"

"Deadly so," she replied.

Delrie rose from behind the desk in the office designated for the head coach. He walked to the window and stared out into space. He kept Niki waiting for more than two minutes.

"I didn't do it," he finally replied.

"Do what?"

"I didn't kill Jimbo. We're friends. At least we were."

"But now, with Billy and Jimbo out of the way, you're in charge. You have a chance to make your mark."

"So?" He shrugged. "That's the luck of the draw. I happen to be in the right spot at the wrong time."

"Coincidence? Is that what you want me to believe?"

"That's the gist of it."

"Then answer my questions. Where were you this morning when Coach Wax was killed?" Niki asked.

Delrie turned back from the window, her face stern. "I can't tell you. I wish I could, but I can't."

"You don't want to give me an alibi that would clear your name? That sounds fishy."

"I don't care how it sounds. I can't tell you where I was this morning." The coach no longer looked at Niki when he spoke.

"Is she eighteen?" Niki watched the man closely for reaction. She was not disappointed. Ricky Delrie was physically shaking, his hands trembling and his lips quivering.

Niki knew the answer to your question without a verbal reply. She went another direction with the probe.

"Do you know John David Slocum?"

"I—uh. Sort of." The words did not come easily for the man.

"What does *sort of* mean? Do you know him?"

"I know who he is. I've had a few casual conversations with him."

"What were those conversations about?"

"Stuff. Just stuff," the coach mumbled.

"Come on. You can do better than that. If you want me to go away, tell me a believable lie."

"He's one of our supporters in the Athletic Association. His daughter is a sophomore and plays on the girls' basketball team."

"His daughter?" This was news to Niki. In her dealings with the Slocums, neither had ever mentioned a daughter. She had to wonder why.

53

ZACHARY

THE GRAY F150 left Zachary and followed the same route as always. John David "Sleazy" Slocum watched the white Ford Explorer pull out of the parking lot soon after he passed. It remained three to four car lengths behind, all the way to Baton Rouge. The driver was good at the shadowing technique.

Sleazy was better. His future depended on his attention to his environment. Too many people considered him to be a permanent enemy, and would continue to do so until he was no longer around.

Slocum pulled into the garage and parked by the bridgeway to the elevators. He waited until the SUV passed, giving no indication he was even remotely aware of its presence.

Then he sprinted down the parking garage stairs to the red sedan. He smiled, knowing that Niki Dupre or one of her investigators was about to spend several frustrating hours searching for him within the confines of the hotel.

When he pulled onto the highway, Slocum watch carefully for a separate trailing car. He saw none. To be sure, the professional took a roundabout route to his destination,

Mansur's on the Boulevard. One more delicious meal he could charge to his mysterious client.

Lisa, the demure hostess, picked up a menu, flashed an alluring smile, and led him through the restaurant to the back room. He was somewhat taken aback when he saw a diner already seated at his favorite table. He thought he might have a word with the manager.

To his surprise, Lisa escorted him to the same table.

"Have a seat, John David." Niki lowered the menu in front of her face with a knowing smile.

The stunned man's mouth dropped. He sat in the chair next to the private investigator, putting much thought into it. Then, as suddenly as his composure had been snatched from him, it returned. He placed the menu to the side.

"What is this all about?" He demanded.

"You were so kind to buy my dinner the last time you were here." Niki's face never lost a smile. "I wanted to return the favor."

"I prefer to dine alone."

"Unfortunately, the place is busy. All the other tables are full, and they have a waiting list. Besides, I've already ordered some spring rolls for appetizers."

Slocum stared at the attractive detective for several minutes. She held his gaze without flinching. Then he instantly relaxed.

"Thank you. It's not often I have the pleasure of such exquisite company. My apologies for my rude manners."

"Accepted. Now, can we talk?"

"I can't talk without a drink in my hands." He snapped his fingers and the waiter immediately disappeared, coming back in less than a minute with a deep red wine.

He held the glass in front of him. "My compliments to a devious young lady."

Niki tapped her class of iced tea against his. "I take that as an honor coming from the master."

Slocum did not sip the wine. He drained it. The waiter immediately refilled the empty glass.

"For what do I owe this pleasure?" He asked.

"I want to ask you a few questions."

Slocum nodded and kept his attention on the disappearing crimson liquid before him. His expression was not revealing.

"Do you know Ricky Delrie?"

"If we are to have this conversation, ask questions to which you don't already know the answers. Our meal will be much more enjoyable if you do."

"How long have you known Delrie?"

Slocum considered his answer for some moments before giving her a reply.

"I don't see where that is pertinent to your investigation."

"What do you know about my investigation?"

"Enough."

"Did you kill the stockbroker, Earl Washington, and try to frame Donna?"

Niki saw absolutely no change in Slocum's expression. No tics. No spasms. No tightening of the facial muscles. No nervous movements of his lips.

"I'm not in that business," he answered.

"That's not what I've heard. Your reputation says you are indeed in that business."

"Ahh." A grin crossed the big man's lips. "My reputation. So that's why you stuck your man on my tail."

"No. Not at the beginning."

"I know."

Niki was the one that was now surprised. Slocum had casually admitted he was aware of the bogus call leading her to believe he was involved. Was he bragging? Was he egotistical?

Why would he admit that so openly? It took a bit for her to regain her thoughts.

"Why? Why did you get us to follow you?"

"I didn't say I did."

"But you said you know. The only way for you to know is if you participated in the setup."

"That is one conclusion you could draw."

Still no denial. Slocum was unlike any other suspect Niki had ever interviewed. The innocent ones were tense and edgy. The guilty ones were more so, but tried to hide it.

"I guess it will do me no good to ask if you killed LaDonne and Coach Wax?"

The big man smiled and picked up the menu, handing it to the waiter. The college student turned to Niki.

"I'll have the Redfish on a Plank," she said.

"Excellent choice,"

Slocum said nothing to the young man, but Niki noticed him writing down two entrées on his pad.

"Did you kill them?"

"No." Slocum did not change expressions. Niki was a keen observer of people. Most, she could read like a dime-store novel. But with Sleazy, his countenance might as well been written in Cantonese or Urdu. The private investigator had no idea what the big man was hiding behind that mask.

"Did you arrange for someone else to kill Washington, LaDonne, or Wax?"

"No." Same non-expression from Slocum.

"How can I believe you?"

"Not my style. I don't hire out my work. Too many loose ends if I did."

That was the first thing Slocum said Niki knew was the gospel. Nowhere in Slocum's past had there been any mention of using partners or subordinates. He worked alone.

"Do you know Carl King?"

Slocum smiled.

"Do you know LJ Wild?"

Another smile.

"Do you know Doug Nicklaus?"

The smile did not fade.

"How many more people have to die to accomplish whatever is the reason you were hired?" Niki's voice rose.

"I haven't said anyone hired to me. I haven't said I killed anyone."

"You're not denying at."

"Nor should I," he smiled. "That would be bad for business."

"Bad for business you can't admit you killed a female student?"

"My business is not that different from yours. People hire me to get results. They really don't care how I get to the bottom line, as long as I get there."

The waiter arrived with the entrées. As good as the food was at the best restaurant in Baton Rouge, Niki could not eat the redfish. She lost her appetite.

54

CENTRAL

"Where do we go from here?" Donna asked at the impromptu meeting at Wildcat Investigators.

"To the unemployment line if we don't get this puzzle solved," Drexel laughed.

"It's not that bad. We'll survive. I should get most of my money back when Bailey turns himself in Friday. We won't be broke." Niki stirred her coffee.

Donna grabbed a second donut, this one with chocolate icing and sprinkles.

"Girl, enjoy that while you're young," Drexel admonished. "A few years from now, every one of those sugar pills will add two pounds to places you don't want to add two pounds."

"Look at Niki," Donna exclaimed, while pointing at the strawberry blonde with her free hand. "She eats them and she weighs the same as she did in high school."

"Only because I work out. Do you know I spend three hours every morning working out?"

"Three hours? Why do you work out that long?"

"Kempo."

"You've mentioned that before," Donna said. "What is it?"

"Martial arts. I spent one hour working on agility and flexibility. We call it the *daily dozen*. Then I spent another hour with the *walking the dog*. That's where I practice the different stances we use. Then I spent the last hour against the speed bags and the heavy bag, using my hands and fists on all the offensive and defensive maneuvers. Then I go for a thirty-minute run."

"I'd rather eat three dozen donuts," Donna said. "That sounds like a lot more fun to me." The hourglass blonde grabbed another donut.

"You'll be a lot skinnier if we don't get through this case and move on to another one generating revenue," Drexel laughed.

"We'll make it," Niki said determinedly. "We don't have a choice."

"How do we close this one?" Donna finished the third sugary treat and picked up a fourth filled with chocolate cream.

"We're down to some basic facts. Flavia Foster is definitely involved. John David Slocum is probably involved. We still don't know who is behind the scenes pulling the strings." Niki said.

"Sleazy won't talk. You tried last night and didn't get far," Drexel offered.

"I agree," she said. "He's been questioned too many times in too many cases to start making mistakes now. We have to get to him through someone else."

"That only leaves Flavia," Drexel looked at Niki.

"Yep. She is the only definite in this deal. Boy, she was really good the first time I talked to her. I almost believed her story."

"We have to put some pressure on her. I'm not sure how, but we need to apply something that will get her attention." Drexel rubbed his chin.

Donna wiped some chocolate from the corner of her mouth. "I know what might help."

Niki cast a surprised look at her partner as the youngster reached for the box of donuts again.

"You have an idea?"

"Yes, Ma'am. Do what every girl does when she's not sure who the father of the baby is. Get a paternity test."

"Don't we have to wait until the baby is born to do one of those?" Drexel questioned.

"How old are you?" Donna scoffed. "Obviously too old to keep up with modern technology. Have you figured how to get your VCR to quit blinking now that they're obsolete?"

"They are?" Drexel deadpanned.

"You'd be amazed. You can actually do more with the phone than say *hello*."

"Okay, you two. She is right. We should get a court order since the results could be crucial for our defense." Niki said.

"I wouldn't rush that if I were you," Drexel cautioned. "What if the results are crucial, but not beneficial? That means the cheerleader wasn't the only one getting screwed by your client. You'll be on that slippery slope of no return."

Niki fell silent. What if Billy was lying to her? The paternity test could prove he had relations with an underage student. He would then be found guilty of rape of a minor and all the other charges. He would spend the rest of his life in jail.

55

CENTRAL

"WE NEED to talk before I go down a path that will put some pressure on Flavia to tell the truth." Niki stared at Billy Bailey in his home.

Sara Sue left the house, presumably for an early choir practice at the church. Niki knew there was no practice, but needed to have this discussion with her husband without her there.

Niki saw the fear and dread creeping into the coach's eyes.

"I want to get a court order for a paternity test. I want to prove Flavia's baby isn't yours."

"Wow. Can we do that?"

"We can and we must. At this point, Flavia will make an extremely sympathetic witness in front of a jury. They will tend to side with her and against you."

Niki watched for a reaction. Bailey did not flinch. Not even a slight indication of hesitance.

"So what are we waiting for? I don't have enough money to pay for one, but I might get a loan against my house."

"That's exactly what I wanted to hear. If this test comes out the wrong way, you don't stand a snowball's chance. You realize that, don't you?"

He held Niki's gaze.

"You don't have to worry for a second about that. That baby isn't mine. It belongs to another man—or boy."

"Are you thinking Steve King?"

"They've been dating for several years. A consensual relationship between teens is not that uncommon. Abortions are tough to get in our conservative state. Flavia would have to come up with a good excuse for being pregnant. That makes sense all around."

"Except I'm not sure she can afford to hire someone like Sleazy Slocum. It takes more than a high school girl's allowance to get his services."

"How about Steve's dad, Carl? I'm not sure exactly what he does, but I get the impression he makes lots of money."

"I've been to his business. I'm still not sure how he makes money, though I'd bet it is not on the up and up. He was evasive when I asked him about it." Niki said.

"No surprise there. Plus, he adores his son. He will do anything for him."

"Are you sure we won't get the wrong answer when they run the tests?"

"Not unless they run it on the wrong female."

Niki was stunned. She struggled to unwind the meaning of the words Billy had spoken.

"Do you mean—?"

A huge grin crossed the entirety of Billy's face, answering the question before it was fully asked.

"Congratulations. How is Sara Sue handling the situation?"

"Until last week, she was walking on cloud nine. Now—" Bailey's voice trailed off.

"She knows how to keep a secret. She never said a word to me."

"We want to tell her parents first. I shouldn't have said anything. But it is too much. I sure hope it's a boy."

"Just pray the baby and Sara Sue stay healthy. Who knows? A girl might be playing quarterback for Central High School when she gets there."

"Not if I'm still the coach," Billy said with certainty.

"We need to make sure that happens. We'll file the motion first thing in the morning."

56

LOUISIANA STATE COURTHOUSE

"WE OBJECT, Your Honor. Why should the victim of the defendant be subjected to an invasive procedure since the reason she is in this condition is because of the defendant?" the prosecutor vehemently opposed Kemp's motion for a paternity test.

"Your Honor, Miss Foster is the alleged victim. We believe this motion will help us prove my client had nothing to do with her present condition." Durwin Kemp was up to his best form.

"How invasive is this procedure?" The judge asked.

"We have an expert in the field. She is in the courtroom, and will be glad to briefly explain the examination and the reliability of the results." Kemp said before the prosecutor could say anything.

The judge nodded and Doctor Brenda Thomas stepped to the microphone.

"What are your qualifications, Doctor Thomas?" The judge asked.

The fiftyish lady with premature gray hair spoke in a clear, crisp voice.

"I am a certified obstetrician, specializing in prenatal care. I have been published in the American Medical Association Journal of Medicine for my research into DNA analysis of the tissues of the unborn."

Doctor Thomas spent another fifteen minutes citing her accomplishments, awards, and peer reviews. She told the judge she had been called as an expert in many trials when the fetus showed some form of irregularity.

She summed up her presentation with a brief sentence, approved prior to the beginning by Kemp.

"The paternity test is a simple procedure, causing the patient no discomfort and very little inconvenience. Through our research, the tests are more than ninety percent accurate. At this point, we do not know of a single inaccurate result."

"Does the prosecution have an objection?" The judge asked, although the tone of the questions suggested such a motion was fruitless.

"No, Your Honor."

"When can the alleged victim be available for the procedure?" The judge asked.

"She will get a break from school around Christmas and New Year's. We can check with her to see if she might be available then. If not, she will have another break in March."

"Your Honor," Kemp stepped back to the microphone. "My client is due back in your court in four more days for you to put him in jail. We believe this test will undermine the entire case against him. We urge the court to schedule the test as soon as possible."

The prosecutor rose quickly. "But Your Honor, the victim should not be inconvenienced by this despicable ploy by the Counselor. She must have the ability to live as normal a life as possible after being victimized by the filthy excuse of a man sitting there."

The judge rapped his gavel. "There are no jurors present. We can refrain from name-calling."

"Your Honor," Kemp spoke. "We can arrange for the alleged victim to be administered the process during her study hall tomorrow. Doctor Thomas has agreed, at our expense, to perform the tests herself. She will have the results by Wednesday morning."

"Your Honor—" The prosecutor yelled.

"Hold your horses, Counselor. I believe the test is vital to both sides, at least the results are." The judge's focus shifted to Kemp. "I assume the results of this procedure will be made available to the prosecutor, even if the results are not favorable to your client."

Kemp swallowed hard. He had discussed this very question with Billy Bailey and Niki prior to the hearing. He warned them they would open a Pandora's box, and would be unable to put the contents back in. The two insisted on going forward despite his objections.

To the judge and the prosecutor, he gave no indication of the doubts he had expressed in private.

"Of course, Your Honor. We will gladly share them with the court and with the prosecutor."

The judge had half a smile. "Why do I get the feeling if the results come out in favor of your client, you will also share them with the media?"

Kemp knew better than respond, but had already put a newspaper reporter on notice.

The judge's frown returned. "By order of the court, Miss Foster will submit to a paternity test no later than the close of school hours tomorrow. The results will be presented to the court no later than Wednesday afternoon."

He hit the gavel and left the room.

57

BLACKWATER ROAD

J<small>OHN</small> D<small>AVID</small> "S<small>LEAZY</small>" Slocum got another email from his anonymous employer. So far, he had followed the vague instructions, and had a nice new gold bar because of it. For someone like himself, depositing large sums of cash in a checking or savings account was problematic at best. Too much of a paper trail.

His affinity for gold and silver bars was more than a way to dodge the government. These precious metals would never be worth nothing like some dotcom companies he invested in previously.

The emails were from a free email service available to the public. Anyone could create a fictitious identity in less than five minutes. The previous emails were sent from local libraries in Central, Denham Springs, and Zachary. The ones received before were thinly veiled codes. A man of Slocum's background and experience had little trouble deciphering their meaning. Once he implemented the instructions, his favorite dealer of gold and silver called to let him know the reward was ready. Slocum never attempted to identify the anonymous employer from the dealer. He knew, if things got more serious, he had ways of tracking down the source of the emails.

With this new email, things had gotten more serious. The instructions were clear. The payment offered was more than adequate. It was more than Slocum would have asked for in direct negotiations.

The hang–up rested with the nature of the order. Slocum had built a well-deserved reputation as a ruthless advocate on behalf of his clients. But, in the past, Slocum always operated under the guise of surprise and secrecy. With Niki Dupre breathing down his neck, he had neither.

Slocum fixed himself a cherry Dr Pepper. Long ago, he gave up the hard liquor, which would have amazed the people he knew in the early stages of his career. There was something about the soda that calmed him and acted as a catalyst for his thought process.

The big man printed out the email, something he almost never did. He was too cautious about leaving any evidence of his involvement in any matter to risk having a hard copy lying around. This time, however, he rolled the paper around and around as he considered his response.

The instructions also unwittingly gave Slocum another clue to the identity of his client. As he pondered the consequences of following the orders, he knew this would be one of the most challenging jobs he had ever accepted.

58

CENTRAL HIGH SCHOOL

Niki slipped into the head coach's office without being noticed. When Ricky Delrie burst into the room to prepare for the football practice, he stopped short at the sight of the private investigator seated in his chair.

"What are you doing here?" He demanded.

"Taking care of business," Niki responded.

"I have to get ready for practice. We have an important game this Friday."

"You have to make a good impression in your debut. Better than Jimbo did. I understand that. Central will want a winner for its next coach."

Delrie walked up to the desk and grabbed two files. Niki knew those had nothing to do with football practice.

"I have to go," he said.

"I think you'd better have a seat. If you don't, you won't like what I will do."

"What are you talking about?"

"You told me Saturday you and a student were involved in a relationship."

"I never said that," Delrie responded, his body language showing nothing but fear and dread despite his verbal denial.

"You might as well have. Just like now, I can read you like the Sunday comics. Large print and full-color."

Delrie sank in a visitor's chair. He placed the two folders back on the desk without bothering with the loose papers that fell out of them.

"You can't prove anything," he mumbled.

"I don't have to prove anything. After this fiasco with Billy, don't you think an anonymous tip to the school board will be taken seriously? In my experience, at first a relationship like yours is very low key. Then one or both of you get careless. You send an email or a text telling her how you can't wait to see her. She responds on her tablet or phone about how much she is looking forward to it."

Delrie turned the color of an oyster. A pale whitish gray. His expression looked as if he had eaten one of the slimy creatures, and it did not go down well.

Niki continued. "With what the school board is facing with Billy, they won't hesitate to subpoena your cell phone, your emails, and tablets. What will they find on those, Ricky?"

"Nothing," he replied, but he could not have convinced a third-grader with his delivery.

"Here's the deal," Niki countered. "Either you fess up or the school board gets an email right after I leave this office."

"Why are you doing this to me?" Delrie's voice weak.

"Because you are taking advantage of a young lady that may or may not have the ability to make an adult decision. Plus, I need to know if your activities involve Flavia Foster."

"No," Delrie shouted. "I didn't get her pregnant. I've never touched her. You can't put that one on me. That's all Billy."

"And he has been arrested, dragged through the mud, and has his integrity in shambles. Do you want to be next?"

255

Delrie staggered backwards. He buried his head in his hand. For several long minutes, he kept it there. When he looked up at Niki, his complexion had turned a dark gray and his eyes had streaks of red running in every direction.

"What do you want me to do?" He finally asked.

"Tell me the name of the girl."

"I can't." The young coach vigorously shook his head. "Let's leave her out of this."

"Too late for that, Coach. You're the one that got her involved. Not me."

"Why do you want to drag her through this mess? She is innocent."

"I agree," Niki nodded. "She is innocent. But she will need professional counseling. She has been raped by someone she respected."

"I didn't—"

"Yes, you did. She is too young to consent to a relationship with you. In this state, it means you raped her. My guess is it wasn't only once. I'm also guessing she wasn't the first."

"But—" Delrie could not think of a viable response. His whole future evaporated in a matter of minutes.

"Who is the girl this time?" Niki insisted.

"He'll kill me if I tell you. He won't hesitate if he finds out what I did with his daughter. I'm a dead man."

Niki did not have to think long to figure out the father of the victim.

"You're having sex with John David Slocum's daughter?" Niki was incredulous.

Delrie nodded, his head once again buried in his hands.

"You are one stupid prick. I wouldn't give you much of a chance of living until the game on Friday. Why did you pick her?"

"Paula. That's her name." Delrie's voice was barely audible. "She's not like most airheads here at Central. She is mature, way beyond her years. We just hit it off. Kinda like it was meant to be. Before I knew it, we crossed the line. I couldn't quit. I tried, but I couldn't."

"You dumb bastard. Maybe you should start thinking with your big head." She paused. "If that is possible for you."

Tears flowed down the macho coach's face.

"I'm totally screwed. Just when I get my big chance, I get screwed."

"You're not the one that got screwed. Literally screwed. Can you stop for one minute feeling sorry for yourself and think how this will affect Paula Slocum? She is the victim in your relationship. Not you."

Delrie had never thought about how a conversation like this might go. He never considered being in this position. But now reality was slapping him in the face with an open palm.

"What do I do? Are you going to the police?" He was silently begging.

"I should. I started to go there this morning. But I needed to make sure Flavia was not involved. Now I'm convinced she isn't."

"Does that mean you won't tell anyone what I've done?" A flicker of hope flashed across Delrie's countenance.

"No, I'm not," Niki said.

"Thank you." Relief suddenly flooded the coach's body. A bit of color returned.

"Don't thank me yet. You haven't heard the terms yet."

"What terms?" The color again faded.

"First, you will enroll in a sexual rehabilitation program. You will have to complete the course in a satisfactory manner. Do you understand?"

"I don't have enough money for that. I'm an assistant football coach at a high school. I can't afford one of those programs."

"I'll give you a loan for a second mortgage on your house. You will pay me back after you graduate from the program."

"Why would you do that?"

"Because you need help. Professional help. I could have you sent directly to Angola, but they would give you a different kind of program."

"Thank you," the coach said.

"Not yet. You haven't heard the rest of the terms."

Delrie blanched. He looked up at the private investigator, saying nothing.

"You will also pay for professional counseling for Paula Slocum. Actually, I will pay for it and you will pay me back."

"I can't—"

"You don't have a choice. You are in no position to negotiate."

"Is that all?" Defeat resonated in his voice.

"No." Niki stared at him. "After you and Paula complete your respective programs, you will go to the district attorney and confess everything you did."

"But they'll still send me to Angola."

"Maybe," Niki nodded. "I can't control that. I believe the DA will look favorably on your voluntary enrollment in a rehabilitation program and your willingness to pay for professional counseling for Paula. But I can't guarantee how favorable his reaction will be."

"What about Sleazy? When he finds out, I won't have a chance. He'll make sure of that."

Niki leaned back.

"I truly haven't thought about it. I only found out he had a daughter at Central High when you told me Saturday. I never dreamed you were stupid enough to get involved with John David Slocum's little girl. I didn't think anyone could be that dumb."

59

CENTRAL

Niki watched the cheerleaders go through their routines. Despite being pregnant, Flavia Foster was superb, flawless in timing, more athletic than any other girl. The teenager saw Niki sitting in the makeshift stands and did her best to ignore the private investigator.

After forty-five minutes, the cheerleader could no longer stand the constant gaze. She grabbed up her pom-poms and raced to the girls' locker room, leaving the other members without explanation. They stared at their leader as she disappeared in the building.

Niki did not follow Flavia into the locker room. She did not need to do so. When Flavia emerged, Niki waited by her car. The strawberry blonde leaned against the driver's side door.

"What do you want?" Flavia's tone was both icy and confrontational.

"We need to talk. Your little game is about to fall apart."

"I'm not playing a game. Coach Bailey abused me, and now he has to pay."

"Flavia, the test tomorrow was show Coach Bailey is not the

father of your child. It will prove he can't be. What will you do then?"

The cheerleader stopped, a dazed look spreading across her forehead. Her hesitant movements indicated to the private investigator that despite her poise, Flavia never planned for this situation.

"The test might be wrong."

"According to our expert, they never have been. DNA is a proven science, better than fingerprints. You and I both know the test tomorrow will exclude Coach Bailey as a possibility of fathering your child."

"It could still be wrong," the teenager had no other argument.

"Why don't you tell me who the real father is? We can avoid some embarrassing moments for you if you tell the truth now."

"I am telling the truth. Why don't you believe me?"

"Because of Coach Bailey's reaction to finding out the test will be performed. Because of your reaction to the same news. It doesn't take a detective to figure out which one wants to see the results."

"You can take your test and shove it. I won't take it. You can't make me."

"You're right. I can't make you, but the judge can. He has ordered for you to comply. You don't get to choose to cooperate. You have to submit to the test."

"Why are you doing this to me? What are you after?"

"The truth," Niki sighed. "A good man may go to jail this Friday unless I can find the truth. That's why I need your help. I don't think you're in this alone. Someone is helping you with the charade."

"I can't help you. I'm telling the truth."

"The test tomorrow will tell the truth. Why don't you end this? Tell me what is going on with your story."

Flavia went to the other side of the Ford Mustang and slid to the other side. She positioned herself behind the steering wheel. In less than one minute, she left a deeply disappointed private investigator alone in the parking lot.

60

ZACHARY

THE GRAY F150 pickup pulled out of Fenwood Drive a little after eight o'clock. Drexel did not try to hide his presence. He drove within two car lengths of the truck and followed the familiar path to Florida Boulevard and then to the hotel.

By the time Drexel reached the parking level where the truck was parked it was empty. He did not spot Slocum at the bridgeway crossing to the hotel. He was not concerned. He knew that he had backup waiting on the street in front of the hotel.

When the familiar sedan pulled out of the garage, Donna fell in behind it. She had changed to a rented Honda Accord, deep gray to blend in with the night. The driver of the sedan showed no signs of knowledge of being followed.

The car left the river area and went back east, away from the Mississippi. When it exited on College Dr., Donna assumed it was heading back to Mansur's on the Boulevard. However, it made a quick right and then a quick left. Donna had to turn left with another car right next to her. By the time she turned around, the red sedan disappeared. She followed the street past four restaurants and a hotel. The street wound around and came out to a four-lane intersection. Donna had no idea which way Sleazy Slocum had taken.

61

CENTRAL HIGH SCHOOL

DOCTOR BRENDA THOMAS followed Niki into the high school principal's office. It had not changed much since Niki was a student several years past. Some of the same pictures still hung in the same places. Murray Daniel was still the leader at the school.

The old man seemed to have aged by decades instead of years when he wobbled into the office. Most of his gray hair was gone, only a strand left here and there atop his wrinkled head. His frame had always been lean. Now it was emaciated. Niki has seen for third world kids in better condition than the leader of the high school.

"Niki, it's always good to see you." His genuine smile was still the same.

"Thank you, Mr. Daniel. This place brings back a lot of memories."

"I trust most of them are good. What brings you back to the old stomping grounds?"

"This is Doctor Brenda Thomas. She has a court order to perform a medical procedure on one of your students."

The doctor pushed the papers across the desk. Daniel took them and spent the next ten minutes carefully reading them. When finished, he took off the thick glasses and set them aside.

"I don't particularly like having the school mixed up in this mess."

"It already is," Niki responded. "When one of your faculty members is accused of inappropriate activity with a minor student on school grounds, Central High School is neck deep."

"Will this open us up to a lawsuit by the student?"

"It depends on the outcome. The tests could go a long way in clearing Coach Bailey and by association, the school of any wrongdoing."

Daniel picked up the papers and read them again. He appeared to be searching for a way out of this predicament. He found none.

"I do not believe the school has much choice. Please note for the records, Niki. We are cooperating despite grave misgivings."

"So noted, Mr. Daniel. Can Doctor Thomas have access to the nurses station?"

"I believe that is appropriate given the circumstances. However, the order only applies to Doctor Thomas. You will have to wait in the visitors' lounge while the test is performed."

Niki walked to the small room adjacent to the principal's office while Daniel escorted Doctor Thomas to the nurse's station. It was far from a lounge. Four uncomfortable chairs. One soda machine. No pictures. No slogans. Bare walls.

The investigator could not relax. The whole case against Billy Bailey could be determined by the outcome. A negative result would not clear the coach, but it would speak volumes about the credibility of the accuser. A positive indication of Bailey's paternity would mean the end of his defense and give the district attorney the impetus to go to trial. She could not lose if that was the result. No plea arrangement. Coach Bailey faced the rest of his life behind bars.

For the first few minutes, Niki tried to sit in one of the unstable folding chairs. After ten minutes, she rose and paced around the small room.

After thirty minutes, she selected a crunchy chocolate bar from the machine. Ten minutes later, a chocolate-covered peanuts package became the object of her desires. She was about to punch the button for jalapeno cheese flavored potato chips when the door opened. Doctor Thomas stepped in.

"Thank God. If you have been much longer, I'd be trading in my size four clothes for some fourteens. How did it go?"

"It didn't," the doctor replied.

"Did she refuse? Did you explain to her she didn't have a choice?"

"I didn't get the chance. She never came to the nurses' station. Mr. Daniel found out she didn't come to school today."

Niki was stunned. This is not one of those scenarios she had considered. As the realization sank in, anger replace astonishment. Flavia Foster had never been at the top of her list, but now she sank to the level of roadkill.

"I'm sorry for wasting your time, Doctor."

"No problem," the distinguished lady responded. "Actually, it's your money we're wasting, not my time. I'll send the bill out tomorrow."

Doctor Thomas left Niki in the small room alone. Now the jalapeno cheese flavored potato chips were not desirable. They were essential.

62

LINDA'S FISH & CHICKEN

"Thanks for coming over here, guys," Niki said to Donna Cross and Drexel Robinson. "I think better when I'm eating Cajun fried chicken livers."

"Haven't had any this good since Mama used to fry èm up." Drexel smacked his lips. "Don't tell Mama, but I think these are better."

"Ugh," Donna moaned. "How can you guys eat the insides of the chicken? Do you know what chickens eat?"

"Do you like boiled crawfish?" Drexel asked the hourglass blonde.

"Of course. Who doesn't like crawfish living in Louisiana?" Donna replied.

"Compared to a crawfish, chickens are picky eaters. Crawfish scavenge for anything dead. The more rotten, the more they like it."

"That's different. There are some parts of the crawfish I don't eat either."

Drexel grinned. "Then you're missing the best parts. Sucking the head of a crawfish is pure heaven."

"Niki," Donna turned her head. "Why did you hire this throwback to the Stone Age?"

"This is between you two," the strawberry blonde replied. "But I agree with him about crawfish heads."

"You guys are impossible. I don't know if I even want to finish my fried chicken."

"If you don't, give it to me." Drexel cast an envious glance at the wings. "I'll take them home for supper. If we don't hurry and finish this case, we'll all be eating other people's leftovers."

"We're getting close." Niki said. "We've got Flavia hiding from us. That means she knows something she doesn't want to tell us."

"By the time we find her, Coach Bailey will be in jail." Donna laid down her fork. "I'm not sure he will survive long in there."

"Me either," Drexel chimed in. "He's not the sort of fellow that will agree to get along. He'll fight back and that doesn't work well behind bars."

"I don't even want to think about it," Niki covered her eyes. "We have to find Flavia before Friday morning."

Niki's cell buzzed. She picked it up and listened intently. Wrinkles formed on the attractive detective's face. When she put the phone back in her bag, she was no longer interested in Cajun fried chicken livers.

"That was Samson Mayeaux. They found Flavia's car abandoned at the maze."

The maze was sixty-two acres of an undeveloped subdivision north of Central. The original owners put in underground water, electricity, phone lines and paved streets before going bankrupt. Now it was a place where weeds and priors had taken over, but still popular with the kids for weekend parties and for adults to dump their trash.

The trio of private investigators dropped their napkins on

the table and sped out. Fifteen minutes later, they arrived at the maze. Samson stood twenty feet from the Mustang.

63

THE MAZE

"I thought you only came out for homicides," Niki greeted her friend and mentor. "You didn't say anything about a body over the phone."

"There isn't one," Mayeaux replied, towering over Niki and the others. "We may be looking at a homicide, anyway."

"Why? What makes you think that?" Niki asked.

"Come look." Samson turned and walked toward the abandoned vehicle without waiting for a response.

All three private investigators followed the huge man up to the driver's side doors.

"Look at that," the chief pointed to a smashed window and blood covering the steering wheel and head rest. Copious amounts of blood.

"Nobody can lose that much blood and still be alive," Niki suggested.

"Exactly," Mayeaux replied. "There is no damage to the car except for the broken window and the stains. It didn't hit anything."

Niki looked at their feet. "There isn't any blood trail leading away from the car, so she didn't walk away looking for help."

"Nope." Came the terse reply. "Somebody moved her after she bled all over everything."

"Have you checked the trunk?" Niki hesitated to ask the seasoned homicide cop, but did anyway.

"Not yet," Samson said. "New mayor. New rules. He wants forensics to be the first so we old-timers don't mess anything up."

"But she might be in there bleeding to death."

"I doubt it. In fact, it's impossible. Too much blood. She would be already dead."

A white cargo van pulled up between Samson's vehicle and the Ford Mustang. Three uniformed technicians unloaded equipment, each carrying a bag and a piece of gear. The oldest, no more than mid-twenties, walked directly to the Mustang. The other two remained by the van.

"Chief, we'll take over the scene now. We'll send you a report."

"Look, you little whippersnapper," Samson erupted. "I've been looking at crime scenes since before you were a bad consequence of two kids having fun. I know how to process it."

"Maybe in the past," the youngster replied. "But we have to keep up with the progress. You're part of the past. I'm the future."

"If you keep talking like that, you ain't gonna have much of a future, Sonny."

The youngster went up to the Mustang and took pictures. After taking two or three, he stopped and stared at the quartet of detectives.

"You people will have to step back. I can't have my crime scene contaminated by careless onlookers," he commanded.

"You—" Mayeaux turned beet red and balled his fists.

Niki grabbed the large man and talked to him until he followed her back toward her Ford SUV. When the four were back in her vehicle, Niki suddenly turned to Samson.

"You've got to stop the tech."

"Why?"

"Something's not right about this whole setup."

Samson looked at her for a second as though she was crazy. Then, without saying a word, he turned and lumbered toward the young technician who had just put the key in the trunk lock.

Samson flew through the air, slamming into the uniformed tech, knocking him to the ground. When he looked up he saw the trunk had cracked open. He jerked the technician, put him on his shoulders and sprinted toward Niki and the other detectives.

As they passed the crime scene van, the explosion turned the sky into a fiery combination of orange, red, and black. A wave of heat blew over Samson and the technician, knocking them to the ground.

The other two technicians were thrown off their feet backwards. Niki, Drexel, and Donna were far enough back to withstand the force of the explosion, but ducked as debris fell from the sky.

When Niki could see through the smoke, she gasped. Samson Mayeaux was still laying face first on the pavement, not moving a single muscle. The technician struggled to get to his knees.

Niki rushed to Samson's side. A slight pulse. No visible external wounds. Unresponsive to oral prompts.

"Call an ambulance," she yelled too loud to Donna and Drexel, who were standing next to her.

"Is he dead?" Fear written all over Donna's face.

"He's alive, but barely," Niki replied.

"Barely, my ass." The whisper came from the prone figure on the ground. Samson tried to get to his knees, but fell back to the pavement.

"You stay right there, you old fart." Niki tried to sound firm, but joy resonated in her voice.

Niki positioned her body so she could look at the remaining embers of the Ford Mustang. The back half of the sports vehicle was obliterated, nothing left but shards of metal. The front half contained larger components of the engine intact.

The strawberry blonde scanned the bits and pieces of the remnants that had fallen from the sky. By the time the sirens approached, she concluded what she didn't see was more important than what she did.

64

CENTRAL

"WHEN DID they start making EMTs who haven't started shaving?" Samson grumbled.

"Be thankful there aren't any broken bones for him to set," Niki replied.

"I feel like I've been kicked by mule that didn't quit until I quit kicking back," Mayeaux moaned, and rubbed a bandaged hand over his ribs.

"Maybe if you didn't play tough like a jackass all the time, you wouldn't get treated like one," Niki laughed.

"I was trying to get that fool kid out of the way before that thing blew."

"You should have let me do it. I'm a tad quicker than you." Niki said.

"He weighs more than you," Samson snorted. "Besides, he would have argued with you, and you'd both been blown to hell. I didn't give him a chance."

"You got halfway there. Two or three steps slower and the devil would have your big butt out."

"It's not the first time I've been rejected. Just ask my first three wives." Mayeaux winced from a sharp pang in his side.

"She wasn't there," Niki blurted.

"Who? Who wasn't where?"

"Flavia wasn't in the trunk when it blew up."

"How can you tell?"

"Look at the debris," Niki pointed at the strewn pieces of mangled metal and twisted plastic. "There are parts of everything from axles to the spare tire, but there aren't any human parts. If Flavia had been in the trunk, we would see parts of her everywhere."

Mayeaux rubbed his eyes. "Helluva observation. If she wasn't back there, why rig the trunk to blow up like that? Me and that idiotic excuse for a tech almost bit the big one."

Niki gave Samson a bottle of water, which he took one sip, then inhaled the rest. He looked at the young private investigator.

"How did you know?"

"Same reason you did or you wouldn't have sprinted to save your new friend."

"Damn kid has to have a chance to learn something before he kills himself. You're right, though. Nobody leaves the keys to an abandoned car sticking out of the lock of the trunk."

"That's what I figured out. For a minute I thought I was too late."

"For a minute? I beg your pardon, but I wish you'd figured it out a lot quicker."

"It wouldn't have mattered other than it would have been you and me instead of you and the tech."

"I'm not following you," Samson said.

"Somebody set that bomb off after they saw you and the tech run away. I'm betting you'll find the remote switch in the mess somewhere."

"Hell," Samson struggled to his feet. "Why would anyone do something crazy like that?"

"To get us off the track. Somebody is trying to distract us."

"I'd say they're doing a fine job of doing just that."

The young technician wandered over by Niki and Samson.

"Sir," he was humbled. "I want to thank you for saving my life. If you hadn't grabbed me, I'd be dead right now."

Samson's gruff features relaxed. "Remember, sometimes experience is a lot more valuable than the latest technology."

"I will, Sir. I apologize for my earlier behavior. I have a newfound respect for our older—I mean, more experienced people now."

Niki and Samson watched the young man shuffle back to the ambulance, and get loaded in the ambulance for the short trip to the hospital.

Niki grinned. "You know, if I'm right, you really didn't save his life. Whoever detonated the bomb was waiting for you guys to get clear. You're just so slow. He pushed the button too soon."

"Shush." Samson held a cut finger to his lips. "I'd rather have that little smart-ass thinking he owes his life to a stone age cop. Don't ruin that for me."

"That's not right. He's got to figure it out after they do the investigation."

"Yeah, but there will always be a healthy doubt in his mind before he tries bossing his elders around again."

65

THE MAZE

THE PICKUP ROARED into the maze, almost striking Niki and Samson before coming to a screeching halt. They took an evasive step behind her Ford Explorer to get out of the way of the irate driver.

Donald Foster emerged from the pickup, his face beet red, his jaws clenched, and his fists rolled up into huge balls. Even the much larger Samson eyed Flavia's father the way he would a coiled cottonmouth.

Foster walked directly to Niki.

"You had my daughter killed," he shouted. "Now it's your turn."

The grieving father took a wild swing at the young investigator as soon as he got within range. Niki easily dodged the errant blow as well as the next two.

Then a pair of my strong arms encircled Foster's body. He struggled mightily, but to no avail. The arms around him were too powerful.

"Thanks, Samson." Niki grinned as the older man. "I thought for a minute there you were getting too old."

"I just wanted to see you dance a little before I stepped in," Samson turned his attention to Donald Foster. "You need to learn to show a little respect to young ladies. Next time, I won't be so nice."

Foster grunted and groaned, but did not quit struggling. His face turned a dark crimson. Samson applied more pressure until Foster had trouble breathing.

"Okay. Okay." The angry father sputtered.

Samson released his grip, and Foster fell to the ground, gasping between curses. He continued to glare at Niki from the pavement. It took three or four minutes for Foster to gather enough strength to regain his footing.

"You killed my daughter. You killed her." His eyes bore lasers at Niki.

"Mr. Foster, I had nothing to do with your daughter's death," she replied.

"I know better. She told me what you were going to make her do today. You had to kill her to keep the world from knowing what that coach did to my baby."

"I don't believe the results of the test would have proven Coach Bailey was the father. We were looking forward to the proof he was not the baby's father."

"I don't believe you," saliva flew out of Foster's mouth with each word.

"I can prove my whereabouts all night and this morning. I was at the school waiting for your daughters to show up until almost noon. She never came this morning."

"Of course not. She is tired of all this. At least, she was."

"Where did she hide out?"

"At a friend's house," Foster spoke more calmly, though his eyes continued to smolder.

"Which friend?"

"Paula Slocum. She's younger than Flavia, but they had become good friends."

Niki's heart almost exploded. Paula's father was John David "Sleazy" Slocum, Central's most notorious man of questionable deeds.

"When did you talk to your daughter last?" Niki asked, trying to keep the dread from her voice.

"Last night," Foster responded. "She came home and told me about you harassing her at school. She said you made a lot of threats."

"I didn't threaten your daughter. I tried to get her to tell the truth without waiting for the test results. Coach Bailey's life is at stake if we don't get some answers soon."

"He won't be getting them now," Foster stared. "Where was he this morning?"

"He—He's home, I'm sure. He no longer leaves this house unless I'm with him."

"Then why did a friend of mine see him drive past the school before it opened this morning? He was alone. Wasn't nobody with him."

"He—" Niki was stunned. "I'm sure your friend saw somebody resembling Coach Bailey this morning. Billy was at home alone."

Foster stuck a fist in Niki's face. Samson took the opportunity to clear his throat with a slight cough to remind the angry father of his presence.

Foster glanced over his shoulder at the behemoth of a policeman and stopped, relaxing his hand. He looked back at Niki.

"You won't have this big bastard around all the time." Foster spat on the ground. "One day it will be you and me."

Foster turned and strode toward his pickup. The tires left

rubber on the pavement when he pulled out, demonstrating his continued anger.

"That boy ain't very bright," Samson shook his massive head.

"He's upset about losing Flavia," she replied. "I would feel the same way."

"That's not what I'm talking about."

Niki gave him a quizzical look.

"When I grabbed him," Samson grinned. "I wasn't trying to protect you. I didn't want him to get his ass kicked right after finding out his daughter got killed. He misunderstood my kindness."

"Don't worry about it." Niki placed a petite hand on his giant forearm. "A lot of people misunderstand your intentions."

66

WATSON

NIKI, Drexel, and Donna gathered at Linda's Chicken & Fish in Watson. None had finished eating when the news about Flavia had come in.

"We're in trouble," Drexel began after tasting his side order of gumbo.

"Yep. No doubt about it," Niki speared a fried chicken liver.

"Why?" Donna asked, preferring to start with a fried dill pickle. "They've got to let Coach Bailey go without Flavia there to testify against him."

"He still has to deal with LaDonne Elgin's murder. He was found over her body with the murder weapon in his hand," Niki responded.

"He was set up. Everybody knows that." Donna poured more salt on the plate of fried dill pickles, as well as her Cajun fries.

"Ahh, the innocence of youth," Drexel sighed.

"What's that supposed to mean?" Donna slammed the salt shaker down.

"Only that adults," Drexel wiggled his finger at himself and

Niki, "we prefer to have facts backup her feelings. So does the judge in a court of law."

"But you know, Niki knows, and I know Coach Bailey is innocent. If we can see it, why can't everyone else?"

"You like crawfish. Right?"

"Of course."

"Would you eat a dog?"

"Are you crazy? Nobody eats dogs."

"Not true," Drexel said. "In many Asian and African cultures, they consider dog meat a delicacy."

"Not by me, it isn't." Donna wrinkled her button nose.

"That's my point. You tried crawfish and love them. Most of the world will never try them because they find the very thought disgusting. You feel the same way about dogs, even though you've never tasted one."

"I still don't get the connection between dogs and Coach Bailey. I think Alzheimer's has already set in on that old brain of yours."

Drexel glanced at Niki. "Today's youth are a bit slow, aren't they?"

"If we're so slow, then why can't you explain that awful story about crawfish and dogs?" Donna fired back.

"You've eaten crawfish and you love them. You hate the thought of tasting dog meat because you've never tried it. People who are involved in the case and don't know Coach Bailey detests the mere thought of him doing bad things to those two girls. Once they've come to an opinion, they won't change it easily."

"Do you teach philosophy on the side?" Niki asked. "Now that the lesson is over, and I pray to God it's over, can we get back to our problem?"

"Sure. We have a man accused of raping one girl who is now dead and killing another one. Our best chance to find the truth got herself blown up this morning." Drexel provided the summary.

"She wasn't in the car when it blew up."

"There was enough blood in it, anyway. I accept your point, but it is irrelevant. If she is dead, it doesn't make any difference how she got that way," he explained.

"Unless—" Niki started.

"Don't tell me. Our client was not at home this morning. Somebody saw him driving by the school." Drexel groaned.

"I couldn't believe it when I called him. He said he thought about going to jail and had to get out and drive around to get some fresh air. He left the house a little after midnight and got back a few minutes ago."

"Where did the fool go?" Drexel asked.

"He said he drove around. He didn't have a plan, just wanted to get out of the house. He drove by the school before it opened this morning."

"The guy is an idiot," Drexel blurted.

"I don't know," Niki ran a hand through her long hair. "I might want to get out and drive around if I was facing being behind bars for the rest of my life. I've never been in that situation, so I don't know how I would react."

"You're no better than your young friend, Niki. Both of you are way too trusting. I bet that sucker knew the test was about to expose all his lies and that's when he killed the girl and blew up the car."

"Whoa," Niki held up a hand. "That's a big leap from acting stupid and killing a girl."

"Not if he's already killed one. Let's not forget LaDonne," Drexel responded.

"And don't forget Coach Wax," Donna added. "Coach Bailey had the motive and the opportunity to kill him."

"Listen to your young friend, Niki. She is considering the facts and not letting emotion and feeling get in the way."

"You're right," Niki said. "You're both right, but I still believe Billy is innocent. I know the circumstances point in the other direction, but I don't think so. Not yet."

"Will you still feel that way when he doesn't show up for the court in three days, and you lose eight hundred thousand dollars?" Drexel asked.

"Don't think I haven't thought about that. I don't know what we would do if Billy doesn't show up Friday morning."

"How do we find Flavia?" Donna asked. "If we can find her, then we may solve a whole bunch of our problems."

"I don't believe visiting with her father right now will get us very far. If she was supposed to spend the night with Paula Slocum, then Sleazy's daughter may know something."

67

CENTRAL HIGH SCHOOL

When Paula Slocum came into the small conference room at the high school, Niki could not help but notice the similarity in her facial features to her father. The same dark hair. The same piercing eyes. The same flawless skin. But unlike her infamous father, Paula had a small frame, almost fragile.

She was barely five feet tall, if that. There was not an ounce of fat on the girl. Niki wondered if the teenager ever ate.

"Paula, I'm Niki Dupre. I'm trying to find Flavia Foster. She supposedly spent the night with you last night."

The teenager nodded, but remained silent. However, her bright eyes focused on the private investigator. Niki guessed the facial features were not the only things Paula inherited from Sleazy Slocum.

"What time did she get to your house last night?"

"About six."

"Did she stay there for the rest of the evening?"

"No, Ma'am."

"What time did she leave?"

"After dinner."

"What time was that?"

"A little after seven," Paula responded.

The young girl was similar to her father, reluctant to expand her answers. Niki realized she would have to ask specific questions to get the information she wanted. Nothing would come easily.

"Did she say where she was going?"

"No, Ma'am."

"What reason did Flavia give for leaving?"

"She said she was going to the library."

Niki sighed. "Did she often go to the library at night?"

"No, Ma'am."

"Why did she go last night?"

"She didn't tell me."

"Aren't you and Flavia good friends?"

"Yes, Ma'am."

"She gave you no hint why she had to go to the library?"

"No, Ma'am."

"Where did she really go?"

"I don't know."

"Have you heard from her since she left to go to the library?"

"Not really."

"What do you mean by '*not really*'? Either you heard from her or you didn't."

"I didn't."

The private investigator remained silent, staring at Paula.

"It's complicated," Paula said, her focus on Niki.

"I've got time," Niki replied. "Tell me how she got in contact with you."

"She didn't."

"But you said, *not really*. When you answer like that, I know you're not telling the whole truth. It tells me you heard from her in some fashion or another."

Paula nodded.

"What was it? How did you hear from Flavia in a roundabout way?"

"My dad."

"Flavia contacted Sle—Your father?"

The first smile from the teenager. "It's okay. I know my dad's nickname. It doesn't bother me in the least."

"Sorry. How did Flavia contact your dad?"

"She sent him a text."

"What did the text say?" Niki asked.

"She wanted to talk to him."

"What did she want to talk about?"

"I don't know. My dad didn't tell me."

"Did your dad talk to her?" The private investigator asked.

"I don't know. He didn't tell me."

"Did you see him on the phone with her?"

"No, Ma'am."

"Do you know if he ever talked to her?"

"No, Ma'am. He left the house."

"What time did he leave?"

"A little after eight."

Niki's head swirled. How did Sleazy Slocum fit into the disappearance of Flavia Foster? What the have to gain by hiding the teenager from the detective and the paternity test? Could he be the father of Flavia's child?

"How long has Flavia known your father?"

"A couple of years."

"What is their relationship like?"

"Good."

"It's Flavia close to your dad? Does she trust him?"

"Yes, Ma'am."

"Are they alone together often?"

"Not often."

"But sometimes? Are they together sometimes was no one else present?"

"Yes, Ma'am."

"How often? Where do they meet?"

"Here at the house."

"Flavia meets your dad here when you're not around? Why would she do that?"

Paula faint smile was replaced with a serious frown. "It's not like that."

"Not like what?" Niki feigned innocence.

"She isn't screwing my dad. They wouldn't do something like that."

"Like you wouldn't do something like that with Coach Delrie?"

"How did you find out about that?" Paula stared at the private investigator with wide eyes.

"I'm a detective. It's my job to find out the relevant facts about people involved with the investigation."

"But Ricky and I are the only ones that know. I didn't even tell Flavia."

"Ricky? Not Coach Delrie?"

"He treated me like an adult. He was Ricky to me."

"You speak like the relationship is over. Did something happen?" Niki asked.

"He told me last night we needed to take a break." For the first time, Sleazy Slocum's daughter showed emotion. Tears rolled down her cheeks. "He wouldn't tell me why."

Niki wondered if she should tell Paula about her conversation with Ricky Delrie the previous morning and her demands on the young coach. She decided it would not be in the best interest of the teenager. At least, the coach had taken the first step she demanded and ended the relationship with a sophomore student.

"Maybe he realized you should see boys closer to your own age."

"But I love Ricky. I don't want any of those idiot guys in high school."

"How old are you, Paula?"

"Sixteen. Almost seventeen."

Niki moved to the same side of the table as the broken teenager.

"Then give it a year. When you turn eighteen and graduate from high school, see if you still feel the same way."

"I know I will," the girl cried. "But what if he finds someone else in the meantime?"

"Then you will also find someone else."

"I don't want to find someone else. All the chickens at school are scared to ask me for a date. They've heard about my dad."

"Do you plan to go to college?"

"Yes, Ma'am."

"Where do you want to go?"

"Dad wants me to go to LSU and stay at home. I want to get as far away as possible from his reputation."

"Do you have good grades?"

The tears stopped, and Paula looked at Niki as if the detective had asked a stupid question without merit.

"Of course. Straight A's."

"Then you can get into any college you want to attend. But you still have over two years to make that decision."

"My dad won't let me go anywhere but LSU."

"I'll talk to him. I might convince your dad to trust you. But you have to earn that trust. No more relationships with the guys ten years older than you."

"Ricky isn't ten years older than me. He's only twenty-four. I don't want anybody but him."

"Then if he feels the same way, he'll still be there in two years. You may not feel the same way by then. Also, you're not doing him any favors."

"I'm not?"

"He's breaking the law and his contract with the school board. If anyone finds out, he may not only lose his job, he may go to jail."

"Like Coach Bailey?"

"Yes. If you're that close to Flavia, then you probably know that she wasn't in a relationship with Coach Bailey."

"I don't know. She never mentioned it."

"Don't you think she would have?"

"Yes, Ma'am," Paula nodded. "I wasn't exactly truthful before. I told her about me and Ricky."

"That might be where she got the idea to blame Billy. Do you have any idea who the real father is?"

"I thought about that," Paul replied. "But I guess I believed her when she said all that stuff about Coach Bailey."

"Do you think your boyfriend may have gotten her pregnant?"

"I don't know. From what Flavia told me, they weren't doing it yet. They wanted to wait until they got married."

"Okay," Niki pause. "I need to talk to your dad. You may have been the last one to talk to Flavia before someone killed her."

"Dad didn't kill Flavia. He liked her too much. Not the same way that Ricky likes me, but more like a daughter. He encouraged me to stay close to Flavia because he respected her."

"I still need to talk to him."

"Will you do me a favor, Miss Niki?"

"Sure. If I can."

"Don't tell my dad about me and Ricky. He will kill him and ground me for life."

68

CENTRAL

"SARA SUE. THIS IS NIKI."

"Hey, Niki. I heard the bad news about Flavia not turning up for the test. Awful, isn't it?"

"It's a setback, for sure. Did Billy tell you?"

"Yeah. He said you were pretty upset with him for leaving last night."

"You bet I was," Niki retorted. "I still am."

"Niki, he's looking at spending the rest of his life in jail after Friday afternoon. He wanted to get out and I can't blame him for that," Sara Sue said. "He might not have many more opportunities unless Flavia shows up."

"He needs to stay at home. It seems like every time he leaves your house, something bad happens. We're trying to help them, but he's got to quit doing stupid things."

"I'll talk to him. I plan to take Thursday off to stay with him all day. Then I'm taking Friday off to go with him to court."

"Good," Niki breathed a sigh of relief. "I'm worried he might not show up for the hearing Friday."

"He'll be there, and I'll be there with him. I know this all looks bad, but I also know my husband is innocent."

"You need to make sure he stays home. One more coincidence, and the judge may not wait until Friday. Billy may not be there Thursday when you take off from work."

"I'll talk to him, Niki. But I have to be honest with you. I can't blame him if he wants a bit of free time before Friday."

"I rather he have a lot of free time to spend with you and his child. Think about it."

69

BLACKWATER ROAD

"WHAT BRINGS you to my humble abode?" The large figure of Sleazy Slocum greeted Niki in the doorway.

"We need to talk," the investigator replied.

"Well, come on in. I hate for you to think I'm inhospitable because you sicced your dogs on me like I was a bunny rabbit."

Niki followed the large man inside the house. Hardly a humble abode, but Slocum's residence did not garner attention. Everything in it was of the best quality, but none of it was garish or overly ornate. Niki wondered how many times Flavia had been within these walls.

Slocum sat in a big man's over-sized recliner. The remote control for the television set was on a small table next to him. Niki saw the morning paper on a lower shelf of the table.

"Have you heard about Flavia?"

"I've heard a little," Slocum answered.

"What do you know?"

"I know if your tub-of-lard detective moved any slower, he and the dumb kid would be making excuses to St. Peter right now."

"Were you there?" Niki's mouth stayed agape.

"Of course not." Slocum gave her an all-knowing smile. "What business would I have at the maze on a Tuesday morning?"

"Burying a body." Niki thought, but did not say. Instead, she was more diplomatic, but not much.

"Somehow, I felt like the whole deal with Flavia's car and the bomb had your signature all over it."

"Sorry to disappoint you. Like they say, imitation is the utmost form of flattery. I might have some fans out there who I'm not aware of."

"So you weren't at the maze this morning?"

"I think I've already answered that. Is there anything else on your mind?"

"Flavia Foster."

"She should be. How does it feel to be responsible for a sweet young girl's death?"

Niki was not prepared for that question voice with such conviction that the premise of her responsibility for Flavia's disappearance was a certainty. She fumbled for a few seconds before answering.

"We're not sure she is dead." Niki tried to sound confident, but failed miserably.

"From what I heard, there wasn't enough left of the car for anyone to survive."

"But we don't know where Flavia was when the car exploded. She wasn't in the car."

"Where was she?"

"I thought you might know. After all, you are one of her best friends."

"Where would you hear something like that?" A bemused smile flitted across the large man's lips.

"I have sources. You're not the only one who can play that game."

"Well, now," Slocum hesitated. "I guess you have me in a corner no matter what I answer. Well done, Miss Dupre. My compliments."

"Then answer the question. How close was your relationship with Flavia Foster?"

"She is a fine young lady. A boatload of talent and potential. She has a tremendous future ahead if she can put this present matter behind her."

"How involved are you in the *present matter?*"

"Oh, I'm on the fringes of most matters in Central." Slocum said without sounding boastful. "Sometimes, I'm more involved than most people think. I prefer to stay in the background."

"Are you in the background in this case? Or maybe a main player and even the basis of everything."

"Miss Dupre, I have every confidence you will ferret out the truth in this affair. Then you will be in a position to answer your own questions."

"Are you working alone or did someone hire you?" The detective searched for any sign of deceit.

"I don't remember saying I was involved at all."

"If you are the father of Flavia's baby, I'd say you are way too involved."

"Our relationship isn't like that. There isn't and never was anything sexual about our feelings for each other."

"What was your relationship with Flavia?"

"More like a crazy uncle with his favorite niece. Maybe like a grandfather. I wanted nothing but the best for Flavia."

"Then tell me who the father of the baby is. That will help her if she is still alive."

"I don't know."

"You don't know who the father is or you don't know if she still alive?"

"I don't know who impregnated Flavia."

"It wasn't my client. It wasn't Billy Bailey," Niki blurted out as if convincing Sleazy Slocum was of the utmost importance.

"I agree with your assessment."

Niki sat in silence, stunned by what she heard from Slocum's lips. The broad man focused on her with a faint trace of a smile, much as his daughter had done a few hours earlier. She was amazed at the similarity of expressions from the father and the daughter.

"Are you saying you don't believe Billy Bailey is guilty of abusing Flavia?"

"You should already know the answer to that."

Niki did not understand what Slocum inferred.

"How was I to know you didn't believe the charges against Billy?"

"He's still alive. That's your proof."

70

CENTRAL

Flavia woke up in a strange bed. She was still wearing the same clothes she had on the previous night; a pair of sweatpants and a Central High School jersey. The covers were pulled up over her shoulders.

Horrible thoughts tore through her mind, but there had been no assault. She was not shackled or confined to the bed any way.

She shoved the covers back and waited to see if she could hear anything. All was quiet in the room. The teenager rose from the bed and tiptoed to the closed door. Putting her ear up against it, she heard nothing. No sound from behind the door.

The cheerleader crept to the window on the other side of the bed. Looking through it, she saw the swamp. Water and scum everywhere she looked. Cypress knees extending out of the shallow water. Larger cypress trees providing an overhead canopy.

She tested the window. To her surprise, it slid up easily. When she leaned out of the window, she looked first right, then left. It was the same in every direction. Nothing but swamp. Flavia thought about climbing out the window and escaping.

But where would she go? What lay in front of the cabin? Who else was in the cabin who might do her harm? What critters were in the swamp?

All these questions made her hesitate before jumping. She looked around the room for some kind of weapon. There was little to choose from. The chairs were intact. No loose legs or backseat slats. She searched in the closet. The nearest thing to an object that might hurt someone was a coat hanger. She took two of them.

Then she took down the curtain over the window and withdrew the rod. It wasn't solid, but she felt better after fashioning the unwound hangers on the end. At least she might thrust them in her captor's eyes. After a couple of practice lunges, she walked to the door. It was time to face her captor.

She expected the door to be locked. It was not. When she peered into the small hallway, she discovered another door farther down and a living area in the other direction. After pausing for more than a minute, she inched out of the bedroom, the makeshift spear in her right hand. Nerves almost forced her back into the room. Her hands trembled. Her heart pounded. Trepidation was her foremost thought.

Slowly, one small step at a time, the teenager edged into the den area, her back against the wall. With shaky knees, she took one more step. She saw a television sitting opposite a couch, a recliner, and a love-seat. On the shelf above the fireplace sat rough candles. It reminded her of the churches she had seen on TV.

Along the wall was a stereo player with stacks of CDs piled on top. Next to the stereo, a bookshelf stood with dozens of paperbacks and magazines. Flavia, not an avid reader, recognized a few of the more famous authors, but not many.

After investigating the den, the teenager searched the kitchenette. Small refrigerator, table with three chairs, sink, stove with an open. When she opened the door to the refrigerator, the cheerleader was pleasantly surprised to find the makings of various types of sandwiches; ham, turkey, bologna.

There were even some soda pops. All the condiments she could want. Mayonnaise, mustard, ketchup, pickles, onions, tomatoes, lettuce. Two jugs of milk and bottled water.

When Flavia inspected the small pantry, she was again surprised to find cereal, pop tarts, oatmeal, potato chips, candy, cookies, and various canned food.

She had no idea what all this meant. Someone had placed her in the middle of the swamp and had not harmed her. Her captor had furnished everything she needed to survive. Why?

Flavia, deciding not to stick around and find out, ran to the front door, yanking it open. She stepped out onto a small front porch, her mouth agape.

Expecting to see a road or at least a driveway, there was nothing but water. Swamp water in every direction she looked. No dry land in front, on either side, or as far back as she could see.

Flavia went back inside and grabbed a broom. She took it back to the porch and turned it upside down. When she stuck the handle and the water, she found it was between two and three feet deep.

Could she wade out? Where was the next isle of safety? How far would she need to go to get help? What could go wrong if she tried?

The answer to the last question was answered when a slithering water moccasin swam by a foot from the front porch. A single bite from the venomous reptile would kill her. She watched its flickering tongue probe for the next meal. The teenager went back inside and sank onto the sofa. She could not stem the tide of tears.

What would happen to her? Who was responsible? Why did they bring her here? These and other thoughts continued to flood her mind until she emitted uncontrollable visceral sobs.

71

CENTRAL

BILLY BAILEY WAS GOING STIR crazy. He felt cooped up in the house with Sara Sue. The television continued to emit flowing images with accompanying sound.

But Billy neither saw nor heard the emissions. He paced back and forth, his mind racing with only two days of freedom remaining before the hearing in front of the judge. It was a dark cloud that followed him to the bedroom, the bathroom, the kitchen. Wherever he went, the cloud engulfed his very being.

Sara Sue, unable to cope with the increasing anxiety, left to go back to her temporary agency. She claimed she was behind on the paperwork. The truth was the business was in financial trouble. Almost everyone in town knew Billy was her husband and did not want to support a child molester or worse.

Sara Sue went to the office to find a way to keep the business open. When Billy was the winning a coach at Central High School, she had trouble keeping up with the demand. Recruiting candidates to fill the flood of openings was her primary objective. Now, finding openings for her stable of temporary workers became her focus. She expanded the scope of potential clients, from Baton Rouge to Denham Springs to Gonzales to Port Allen. She sent brochures to the purchasing and human resource departments with every company in every direction. Sara Sue emailed key contacts in the oilfield industry, the refining industry, the chemical plants, the retail associations, the shipping industry, and the tourist companies.

She offered deep discounts in her fees to a point she was making little money and working twice as hard. She feared if she could not provide opportunities for her temporary workers, they would flee to other agencies.

Billy was not aware how deep the troubles were at Sara Sue's company, but he understood there were problems. He also realized her woes were a result of his predicament, as if he needed additional pressure heaped on his shoulders.

Niki could not have been more adamant about him staying home, out of the glare of publicity and away from any more potential pitfalls. But after an hour of pacing, he could stand it no longer it. He needed to get outside of the shrinking walls.

Billy drove straight to Linda's Chicken & Fish in Watson. He left at almost nine o'clock and many of the locals had already eaten when he entered. Most of the tables sat unoccupied. A group of high school boys surrounded two pretty girls at one table. A family of four finished a bucket of fried chicken at another.

He took a seat in the back corner after placing his order for chicken livers with sides of gumbo and fried dill pickles. He figured those were part of the local cuisine he would miss the most imprisoned.

When the young girl brought his tray of food to the table, she hesitated.

"You're Coach Bailey?" More of a question instead of a statement.

Billy nodded, dreading what might happen next. He was

trying to escape the cloud that followed him everywhere, and this girl was about to darken it.

"Can I tell you something?"

Billy nodded, knowing there was no escape.

"Most of us over here think you're getting the shaft for all this junk. We don't believe you did anything wrong."

At first, Billy could not respond. The girl's words were the last thing he expected to hear. He had guarded his thoughts for abasement.

"Why—uh, thank you."

"Most of us know Flavia," she continued. "We don't believe anything she says. Our guys on the football team say you're a stand-up kinda guy."

"I don't know what to say," Billy replied, looking up at her tender face for the first time. "You're right. I didn't do anything with Flavia or any other student."

The girl nodded toward the counter. "The manager said to tell you the meal is compliments of Linda's. We all want you to know we respect you."

Billy was speechless. He wanted to hug the young lady, but did not dare touch her. He sat there, a confused expression evident to all around. He finally uttered an unintelligible thanks.

The girl left the table. Billy sat in stunned silence. Then he realized two of the high school boys stood by his table. When he focused on them, they looked nervous, unable to stand still.

"May I help you?" He asked.

"We wanted to tell you you're the best. Our coach talked to us yesterday. He said you were a role model to look up to."

"He said he didn't know all the facts," the other teenager interjected. "He said when all the facts come out, everyone will respect you for the man you are."

Billy was overcome with emotion. On an impulse, he rose

and gave a firm handshake to each young man. Then he gave both a big hug.

"Please tell your coach I appreciate his words," Billy said. "I don't know how long it will take for the truth to come out, but I know one day it will."

The two boys ambled back to the other table. The two girls gave them a hug and a kiss on their cheeks. Billy gave them a thumbs-up.

The food suddenly became appetizing, like every other time he had eaten at this restaurant. The black cloud has some holes in it. As he placed a scrumptious liver coated with ketchup and Tabasco sauce in his mouth, he thought about what a fool Niki Dupre was to tell him to stay within the confines of his house.

Billy savored every liver, every dill pickle with lots of salt, and every spoonful of gumbo spiked with the hot condiment. He did not want to be reminded this might be the last time in his life he would enjoy this type of seasoned cuisine. From what he heard, prison food was not something to which he would look forward.

When he finished the food on the table, the young waitress appeared at his side. In her hands was a mountain of ice cream with chocolate syrup dripping down the sides.

"Compliments of the manager," she said. "Us too."

Billy took the bold of deliciousness and gave her the biggest smile of his life. The night was one he would remember for a long time. The coach took his time, savoring each sweet bite, the chocolate soothing the edges of his nerves.

When he finished, he went to the front and thanked the manager. He was shocked when the workers came from behind the counter. A cashier held a long stick with her phone on one end. After taking several selfies, they each patted him on the back and affirmed their support for him.

He could think of nothing else but the kindness of the staff at the restaurant on the drive back to Central. Before he realized it, he was in his own driveway. Sara Sue's car was not in the garage. Maybe he would not have to tell her he broke his promise to Niki to stay home. He saw no reason to cause an additional source of tension when no harm happened during his brief excursion to Watson.

The coach whistled, the boatload of chocolate boosting his mood. He put the door key into the lock and twisted. He heard the lock click open and then heard another soft sound.

He saw nothing but a hand across his face. A rag closed around his nostrils and an acrid odor attacked his senses. Billy grabbed the arm of the hand holding the rag, but despite his powerful muscles, he could not budge it. The arm was too strong. Blackness closed in about him. His last thought of consciousness was Niki Dupre was right.

72

CENTRAL

"He's not here." Sara Sue's voice exposed the panic she was feeling.

"Slow down," Niki responded, trying to collect her own thoughts of the early hour.

"He's not here," Sara Sue repeated.

"Are you talking about Billy?"

"Yes. His truck is here and there's blood everywhere. Billy is gone."

"I'll be there in a minute." Niki gathered her wits and her clothes. "I'll call Samson and get him to meet me there."

"Hurry. Please hurry. Something's happened." Sara Sue was now fanatic.

73

HOME OF BILLY BAILEY

"When did you last see your husband?" Samson asked after inspecting the garage.

"Tonight. I mean last night. He was here when I left for work. I had to catch up some small stuff there." Sara responded.

"What kind of mood was he in when you left?" Niki asked.

"He—He was antsy. With the hearing coming up, he's feeling the pressure. Me too." Sara Sue could not sit. She placed in the confined living area like a caged tiger.

"Did he say anything about going anywhere?" Samson kept his voice calm.

"No. He wouldn't go anywhere. Billy promised Niki he would stay home until the hearing on Friday. He never breaks a promise. I can swear to that."

"When was the last time he ate at Linda's in Watson?"

"I—" Sara stopped pacing. "We went there a week ago. Why?"

"There's a soda cup from Linda's in the car. It still has some liquid in it." Samson paused. "No way it's been in his truck for a week."

"But he was staying home."

"How did the cup get into the truck?"

"I don't know," Sara shrugged. "He might have swung by there to pick up some livers. He loves them."

"Was there an empty box in the trash? I didn't see one."

Sara ran to the garbage disposal in the kitchen. After a brief inspection, she raced to the garage and lifted the lid to the garbage can. There was no box in either.

When she came back inside the house, she flopped down in the rocking chair, all energy drained. Sara folded her arms across her chest, a move Niki recognized as a protective reflex, trying to shield out the world.

Niki moved her chair next to the rocker. She reached a hand over to Sara's shoulder.

"We'll find him. Samson is the best in the business. If anyone can find Billy, then Samson can."

Tears rolled down Sara's cheeks onto her folded arms. When she spoke, her voice cracked.

"What—About—The—Blood?"

"He might have cut himself," Niki replied. "He could have gotten a ride to the hospital. Samson has his guys checking the emergency rooms to see if he showed up at one."

"The blood is in an irregular pattern," Samson interjected. "It seems to be strewn in a random manner. I'm not sure what to make of it."

"It means Billy is hurt," Sara Sue wailed. "What other meaning could there be?"

Samson motioned for Niki to follow him to the garage. Bright red splatters splashed against the truck, the walls, and the floor. He pointed to each display of blood.

"Look here," he pointed at the truck.

Niki did as he said, but saw nothing that stood out except the blood was fresh.

"Now, look here." Samson pointed at the blood on the floor.

"Now here," the chief motioned to the wall.

"What are you seeing that I'm not?"

"Three separate instances of blood splatter. Nothing in between," Samson paused. "If Billy was bleeding that much, what caused him to stop bleeding all the way from one place to the other?"

Niki looked again. She saw the spaces on the floor without a speck of blood. But there was plenty of it everywhere else.

"He could have wrapped the cut and then took the bandage off," Niki suggested.

"Okay," Samson nodded. "Where does the blood trail lead?"

"To the truck." Niki did not understand the significance of the question.

"Where does it lead after the truck? Where did he go from there?"

Niki realized what the seasoned chief of police was seeing. Or rather, not saying.

"It doesn't go anywhere. There is no trail away from the pickup."

"That's right," Samson nodded. "And we know he didn't take the truck. It's still here."

"If someone picked him up outside, there should be a blood trail from the truck to the driveway."

Niki searched the ground outside of the garage before continuing. "There is no blood anywhere out here."

Mayeaux retraced his steps from the door to the outside of the garage. Niki waited until he completed his the renewed search.

"What do you make of it, Samson?"

"The only logical reason I can come up with," another pause for the chief to re-calibrate his thoughts, "the blood evidence is planted."

"But there's so much of it," Niki protested. "Nobody could lose that much blood and still be alive."

"It only looks like a lot," Mayeaux responded. "But if you look closely, it's a little blood spread across three areas."

"Looks like a lot to me." She gave another glance at the three separate patterns.

"Have you ever had blood drawn for health reasons?"

"Sure," Niki replied.

"How much did they take?"

"Five or six of those little vials."

"There is more in each of those then you realize," he said. "Each vial could amount to enough to account for one of those splatters, at least."

Niki caught the implication of where Mayeaux was going with this theory.

"You think Billy planted the blood and took off?"

"Yep." Mayeaux nodded. "I don't see any other logical explanation."

"But why? Why would he do something so foolish?" Niki asked, although she already knew the answer.

"Because your client is guilty."

Niki's knees quivered. Her stomach roiled. She had believed in Bill *Billy* Bailey. She had given him her time and money to prove his innocence. Now he was on the run. The only reason to go on the lam was to avoid the hearing on Friday. The only reason to avoid the hearing was because Billy Bailey was guilty. He had molested Flavia. He had killed LaDonne. He had killed Earl Washington. He had killed Jimbo Wax. He had killed Flavia and blown up her car.

The facts hit her harder than a punch to the stomach. She found herself leaning over the flower bed, throwing up on the beautiful plants.

"I would say," Mayeaux chuckled, "that you are contaminating the scene of the crime."

Niki gave him a brief glance, then bent over one more time.

74

BATON ROUGE COURTHOUSE

"But, Your Honor, the primary witness has also disappeared. The defendant is not the only one missing." Durwin Kemp desperately tried to get an extension for the Friday hearing.

"If I am to understand the testimony from Chief Mayeaux, there was much too much blood at the scene of the car explosion for anyone to live with that kind of loss. Is that correct, Counselor?"

"The alleged victim has not been located. We can't assume she is dead. In either case, my client has the right to face his accuser. We have the right to cross-examine any testimony she may give." Kemp countered.

The judge leaned back in his chair and removed his glasses. He seemed to be weighing the logic of the attorney's argument.

"Your Honor," the prosecutor jumped to her feet. "You cannot allow this travesty of justice. You cannot allow the defendant to kill the key witness and then fake his own death to get away from spending time in jail. This is a mockery of our system."

"How do you know the killed the witness? How do you know he faked his own death?"

"Because there is no other logical sequence of events, Your Honor." The counselor said.

"Then why haven't you brought charges against the defendant for the murder of Flavia Foster?"

"We—We are considering that possibility, Your Honor. We haven't gathered enough evidence to file yet."

The judge broke into a slight smile.

"Do you have enough evidence showing Mr. Bailey faked his own death?"

"The police," the prosecutor began, "they are still collecting evidence from the crime scene. We hope to have the report no later than Friday."

"Then tell me, Counselor," the judge stared at the prosecutor. "Why is this a one-way street?"

"I don't get it," the prosecutor mumbled. "I mean, I don't understand what Your Honor is saying."

"The let me be perfectly clear," the judge fingered the glasses in his hand. "You say the only scenario is the defendant killed the key witness, who was supposed to subject herself to a paternity test. And then he faked his own death and disappeared."

"That's right, Your Honor. We believe the evidence, when we get it, will support that theory."

"So you don't know what the evidence will tell you?"

"We have a good idea, Your Honor."

"It seems to me a parallel theory could also be postulated. Why does the evidence not say the key witness faked her own death and then disappeared to avoid the tests? Why is it impossible that she did not murder the defendant?"

"Your Honor," the prosecutor scrambled. "We are sure the evidence, when gathered, will refute that possibility."

"What you are telling me, Counselor, is you don't know diddly squat without the crime scene reports. And yes, before you start filing appeals, *diddly squat* is an accurate description in my court."

"I must object, Your Honor."

"Good for you. Objection denied. I order an extension of the hearing for one additional week. That both sides will have ample opportunity to obtain and review the necessary reports from our Police Department. Any questions?"

"Your Honor," the prosecutor did not want to give up easily. "The people believe this will set such an egregious precedent for future cases. I asked Your Honor to take a moment to carefully consider the dire ramifications of such an order before he makes it final."

"Big words like *egregious* and *dire ramifications* do not impress me, Counselor. Evidence impresses me and you seem to have a dire shortage of that in my courtroom."

The prosecutor whispered into her assistant's ear. He merely shrugged, having no quick answers for his boss.

The judge turned his attention to the defendant's table.

"Mr. Kemp."

"Yes, Your Honor." Durwin answered.

"I don't want to be made a fool. If I find any shenanigans on behalf of the defense, I will not be happy."

"Yes, Your Honor. I assure you that you will find no conduct unbecoming the court on our side."

"Good," the judge responded. "Unless you find out where your client, yes, I will revoke bail at the hearing a week from Friday. Just so we're clear as to what I mean, your client will relinquish all funds and assets he put up for bail at that time unless he is seated in the chair next to you or found dead. Do you understand?"

"Yes, Your Honor," Durwin stated.

Niki, sitting in the first row behind Durwin Kemp, wanted to go outside and throw up again. Then she barely caught a movement in the back of the courtroom, which made her inhale sharply.

A figure glided out of the door like a ghost. It was large. Ominous. Threatening. It was the shadowy figure of John David "Sleazy" Slocum.

75

ATCHAFALAYA BASIN

BILLY BAILEY WOKE WITH A START. The last thing the football coach remembered was being in his own garage with a hand wrapped around his face. Now, he was in a small bed in a room he had never seen before.

"Thought you'd never wake up," the feminine voice floated through the air.

"Huh? What?" Billy tried to focus his blurry eyes on the source of the sound.

"I was beginning to worry about you," the girl stated.

His eyes gained clarity, enough to make out the face of Flavia Foster. Of all the people in the world he did not expect to see in the same room, the cheerleader was at the top of the list.

"Where are we?" He asked, though his mouth fell like it was full of dirt.

"Somewhere in a swamp. I can't tell you exactly where."

"How did I get here?"

"Probably the same way I did," Flavia answered. "All I know is I heard a boat come up to the camp sometime after midnight.

Then it left. When I opened the door, you were laying on the porch."

She handed Billy a bottle of water. He drank almost the whole thing in one gulp. Then he was wide awake.

"How did I get into bed?" He asked.

"I put you there. Actually, I kinda dragged you there. You helped a little."

"I don't remember."

"Don't worry," Flavia smiled. "I don't remember my trip either."

"You're supposed to be dead."

"I guess someone forgot to tell the fellow that put me here. At least for now, anyway."

"Gee," Billy rubbed his head. "Your car blew up. There was blood everywhere. Everybody thinks the worst."

"I'm sure some people are hoping for that to happen. I guess I really can't blame them."

Billy noticed the bandage taped to the inside of his elbow for the first time. When he peeled it off, a needle mark with a bit of bruising was revealed.

"Do you know anything about this?" Billy asked while pointing at the needle mark.

"Nope." Flavia replied. "I was more concerned with you continuing to breathe. Everything else was kinda secondary."

"Don't you want me dead? Isn't that why you made up the stories about me?"

"No." Flavia stood and walked to the small window overlooking the swamp. "I know you probably won't believe this, but I had no choice."

76

WILDCAT INVESTIGATIONS

"What do we do now?" Niki asked.

Drexel glanced at Donna before volunteering an answer. "We need to find Billy or you will be out some serious cash in a little over a week."

Niki slammed her hand on the desk. Anger perforated the space between the trio. Her eyes fired darts at both Drexel and Donna.

"Why did I trust him? I'm the biggest fool in Central."

"It's not your fault, Miss Niki," Donna tried to calm her down. "We all believed he was innocent."

"He fooled us all. No matter what the judge said, I don't believe Flavia staged her own death, then somehow murdered Billy without a trace. That didn't happen."

"Why did he bend over backwards to help him out?" Drexel asked. "Does he owe you a favor or something?"

"You've got me," Niki responded. "Durwin was more surprised than the prosecutor. He said the ruling came out of left field. He thinks we should all go down to the boats and try our luck at the blackjack tables while we're on a hot streak."

"It was odd. You have to admit that," Drexel offered.

"Two odd. Something is going on behind the scenes we know nothing about."

"What do you think it is?" Donna asked.

"I have no idea. But I've got a feeling I know who does."

"Not him," Drexel groaned.

"Yep," Niki glared. "Sleazy Slocum was in that courtroom this morning. I don't think he just happened to be passing by."

77

ZACHARY

"Why were you in the courthouse this morning?" Niki demanded as soon as Slocum opened the door.

"And *hello* to you too," Slocum responded.

"I don't have a lot of time for civility."

"Billy is missing or dead. Someone you said you cared for is missing or dead. Why do I think you know more than your telling?"

"Come in. I'd rather have this discussion in the privacy of my home with you if don't mind."

The large man walked directly to his favorite recliner without looking back. Niki had no choice but to follow him. She remained standing instead of taking a seat.

"Why were you there?" She demanded again.

"I was in the neighborhood. I wanted to get up to date on the case. As you said, I care for Flavia."

"I don't believe you. Why would you be in the area?"

"I like to collect rare mental." Slocum took a sip of cherry Dr Pepper. "Sometimes I collect my fees in that form. I had a payment due from a client this morning."

"Would that be a payment for the disappearance of Billy Bailey?"

"Just like you," Slocum smiled. "I keep the confidentiality of my clients at all times. I can't discuss the details of my contribution to my client's cause."

"I'd be willing to bet that was the second time you've been paid this week. Why don't admit it?"

"I collect fees for my accomplishments. You can charge by the hour whether you're making progress in a case or not. I have to produce results to get paid."

Niki could not believe this man was telling her this. This was more open than he had ever been with anyone, including his wife and daughter. She wondered why.

"What results did you get to be paid off in gold and silver?"

"It all depends on your point of view."

"That's double talk. You're being open with me. Why can't you tell me everything?"

"Time heals all wounds. As the Good Book says, there is a season for all things. Your understanding will grow with time."

"I like straight talk, not fortune cookie phrases. Talk to me in terms I can understand."

"Niki, sometimes your friends are your enemies. Sometimes your enemies are your friends. Only the facts, when revealed, will tell you which one is your enemy and which one is your friend."

"Sleazy, you've never been anyone's friend. All of your life, you've played the game only to benefit yourself."

"That's true." Slocum took another sip of soda. "I don't apologize for the things I've done."

"Did you have anything to do with that weird ruling this morning?"

"That doesn't really matter, does it? The important thing is that you won and now you have time to solve this poser."

Niki studied Slocum's facial features. He would have made a great poker player. He gave nothing away with his stoic expressions.

"Okay," she said. "Let's assume you rigged the hearing. The judge owed you some kind of favor. Now I have to ask why you wanted to give me more time."

"Maybe you know something I need to know. Since you believe I helped you, then you might be willing to help me."

"I don't know," Niki hesitated. "I try to keep my cases aboveboard and legit. I'm not sure you do the same."

"It is justice we both seek?"

"Yours or mine?"

"In this case," Slocum replied, "let's assume it is one and the same."

"So you want me to find out who molested Flavia? You don't think it was Billy, do you?"

"The important thing is for you to discover the truth. You are in a much better position to have the legal system bring justice than me."

Niki believed the underworld figure. Something about his tone, his demeanor, his eyes, told her he was now on her side. She was also certain he had taken some action that might be frowned upon by the authorities.

"What is it you want from me?" Niki asked, though she feared hearing the answer.

"I need the truth. The simple truth."

"If I can, I will tell you the truth. As long as it doesn't break the confidentiality of my client."

"Fair enough. The question I have for you has nothing to do with Billy Bailey."

Now Niki was truly concerned. She knew what was coming, but helpless to prevent it. Sleazy Slocum was not about to ask a question as the shadowy figure supported by his reputation. He was about to ask a question as a father.

"Go ahead, but I don't want to disclose anything someone close to you said either."

Slocum's smile froze on his face. It generated more cruelty than friendliness. "I'll ask the question. If the answer is yes, then you say nothing. If the answer is no, then you can tell me."

"But I—"

Slocum held a hand out. There would be no further discussion of the terms of the question.

"Is Ricky Delrie molesting my daughter or has he been in the last few months?"

Niki tried to figure out some way out of answering the question. She came up with nothing.

"Thank you, Miss Dupre." Slocum leaned back in the recliner. "You have answered the question to my satisfaction."

"But that's not fair. I didn't say anything. How am I to know what is going on in your daughter's life?"

"Niki, Niki," Slocum gave a clicking sound. "Your weakness is your honesty. You want people to believe in you and trust you. I am not constrained by those sensitivities."

"Hold on." Niki stepped closer to him. "Don't go and do something stupid because I didn't say anything. I don't need that on my conscience."

"Whatever happens next would have nothing to do with you. As we spoke before, we are both seeking the same thing. Justice."

"But my kind of justice is within the system of government. My kind of justice is legal. I'm not sure yours is."

"I suppose," Slocum began, "that's something dreadful happened to Miss Cross, your partner. Would you stay within your strict constraints to ensure you would see her again?"

"That's not fair. You've given me an extreme hypothetical. Nothing has happened to Donna."

Slocum smiled. "Not yet."

"What the hell is that supposed to mean?"

"Only that we cannot protect the ones we love from every circumstance."

"Listen." Niki moved to right in his face. "If you know something about to happen to Donna, I want to know. This may be a big game to you, but it's not to me."

"The way you can help your friend is to solve the case."

"Do you know who is behind this?"

"I—" Slocum hesitated. "Let's say I have a clue, but I'm not in a position to reveal what I know."

"You—" Niki turned red, boiling with rage. Then she settled down. What good would flying off the handle do at this point? She opted for a different approach. "How do you suggest I figure out what you know? How do I get there from here?"

"Go back to the beginning," Slocum said. "Go back to the very beginning."

78

CENTRAL

"Hey, it's Niki."

"What are you doing out this time of night? I thought all you old-timers went to bed at dark," Donna laughed.

"I'm not that much older than you. You're confusing me with Drexel."

"I get all you old geezer's mixed up. You all sound the same to me."

"Well, this old geezer has some advice for you."

"Imagine that," Donna continued to laugh.

"Listen for change. If you're not in your apartment, don't go there. Come directly to my townhome."

"Geez. You see him like my mom. I know how to take care of myself."

"Not tonight." Niki tried to remain sedate, but her young partner was making it difficult. "You need to stay at my place tonight."

"What's happening?" Suddenly, Donna was serious.

"Somebody, and I don't know who, intends to harm you. My feeling is they plan to do something soon."

327

"Oh, my God." Donna turned down the CD player. "What do they want to do to me? Why me?"

"My best guess is they want to distract me. The best way to do that is to have something bad happen to you."

"Oh, sweet Jesus. You never told me working for you could be dangerous to my health."

"Unfortunately, it seems that way."

"What can we do?"

"Try to keep you safe and sound and solve the case," Niki responded.

"How do that?"

"According to my source, the answers all at the beginning."

"What beginning?" Donna expressed.

"I wish I knew."

79

BATON ROUGE

Ricky Delrie staggered and almost fell. He had passed his limit for the consumption of alcohol more than two hours ago. But he kept drinking. He kept trying to escape. One more drink might help them forget about Niki Dupre. Forget about Paula Slocum. Forget about Sleazy Slocum.

Delrie had called in sick for school since his discussion with Niki. But he had not yet decided to do everything she demanded of him. He was not ready to give up his job. He was not ready to seek counseling. He was not ready to admit to the authorities or anyone else about his relationship with Paula.

Why was that nosy private investigator getting into his business? Did she not have better things to do? Her client was about to go to jail. If she could find him. Just because Ricky was away from the school did not mean he did not hear the scuttlebutt about Billy Bailey. That guy had a lot more problems than Ricky Delrie.

Delrie finished the drink. Gin, Vodka, Rum. He was not quite sure what it was at this point. The acting head coach stumbled to his car, and only by the miracle of his guardian angels did he drive to Niki's townhome complex without killing himself or someone else.

He dragged himself to her door and banged on it. A neighbor came out of his townhome and glared at the drunk man. Delrie tried to flip him the finger, but his coordination was gone. It looked like he was waving at the irate man in his boxer shorts.

When Niki opened the door, to say she was surprised would have been an understatement of monumental proportions. She was not quite sure what to make of the drunk standing before her. He could barely remain erect.

"May I help you?" Niki asked.

"You betcha your little butt," the drunk replied.

"Ricky, you're drunk. You need to leave before I call the police." She started to close the door.

Delrie rushed inside, or stumbled inside, depending on which point of view. In his troubled mind, he was racing at full speed. Niki saw him almost trip over his own feet. His aim missed the target, and he ended up flat on his face.

Niki helped him to his feet.

"You need some coffee, Ricky. Black, hot, and strong. Either that or I need to call an ambulance for you."

"Don't want no coffee," he muttered.

"Then I'll call you an ambulance."

"Nope. I—I am—Leaving."

She chuckled. The man was in no condition to walk, much less drive.

"What did you have to drink?"

"One beer," he said.

Niki laughed out loud. "Was that before or after the other two six-packs?"

"Just one," he slurred.

"Right. And you only talked to Paula."

At the mention of Slocum's daughter, the inebriated coach stood erect as if made of stone.

"What you talking about?"

"We've had this discussion, Ricky. When will you go into counseling?"

"I'm not. I—Decided not to."

"That wasn't our ideal. Do you want me to tell the authorities?"

"I ain't scared of them."

"Maybe you should be. You should also be worried about Sleazy. He was asking about you."

Panic took over Delrie's whole body. Then he urinated on himself.

"I ain't scared of him neither." His words did not jibe with his bodily function.

"Ricky, you're making a mess on my floor. Move over to the couch. Wait. Let me put something down first."

Niki grabbed some garbage bags and split them down the sides. She laid them on the couch and laid some old sheets on top. She then helped Delrie lie down. He was asleep almost before he was prone. The coach snored while Niki locked her door. The private investigator covered Delrie with two blankets and propped a pillow under his head. The snoring continued uninterrupted, no matter how much she moved him around. Then the investigator cleaned the messy spot on the floor and threw the rags into the washer.

Niki left him on the couch and went back to bed. If she made him leave, there would be little chance of the coach finding his way home without harm. She went to her bedroom, locked the door, and went to bed.

80

ATCHAFALAYA BASIN

"What should we do now? Flavia asked.

"We have little choice. Unless you know a way out of this one I don't." Billy Bailey replied.

"We've got to try. Otherwise, whoever brought us here will come back to kill us."

"I'm not sure." Billy walked to the front door the cabin. "If they wanted to kill us, why bring us here and provide us all the food? I'm still trying to figure it all out."

"Well, I'm leaving." Flavia pushed by him to the front porch.

"Wait. It's not safe."

"It's not safe to stay here. I've at least got to try."

"Please don't." Billy tried to grab her arm.

She pulled away and jumped off the porch. The water was not that deep, coming up to her waist.

"See, is safe. It looks like the boat came through that opening. I'll follow it."

Billy watched the cheerleader turn and wade away from the cabin. Out of the corner of his eye, he saw movement. He turned and his mouth fell open. A huge alligator slid off a log on a slow approach toward Flavia.

Billy leapt off the porch. At the sound of the splash, when the coach hit the water, Flavia stopped and turned. She saw Billy churning through the water and mistakenly thought he had decided to join her. She turned away from him and kept wading.

Billy caught up with the cheerleader just as they reached a fallen Cypress tree. He turned and saw the swirl of water closing in on them. The coach grabbed the teenager around her waist and slung her up in the treetop. Then he pulled himself up right behind her.

The alligator erupted, half of its body out of the water. Its teeth closed in on the bottom of Billy's shoe, ripping it from his foot. The edge of the creature's teeth left deep grooves in his flesh.

Billy screamed with pain. The alligator fell back into the muddy mire. Flavia shrieked before sobbing uncontrollably. Blood poured out of the bottom of Billy's left foot and the red liquid fell into the water, further energizing the large reptile.

It lurched again. The mighty jaw snapped closed, only an inch below the coach's bloody foot. He and Flavia scrambled higher in the treetop. After three more feet of ascent, Billy relaxed a little.

Then Flavia shrieked again. Not four feet away from her head, a massive cottonmouth hissed its displeasure at being disturbed from its morning sunning. Being one of the most territorial animals on the planet, the venomous snake was not willing to share its favorite spot, no matter how big the intruder might be.

The forked tongue flickered out, and the snake coiled into a striking position. Billy jerked Flavia back to him and saved her life by his instinctive reaction. The stake struck, displaying the pure white mouth which was the source of its nickname. The strike fell short, and the reptile coiled again.

Billy broke off a limb and inched himself between Flavia and the snake. The pain in his foot sent sharp jolts with each small effort. He positioned himself as best he could on the fallen tree trunk.

The coach raised the lamb and slashed down on the snake. He missed. The reptile was now more upset and vile than before. It slithered closer to Billy. One last chance.

The coach ignored the searing pain shooting up his leg and struck the final blow. The snake, stunned by the direct hit to its head, fell off the tree trunk directly into the pool of blood beneath caused by the gashes in Billy's foot.

The massive alligator made a quick lurch and emerged from the dark water, parts of the water moccasin hanging from each side of its enormous mouth. The armored reptile was satisfied. He swam back to the log and climbed up before swallowing its breakfast.

Billy shoved Flavia into the water.

"Run." He shouted. "Run back to the cabin."

He jumped in behind her and waded on one foot. He was unsuccessful and fell face first into the miry liquid. When he surfaced, he saw Flavia stop and look back at him.

"Run. You have to make it to the cabin. You don't have much time." She glanced at the alligator on the log. With one mighty gulp, it swallowed the large cottonmouth. Then the creature turned its massive head toward the pair in the swampy water.

"Run." Billy repeated.

Instead, Flavia waded back to the coach and helped him to his feet. More accurately, to his good foot. She put one of his arms over her shoulder and they made slow, unsteady progress toward the porch.

Billy glanced at the alligator. It remained on the log, evidently satisfied with the bit of appetizer. He breathed a sigh of relief, but his relief was short–lived.

Another swirl emerged from the swamp. It was immediately followed by another. Then another. All the swirls converged on the bloody mess under the fallen Cypress.

Billy realized the animals were attracted to the blood. He was still bleeding.

"You have to leave me behind and get to the porch," he yelled much too loud than required.

She ignored him. He tried to help despite the unimaginable pain. They reached the porch and climbed up. Flavia had to help Billy with the last push.

He laid on the porch and rolled over. He wished he had not. Another alligator was coming out of the water onto the porch.

"Get inside," he yelled at Flavia.

She flung the door open and dragged the coach inside. Flavia slammed the door on the long snout of the reptile. Another was just climbing up to join its hunting buddy. The cheerleader locked the door and shoved a chair under the knob. She then turned back to Billy.

The teenager raced to the bathroom and returned with a first aid kit. In minutes, Flavia sterilized the gashes, applied antibiotic cream, and wrapped his foot with gauze. She said nothing the entire time she worked on him.

"Thanks," he said when she backed away.

"You're welcome," she replied. "It's the least I can do after all the trouble I've caused you."

"Do you want to talk about it?"

"Yes, Sir. But I can't," Flavia replied.

"Why not?" He tried to chuckle. "It's not like I'm in a position to tell anyone."

"I just can't," she repeated. "I made a promise and I can't break my promise."

"Will you do me a favor?"

"Uh—" Flavia hesitated "I don't know. What do you want me to do?"

"Write a letter to Sara Sue. Tell her I am innocent of the charges. Tell her I didn't do the things you accused me of doing."

"Why? Neither of us has much of a chance of living through this."

"Because I love my wife. Because I feel like I let her down. Because I want her to know the truth."

"But you didn't do anything. All of this is my fault. Not yours."

"She may never get the letter, but it's the best I can do under the circumstances. I'll put it in a plastic bag and hide it under my clothes."

"A lot of good that'll do." Flavia laughed out loud. "Unless one of those alligators out there poops it out after eating you, then nobody will ever know."

"I have a feeling," Billy replied. "Whoever put us here doesn't want us dead or we would already be that way."

"Then why are we here?" Flavia asked.

"To have some breakfast. I'm hungry."

81

NIKI'S TOWNHOME

"Good morning, Ricky," Niki hollered as she came into the living room. She had overslept.

There was no response from the couch. She walked over and poked the blankets. No response. She pulled the covers back from Ricky's head and gasped.

He was stripped naked. Tape covered his mouth. Small cuts covered his entire body. Niki knew immediately the young football coach was dead.

"What is it, Miss Niki?"

In all the excitement, Niki had forgotten Donna spent the night in her spare bedroom. The youngster was now standing in the opening to the hallway in a robe.

"Call Samson. Somebody killed Coach Delrie," she said, without taking her eyes off the coach.

82

NIKI'S TOWNHOME

"There is little doubt about the cause of death," the large chief of homicide pronounced.

"Were any of the cuts deep enough to kill him?" Niki asked.

"Nope. All they were meant to do was to inflict pain and terror. I imagine they were successful on both parts." Samson replied.

"What killed him?" Donna was now dressed in jeans and a pullover shirt.

"He choked to death."

Both ladies frowned. Samson answered the unspoken question.

"Somebody cut off his private parts and shoved them down his throat."

Donna gasped. Niki immediately knew who was responsible for the death of Ricky Delrie, but also knew there would never be any solid proof.

How did Slocum know the coach would be in her townhome? She did not know until he arrived and was too drunk to send home. She doubted if Delrie knew he would end up spending the night on Niki's couch. If he did this to Ricky, what did he do to Flavia and Billy?

"Do you know something?" Samson asked, looking closely at Niki expression.

"Too much," she replied. "And not enough."

83

NIKI'S TOWNHOME

THE FORENSICS TEAM WAS GONE. So was Niki's couch, sheets, and blankets. All the mess was cleaned up, and the room felt empty without the biggest piece of furniture.

Neither Niki nor Donna had much of an appetite. Drexel Robinson showed up with po'boys. One shrimp, one oyster, and one combination.

"Come on, girls. Y'all gotta eat," he said.

"You can have mine," Niki responded. "I'm still not hungry."

"I'll take hers. With all the stuff going on, we didn't eat breakfast." Donna raced to take two of the sandwiches out of Drexel's hands.

Drexel kept the combination, sharing the other two sandwiches with Donna.

Niki walked over to the door opening to her balcony and stared outside.

"What's on your mind?" Drexel asked.

Niki turned. "How did he do that to Ricky and not wake up either of us?" She pointed at Donna.

"He couldn't have put anything in your drink or food. Donna was already snoring when Delrie came by."

"Then he must have given us something after we were asleep," Niki responded.

"I've heard of those kinds of drugs. Just spray a little up your nose, and it puts you in a deep slumber."

"I've heard of those also, Drexel." Niki walked back to the center of the room. "Before now, I thought they were a myth."

"Mr. Slocum drugged us while we were asleep?" Donna expressed shock. "I don't believe it."

"Then how do you explain a man was brutally tortured in this room and neither of you heard a thing?" Drexel asked.

"Beats me," she replied. "That's scary."

"Not as much for us as it was for Ricky," Niki replied.

"One thing about Slocum. I don't know what kind of grudge he had against the late Mr. Delrie," Drexel paused, "but he doesn't hold it inside. He lets it out."

"What do we do, Miss Niki?" Donna had lost some of her appetite.

"We let the deal between Slocum and Delrie alone. We'll let Samson sort that out."

"But we know who did it," Donna retorted.

"No, we suspect someone. We have no proof. Absolutely none. We're not even sure we were drugged. I imagine whatever he used is completely out of our systems by now."

"So where does that leave us?" Drexel asked.

"The last time I met with Sleazy, I was almost positive he knew who was responsible for the murders."

"So do we call him up and ask him?"

"No." Niki shook her head. "He would only deny it."

"So we're back to nothing," Donna picked a fried oyster from her po'boy.

"He gave me a hint. He said to go back to the beginning and I would find the answer."

"It's been so long. What was the beginning?" Drexel asked.

"The Friday night game," Niki said without enthusiasm. "It all started with those two photographs of Billy with Flavia and LaDonne."

"I know." Donna almost spat out an oyster.

"What does that young, nimble mind of yours know?" Drexel grinned.

"He was telling Niki to go back and look at the film of the game."

Niki and Drexel nodded. The strawberry blonde pulled the disc from her bag and loaded it.

"Forward it to after the game, when the celebration started," Donna instructed.

"What are we looking for?" Drexel queried.

"One of the fathers. It has to be one of them. Either Carl King, LJ Wild, our Paul Nicklaus. It has to be one of them. Everybody else is dead."

They reviewed the celebration on the football field after the game in detail, rewinding whenever they lost one of these three suspects in the crowd. At the end, they had nothing.

"Maybe I was wrong," Donna said.

"He might not have been talking about the film after all."

"I want to see it one more time," Niki said.

Donna went to the kitchen to get another soda to finish the shrimp po'boy. Niki and Drexel leaned back in their chairs and played the film once again. This time, they let it play straight through.

"We don't have diddly, to quote the judge," Drexel announced.

"One more time," Niki said.

She sat alone, going through the footage for the fifth time.

Donna and Drexel went outside to get some fresh air, trying to figure out what steps should follow.

"I've got it."

Drexel and Donna heard the shout from outside. They rushed inside toward Niki.

"What have you got?" Drexel asked.

"I know who we're looking for. It all makes sense now."

84

BLACKWATER ROAD

Niki watched the man get out of his truck. He walked toward the door of his house. She pulled her Ford Explorer into the driveway right behind his pickup.

He stopped and glared at the detective.

"What are you doing here? Haven't you done enough already?"

"No, not yet," Niki answered.

"What do you want? I'm tired, and I'm hungry," the man said.

"Don't worry. When you go to prison, they'll feed you three times a day. From what I understand, the food isn't that great, but you won't starve to death."

The man shot an icy look at the slim detective and took a menacing step in her direction.

"What are you talking about? Have you lost your mind?" He demanded.

"Not yet. But I think you have if you thought you could get away with murdering Earl Washington, LaDonne Elgin, and

Jimbo Wax. Not to mention raping your own daughter, Mr. Foster."

Donald Foster turned blood red. His hands clenched, muscles tightening. He closed the distance between them.

"If I were you, I'd be a lot more careful about what you say." His face now was inches away from Niki's.

"Or what? I'm not a teenage cheerleader. What do you plan to do to me?"

"Keep talking and you'll see."

Niki recoiled slightly at Foster's breath, a combination of alcohol and onions. The big man mistook the reflex action as a sign of weakness. He lunged at the detective.

She was ready, but Foster was faster and stronger than she anticipated. His right fist missed her face, but his left caught her flush in the side.

A sharp pang shot through her body. Her breaths became ragged and difficult. Seizing on her weakness, Foster deftly positioned a powerful forearm under her chin and pivoted her body until he was behind the detective.

"I'm going to break your pretty little neck," he hissed.

"Where—Flavia—Billy?" She gasped under the increased pressure to her throat.

Foster eased up on the force, knowing he was in a commanding position.

"In a place you'll never find them. Neither will anyone else. They're dead."

A ripple of sadness filtered through Niki. Her hope was gone.

"Yeah, I did the little bitch," Foster said proudly. "She was my stepdaughter. No relation. No incest. She liked it."

"I'm sure," Niki gasped. "Every seventeen-year-old beauty dreams of an over-the-hill loser like you."

Foster tightened his grip. Niki struggled to inhale small pockets of air.

"I did the stupid stockbroker. It was supposed to be you who found him."

"You wanted to distract me. I get that. Why Jimbo?"

"Because that's stupid whore talked to him. She couldn't keep her big mouth shut."

"Don't worry. The baby's DNA will prove you raped Flavia."

"Huh?" More onion and beer breath. "They will never find it. Goodbye, Miss Dupre."

The iron-like forearms tightened. Niki reached back with both hands and slapped his ears. At the same time she kicked backwards, cracking his knee.

Foster yelled out in pain, and the vise-like grip loosened. Then the detective did the unexpected. She used his grip to leverage her body and flipped backwards over his head. She ended up directly behind the big man, out of breath with sharp knife-like pains in her midsection.

She kicked the same sore knee the from the back. Foster howled again. Then Niki delivered three quick straight jab to the large man's kidneys. He crumbled like a rag doll.

Niki jumped on top of him in an instant, the internal rage driving her. She pummeled him nonstop until he looked like a tattered, bloody corpse.

A pair of oxen–sized arms grabbed her from behind.

A new attack? Who was coming to Donald Foster's defense? The detective struggled against an ungiving force.

"Calm down, Niki?" Samson said. "You don't want to kill him."

"Yes, I do," she spat, the rage refusing to quell.

The massive chief of homicide embraced her body and lifted her away from the fallen stepfather. When her feet hit the ground, she twisted with all her might. It didn't help. Samson just smiled.

"Leave me alone," she yelled. "He killed everybody. He got Flavia pregnant."

"I know," Samson replied. "I've got it all on tape."

85

CENTRAL HIGH SCHOOL
FOOTBALL FIELD

"HERE. THESE WILL BRING THEM BACK," Sleazy Slocum said, handing Niki two needles. He pointed at the unconscious bodies of Billy Bailey and Flavia Foster at the fifty yard line.

"You drugged them?" Niki asked.

"Had to. Otherwise, they would have recognized me. I can't afford that."

"Why did you take them?"

"Foster gave ordered me to kill them. Donna as well. I decided the best way out of this was to make him think they were dead until you figured it out."

"If you knew, why didn't you tell me?"

"Couldn't," Slocum replied. "That would've been a conflict of interest. Bad for my future business."

"He paid you?"

"Don't worry. He won't need the money where he's going. I'll use it to help Flavia. She will need lots of help, I'm afraid."

"So you were coming to get Donna in my townhouse when you found Ricky Delrie?"

"Talk about a stroke of luck," the big man laughed. "For me and for Donna."

"How did you know she was there?"

"Because I warned you, and I knew you would be true to your mother-hen nature and bring her back to the nest right under your wings."

"What about Ricky Delrie?"

"He finally did something useful. He became part of the food chain. The grubs and worms will find him quite tasty."

"You know I should report you to the police."

"But you won't. You know I saved those two there on the field." He nodded at Flavia and Billy. "Think of it as protective custody instead of kidnapping."

"What should I tell them about Delrie?"

"He is helping the beautiful wildlife of Louisiana get stronger," Slocum shrugged. "That's more than he did for the people he met."

Niki did not know how to respond. She rose and walked down the stairs toward Flavia and Billy. When she reached the field, Niki turned to wave at Slocum. He was not there.

John David "Sleazy" Slocum faded into the dark Louisiana night.

Dear reader,

We hope you enjoyed reading *Murder & Billy Bailey*. Please take a moment to leave a review, even if it's a short one. Your opinion is important to us.

Discover more books by Jim Riley at https://www.nextchapter. pub/authors/jim-riley

Want to know when one of our books is free or discounted? Join the newsletter at http://eepurl.com/bqqB3H

Best regards,

Jim Riley and the Next Chapter Team

You might also like:
Murder in Louisiana Politics by Jim Riley

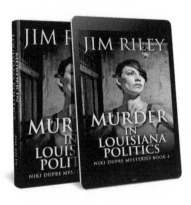

To read the first chapter for free, please head to:
https://www.nextchapter.pub/books/murder-in-louisiana-politics

Murder & Billy Bailey
ISBN: 978-4-86750-201-3

Published by
Next Chapter
1-60-20 Minami-Otsuka
170-0005 Toshima-Ku, Tokyo
+818035793528

4th June 2021